COME HOME TO DEATH

by

Marilyn Levinson

OTHER TITLES BY MARILYN LEVINSON:

CHAPTER ONE

Terry wasn't back! No sign of his shiny black motorcycle flaunting Mrs. Bressler's steadfast rule that no tenant was permitted to park in her driveway. And that especially included—as she told Erica often enough—the fancy Mr. Terry Parker and his noisy, fume-polluting Harley Davidson.

Erica switched off the ignition and stared out the rain-streaked windshield. The April shower was over, leaving the sky a few shades lighter than the drab sidewalk. She was too overcome by disappointment to wonder why a late model blue Lincoln Continental was parked in front of her boarding house in this shabby though respectable neighborhood. Silly to expect Terry to have miraculously reappeared in the two hours she'd been out doing the Saturday marketing.

A blanket of despair settled about her so that she felt a part of the bleak, sunless landscape in this small town in upstate New York. Until this moment, she hadn't realized how much she'd banked on Terry's coming home this morning in spite of the fact that he always returned after one of his long, unexplained absences at dusk or late at night.

Work had gotten her through the week. As usual, the magazine where she was senior editor was late going to press, keeping her at the office until all hours with last minute changes and problems to solve. She'd had no time to eat lunch, much less dwell on her personal worries. She came home exhausted, downed a carton of yogurt and a banana, then turned on her laptop and forced herself to work on next month's feature article: "Fifteen Fabulous Places to Meet the Man of Your Dreams."

Each night, she willed herself to fall into a deep and dreamless sleep, successfully warding off useless speculation as to where Terry could be. After all, this wasn't the first time he'd gone off during the nine months of their erratic yet passionate marriage. He told her not to worry often enough, that his sudden departures had nothing to do with their relationship.

"I've told you, it's work," he'd say when she pressed him for information. "My job has me traveling all over to learn about the new products, then I gotta help out with training sessions. Nothing for you to be concerned about." And when she asked why he couldn't text or call more often, he'd roll his eyes and say he wasn't a text or calling kind of guy. Still, all sorts of disturbing ideas swarmed about in her head, ideas Terry laughed at whenever she summoned up enough nerve to voice them. "In trouble? Me? Erica, sweetheart, you have to be kidding."

Erica hoisted the groceries, a bag in each arm, and slammed the car door shut with her hip. She was a good deal sturdier than her petite, boyish figure led one to believe. The oversized glasses and cropped blonde hair gave her a perennial schoolgirl appearance, which a penchant for baggy sweaters and long, gauzy skirts did nothing to dispel. But the staff at *Today's Woman* knew her to be competent and dependable, and turned to Erica to untangle impossible situations. She'd been self-reliant, as well, until Terry had come crashing into her life.

Head bowed, Erica climbed the steps to the screened-in porch that fronted Mrs. Bressler's rambling wooden-framed house. She was about to put the key in the lock when the door flew open. The landlady's bulky frame filled the doorway, her ample bosom heaving with distress as she struggled to reduce her normally strident voice to a whisper.

"Erica, dear, two men are upstairs waiting for you. I had to let them in. He near knocked me down, the fat one did."

"Who are they? What do they want? I don't know—"

"They want Terry, of course. And when I told them he was away, they said they wanted to talk to you." Mrs. Bressler jerked her double chin upward. "They're most likely watching for you. Through your bedroom window." She almost whined. "They made me unlock your door. I didn't want to, God knows, but I thought, for your sake, it would be worse if I called the police."

The police? Erica clutched the groceries to her chest. Her mouth was dry as she whispered, "What do they want with Terry?"

"Couldn't tell you, I'm sure." The landlady sniffed. "I never saw the likes of them before. They look like a couple of gangsters, if you ask me."

Erica stood, too frozen to move. Her eyes traveled past the open door, up the staircase leading to the cozy, makeshift apartment that had been her home for three years.

Mrs. Bressler watched her. The older woman spoke, her tone softer, "Come into my kitchen, Erica. Call the police, if you think that's the wisest thing to do." She sighed deeply. "Truth is, sometimes I sit up nights, worrying about you and that Terry you married. Only knew him a month, you did. It's not my place to say so, but maybe you should have waited a bit. Got to know him before you took the big step."

But Erica wasn't listening. She suddenly remembered the blue Continental parked a few feet away. Her Honda was no match for it. She had to get away! The two packages slipped from her grasp as she turned and raced down the block.

She headed for Old Main Street, where a few rundown stores still remained in the center of town. She crossed to the Sweet Shoppe, its faded Dolly Madison sign adorning the grimy window. The familiar, dimly lit luncheonette, with its long counter and patched red vinyl booths, was empty. She huddled into the corner booth.

What do they want? What do they want from Terry? droned on and on in her head.

Charlie, the owner and counterman, came over, his customary good-natured grin on his face. "What's your pleasure, Erica?"

"Coffee, just coffee," she mumbled.

Charlie nodded and went to get it. He never asked questions. Never seemed to find it odd that one evening she'd walk in, arm-in-arm with Terry, all lit up, then show up a few nights later, alone and glum. Erica found his lack of curiosity a comfort. Charlie obviously accepted that life was both happy and sad, good and bad—a pleasant respite from Mrs. Bressler, whose worrying about her seemed to have taken over where her aunts' had left off.

She sipped, scalding her lips on the steaming coffee.

"Mrs. Parker."

The deep, commanding voice startled Erica. The cup slipped from her hand. Coffee spilled onto the table.

"Didn't mean to frighten you."

But he had, she knew. Meant to frighten her. The voice belonged to the taller of the two men. He was tanned and had the fit good looks of a professional tennis player. But his eyes were cold, his expression severe. His gray sports jacket looked expensive—camel's hair or cashmere, Erica guessed. Without invitation, he slid into the seat opposite her. The shorter, stocky man stood glowering at the end of the table. Erica couldn't stop staring at him. He seemed on the verge of striking her.

The seated man spoke again. "Take a load off your feet, Andy. We found her, didn't we? She's not going to run away. But first, be a good boy and get us some coffee."

"Aw, Sean, I don't—"

Sean's frown cut short his companion's complaint, and Andy lumbered off to do as he was ordered.

"Silly to run away, Mrs. Parker." Sean's tone was conversational. "We won't harm you. As your landlady must have told you, we're looking for your husband."

Running had been stupid. As usual, she hadn't stopped to think. They had obviously seen her running down the street and now supposed she had something to hide.

She did her best to keep her voice steady. "What do you want with Terry?"

"Come, now. You really have no idea?" He sounded amused.

"How could I?" she asked defensively. "I don't know very much about my husband's work."

"His work?" A genuine chuckle escaped his even white teeth. "Hey, that's very funny."

Her cheeks heated. She should have made Terry tell her exactly how he earned his living. The truth was, after a while, she didn't want to know. Something in Terry's tone implied that knowing would unearth unpleasantness, and Erica shunned unpleasantness at all costs.

Charlie came over, a cup of coffee in each hand, followed by the sheepish Andy. "Anything else I can get you, gentlemen?"

"This is fine, thanks." Sean's voice, though soft, was somehow threatening. He tossed a five-dollar bill on the table. "What we would like is some privacy." His eyes narrowed, giving him a foxlike appearance.

Charlie remained unperturbed. "Are you going to be all right, Erica?"

The quiet voice, the steady gaze calmed her, reminding her that she was in a public place. Charlie wouldn't stand by and let anything happen to her. She took a deep breath and shed some of her fright, and understood she'd fled, not from fear for her own safety, but because these men were about to bring an end to her willful blindness. Once she learned what they had to tell her, life with Terry could never be the same.

"Thanks, Charlie," she said softly. "I'm all right."

It was the right thing to say. Sean's manner became less aggressive. "Mrs. Parker, we're looking for your husband. He owes our boss a lot of money."

The other man sipped his coffee while Sean continued to study her. He must have seen her eyes widen and fill with tears because his tone softened. He hunched closer to her across the table.

"Terry lost it gambling Sunday night. He promised to pay it back by last night. He didn't. He took off instead. He never did that before, and frankly, Mr. B is a little bit put out."

"Oh." A deep sigh reverberated through her taut body as she struggled to absorb what Sean's few sentences had revealed. So that was Terry's "work." He was a gambler, and God knew what else. He had lied to her, just she had suspected in the deepest recesses of her mind. She hesitated, then asked, "How much does my husband owe?" It was better to find out the worst.

"With the interest, twenty thousand dollars."

"My God! So much? What are we going to do?"

Erica lowered her head in an attempt to hide the tears streaming down her face behind her glasses. She flinched when a tanned hand reached across and gripped her shoulder.

"Hey, Mrs. Parker. Erica. I had no idea Terry kept you in the dark. He did say...but then you don't look..."

Erica dried her eyes with a paper napkin, noting the uncertainty in the man's voice. What could Terry have told him about her? She, too, was puzzled.

Sean leaned back and regained control of the situation. "Tell me about the last time you saw Terry. Was it Sunday night?"

"More like Monday morning. Close to four o'clock. He came in and woke me up. He reeked of liquor. I asked what was wrong and he said he needed money."

"Go on."

She sighed with exhaustion, no longer afraid. She now knew the worst and, horrible as it was, it was better than the nameless, shapeless horrors that flickered through her mind whenever Terry disappeared or refused to answer her questions.

"Terry thinks I'm wealthy," she continued, "because I receive monthly checks from my parents' estate. But I can't get the capital. I've told him so again and again. And everything I've saved these last three years is...gone."

"So, he cleaned you out already," Andy commented between slurps of coffee. "Some nice guy."

"You don't understand!" Erica protested shrilly, angrily. "He was good to me. The only one who cared. Cares."

She could have bitten her tongue. Why had she used the past tense? And why was she bothering to explain to these mobsters about Terry? It was none of their business what she did with her money.

"Did he take off that night?" Sean asked.

Erica hesitated, then shrugged. Sean might not have the right to question her, but refusing to answer could only make for more trouble.

"He kept after me, as though I were hiding something from him. I told him I could borrow some money from Rob Fenley, who owns the magazine I work for, but Terry just laughed. Then he got angry. He said something about keeping an agreement. I didn't know what he was talking about. Finally, he fell asleep. When I got home from work Monday night, he was gone. His note said he'd be away for a few days on business, and not to worry. Mrs. Bressler said he left around noon."

"Do you have the note?" Sean persisted.

She reached into her pocketbook, feeling herself blush. How stupid to keep the note, but it had been a bitter quarrel, and it was something of Terry's.

Lips pursed, Sean read the torn sheet of paper, then returned it to Erica.

"Where do you think he could have gone? You must have some idea."

He sounds like a prosecuting attorney on a TV show, Erica thought. Hammering away single-mindedly at the truth. She almost giggled aloud at the absurdity of the comparison, at the absurdity of her situation. These two men had dropped a bombshell on her life, and now they expected her to help them locate Terry. Well, she wouldn't! For once, she was glad she didn't know where he was.

"I have nothing else to tell you." She folded her hands in her lap. "Terry never told me anything. Never brought any of his friends around."

"I'm sure he didn't," Sean said grimly.

He believed her, Erica realized, when he handed her a business card.

"Here's a number where you can reach me if Terry comes back." He ignored her wince. "Either you call me or have him call. Don't forget. Tell him terms can be arranged." Sean leaned across, gray eyes glinting into hers. "Because if he doesn't, he'll regret it. I can promise you that."

The two men rose and left the Sweet Shoppe. Minutes later, Erica was outside, too, her mind churning so she almost forgot to pay for her coffee. She nodded automatically to Charlie when he handed her the change.

Anger, outrage, and the need to help Terry whirled about in her mind, each emotion elbowing the others in an attempt to gain dominance. Unpleasant memories thrust themselves forward for reinterpretation. The times he'd "borrowed" money for old medical bills, for motorcycle repairs. All lies. She hated the thought that he'd deceived her so he could pay off his gambling debts.

But he could be wonderful, she reminded herself. Tender and caring. Buying her roses in the middle of January. Nursing her day and night when she was bedridden with the flu. He probably didn't tell her he was a gambler for fear she wouldn't marry him if she knew.

And he'd wanted to marry her. The thought warmed her heart for a block, but had no power to check the realization that, though he made her feel desired and happy, Erica didn't know her husband very well. She had no idea how he spent his days or how he earned his living. Which was why she was left in this humiliating and foolish position. It was the steep price one paid for willful ignorance. For relinquishing her responsibility to herself. She could hear Aunt Constance's booming voice reprimanding her, "So this is the kind of mess our girl gets herself into when we're not around."

Still, it was *her* mess, damn it. Hers and Terry's. If he didn't raise the money, those men would hurt him. That much was clear.

The sun came out as she reached Mrs. Bressler's house. She began climbing the stairs when a male voice asked, "Are you Erica Parker?"

She spun around as a man stepped out of a blue BMW and walked toward her.

"I am," she said, almost defiantly. She had had her fill of strange men hassling her. "And who are you?"

"My name's Doug Remsen. I'm a friend of your husband's."

"Oh." The air left her body like a deflated balloon. "I thought..." She didn't quite know what she thought, aside from being glad Terry had a friend. "I don't know where Terry is, as I explained to the two thugs who just told me he owes their boss a lot of money."

"That wouldn't be Sean and Andy, by any chance? I thought I recognized Sean's car."

Erica nodded. "They scared me half to death."

"I'm sorry. They had no business doing that." Doug's voice sounded harsh, but his gray eyes were filled with sympathy.

"Thank you." For the first time, she noticed he was rather good-looking and fit, about ten years older than her husband. "It all came as a shock. I had no idea Terry gambled. He led me to believe..." She couldn't bring herself to tell him what a fool she had been.

Doug smiled. "Don't beat yourself up. Terry is a charmer and quite adept at hiding his faults from the people he cares about."

She found herself returning his smile. "It sounds like you know him well."

"Well enough. Since Terry's not here, I'll try texting him again." Doug reached inside his jacket pocket. "It was nice meeting you, Erica. Here's my card with my number. In case you need to contact me."

Why would I need to contact you? she wondered as she watched him drive away.

Her short conversation with Doug Remsen had helped restore her equilibrium. She climbed the steps, filled with determination. Now that she'd decided to act, she knew what she had to do.

She went straight to the small bedroom under the eaves and hauled down her suitcase from the closet shelf. She emptied the drawers and closet of her skirts and sweaters, blouses, jeans, and underwear. There wasn't very much. She'd deliberately kept her possessions to a minimum. She grabbed her lipstick, toothbrush, and hairbrush from the bathroom and left the rest. Then she closed her laptop and scribbled off a short note to her boss, which she stuffed, along with the article she'd almost finished, into an envelope. Rob was going to scream the office down for her taking off like this, but she had no time to worry about that.

The letter to Terry took more thought. She decided to be forthright and brief.

Dear Terry,

Two thugs named Sean and Andy came here today looking for you. Sean told me all about your debt. I'm driving down to Long Island to try to get the money you owe. Call Sean, please. He says terms can be worked out.

I love you,

Erica.

P.S. Doug Remsen also stopped by to see you.

She included directions to the house on Long Island, the telephone number, and the number Sean had left her. Not knowing why, she put the card with Doug's number in the zippered compartment of her pocketbook next to Terry's note.

Erica trudged downstairs with her belongings and dropped them in the hall as she went to find Mrs. Bressler. Her landlady was sitting in the kitchen, sipping a cup of coffee, and wolfing down a large Danish. With great effort, she rose to her feet.

"Erica, honey, are you all right? I've been worried sick about you. Almost called the cops, but I wasn't sure if you wanted that. Did those men hurt you?"

Erica shook her arm free of Mrs. Bressler's frantic grip. Why did she have the bad luck of finding a landlady who reminded her so much of Aunt Constance? Several times in the last three years, she'd been on the verge of moving out, but she always decided against it. The rent was cheap, and Mrs. Bressler meant well, although her occasional emotional outbursts on Erica's behalf sent her shuddering with distaste.

It took great effort to answer civilly. "Nothing happened, Mrs. Bressler. They wanted to talk to me about Terry. That was all."

"Thank God." Mrs. Bressler gave a deep sigh of relief.

Erica forced some warmth into her voice. "I appreciate your concern and all that you've done for me. I'm going away for a few days." She handed the older woman a slip of paper. "This is where I'll be staying. I left a letter for Terry in the apartment." She hesitated, hating to involve Mrs. Bressler in her private affairs, but feeling she had little choice. "Please remind him to call the phone number inside. It's very, very important. About his, er, work."

Mrs. Bressler grew agitated. She pulled Erica's head to her large bosom. "Where are you going? Let me help you. I can lend you money. I know you're a good girl and you'll pay me back."

Fiercely, Erica pulled away. She knew she should be touched by this kind gesture, but it only irritated her. "I'm fine, really. Thank you, Mrs. Bressler, but I don't need anything."

She saw the hurt look on her landlady's face and she made herself smile. It felt like a grimace. "Good-bye, Mrs. Bressler."

Erica carried her belongings out to her car and got behind the wheel. She sighed deeply as she turned on the ignition and the Honda came to life. A feeling of apprehension came over her at the thought of the four-hour drive before her. But it wasn't the long ride that bothered her. *I'm doing it for Terry*, she told herself again and again, like a mother coaxing a reluctant child.

For, as much as Erica was determined to help her husband, she dreaded reaching her destination. She was going home to Manordale, the one place she swore she'd never set eyes on again.

Erica sped down the thruway, skillfully maneuvering past the cars and trucks sharing her route southward. Now that she'd set her plan into action, fear and anxiety evaporated as naturally as a snake shedding its outgrown skin. The ominous overtones of the morning's encounter faded, leaving only the urgent need to raise the money for Terry as soon as possible. Surely those men wouldn't kill him! The thought made her shudder. But maybe they broke arms and legs.

Erica shook her head vigorously. No point in scaring herself silly.

Nonetheless, she couldn't stop thinking about Terry. They were both twenty-four, but Terry had obviously seen more of the seamy side of life. His dark eyes glinted with a streetwise savvy. He was often suspicious of people, even of Mrs. Bressler. But Erica had never given that much thought. She was too taken with the catlike grace of his lean, muscular body, with his outrageous handsomeness, and—best of all—the flashes of tenderness that occasionally showed through his macho stance. Not many of those lately. This past month, he'd behaved like a teenager who had to be cajoled out of the sulks.

Doug Remsen would never behave so immaturely. Erica shivered with guilty delight as the image of Doug Remsen worked its way into her musings. Now that the unpleasantness of the encounter with the two thugs had worn off, she remembered Doug's kindness. The sympathy he'd shown when she admitted that she hadn't known Terry liked to gamble. Blushing, she felt a stab of pleasure because he'd given her his card, now secure in her pocketbook on the passenger's seat.

Erica sighed as, once again, her thoughts were focused on Terry. Bad as this morning's revelation had been, it was a relief to finally know the worst. A sudden chill crept up her spine. Would Terry feel desperate enough to rob a bank or hold up a store? She gunned the gas pedal, not realizing how fast she was moving until she passed three cars in as many seconds. She slowed down to sixty. *My God*, she thought. *What if Terry keeps on gambling?* She was at the end of her resources.

But was she? Erica suddenly remembered the house in Manordale and the cottage out at Montauk. They were both hers. Could she give them up for Terry? A wave of nostalgia swept over her. Images of beach picnics, family gatherings, her parents' celebrated cocktail parties, flitted through her mind. Her barriers were down. The need for expediency sent her hurtling back to her past life, uncovering the painful memories she had carefully erased from all conscious thought for so long.

Erica chuckled wryly. To think she was driving straight into the arms of Aunt Constance and Aunt Betty, the very people she'd fled three years ago. Only three years? It seemed more like twenty.

As the miles flew by, Erica allowed herself to remember the happy years with her parents. She'd just turned eleven when they were killed in a plane crash. Her own life had nearly crashed, as well. Bossy, blustery Aunt Constance, her father's older sister, and her gentle husband came to live with Erica. To run her life, was more like it.

"We don't need a housekeeper," Aunt Constance had declared, and dismissed Missy, who had been with Erica since she was born. Another loss. Devastated, Erica grieved in the privacy of her bedroom, which didn't suit Aunt Constance one bit.

"Come and watch television with your Uncle Leonard and me, Erica. We're a family now. We have to stick together."

You're not my family, Erica thought, but she'd followed her aunt downstairs. There was no point in putting up a fight. Aunt Constance would keep after her until she got her way.

Uncle Leonard had died when Erica was in high school. A week later, Erica's mother's sister moved in. Petite and determinedly cheerful, Aunt Betty was every bit as intrusive and controlling as her good friend Constance. Aunt Betty was a high school business teacher and considered herself an expert on teenagers. She'd tried to supervise Erica's wardrobe, her social life, and her future.

"I can't stand it! They're driving me crazy!" Erica would complain to her best friend, Jason Hartley. Jason was two years older than her, a gangly redhead whom the neighborhood boys alternately teased and shunned for being a loser. Erica didn't care how badly Jason played ball. She appreciated his gentle nature, his ability to understand what she was going through.

"Relax, Ricky," he'd told her often enough. "Just nod and smile and tune them out. You'll be going off to college soon enough."

"Yay! To freedom!" Erica shouted, thrusting her fist in the air. She could hardly wait.

Then, Jason's mother had died, and it was Erica's turn to comfort him, to listen to his tirades against his father for marrying his secretary six months later.

Erica had her own bad news to bear, as well. She'd nearly wept when her aunts had sat her down and told her she wouldn't be going to an out-of-town college, after all.

"Sorry, Erica. I know you've been looking forward to going away, but we simply haven't the money," Aunt Constance said gruffly.

Aunt Betty patted Erica's arm. "It won't be so bad. We're getting you a car." She beamed at her niece. "And this way, we'll all be together for four more years."

Four more years. Erica didn't think she could take it. Still, she'd enrolled in a local university and majored in accounting. She'd found figures and bookkeeping boring, but she was determined to get a position that would enable her to earn enough money to live on her own.

Just before her twenty-first birthday, Jason's father, Sherman, who was also the family lawyer, had called Erica into his office. He'd informed her that she would be receiving fifteen hundred dollars each month from her parents' estate. Erica was delighted. She'd worked hard in her senior year and secured a good job for the fall.

After graduation, she was about to set out on the cross-country vacation she'd been planning for years when her aunts tried to convince her to cancel her trip.

"It's plain dangerous for a young woman to be traveling all over the country by herself," Aunt Constance insisted.

Aunt Betty tittered. "Erica, dear, there are so many nice resorts where you could swim and play tennis and rest in the sun." She gave Erica a sly look. "And you've a better chance of meeting young men at a resort."

It had been the last straw. Erica drove off, determined to start a new life. She hadn't a destination in mind, except that it be far from Long Island. When she finally settled down, she made no attempt to contact her aunts. Of course, she had to write to Sherman to tell him where to send her monthly checks. But she asked him to keep her whereabouts confidential. As far as she could judge, he had.

"And here I am again," she said out loud as she turned off the highway and onto the four-lane road leading to Manordale.

Soon, she was on Main Street, her Main Street of twenty-two years. It looked the same except for a few changes. A boutique stood where the travel agency used to be. There was a new health food store now, and a two-story Tudor-style mini-mall. She drove past a condominium that hadn't been there when she'd left.

Automatically, she made the necessary turns, left, right, then right again, until she reached the white brick house on Chestnut Drive. Her heartbeat accelerated as she pulled into the driveway behind a blue Toyota Camry. She noticed the lawn was overgrown and patchy. An upstairs shutter was missing.

She made her way up the walk.

Suddenly, she was trembling, her anticipation turning to terror. She fought to control the preposterous thought that the house was about to swallow her up, and she'd never see daylight again.□

CHAPTER TWO

The hardest part was not racing back to her car after she rang the bell. Erica glanced at her watch. Five-thirty. Both her aunts were usually home by now. Unless, she thought in sudden alarm, one of them had died. Or they'd moved away after she'd left. Neither possibility had occurred to her the entire trip south.

"What you don't like to think about, you shut clear out of your mind," Aunt Constance had told her often enough. Maybe her aunt was right. To avoid further speculation, she jabbed the doorbell again.

As though responding to the emotion behind the ring, Aunt Constance's voice began bellowing from inside. "Coming, coming. Hold your horses. I'm—" She opened the door, puffing from her exertions, then stared, mouth agape, at the sight of her unexpected visitor.

"Hello, Aunt Constance." Erica's calm voice belied her racing heart.

"Why, Erica!" She remained riveted to the floor, her arms reaching out from her large and shapeless figure.

"I hope you don't mind. I should have called, I suppose."

In answer, Erica was engulfed in her aunt's fierce embrace. At fifty-eight, Aunt Constance looked more like seventy. She'd grown grayer and wider, her features encased in wrinkles.

"I knew you'd come back. I just knew it! Why, I was just telling Betty the other day—"

"What were you telling me? And who are you—Erica!"

Aunt Betty hadn't changed. Determined, clawlike hands grasped Erica to her scrawny bosom, then held her away so the shrewd blue eyes behind their steel-rimmed glasses could scrutinize her.

"My dear, you look wonderful! I love your hair short. But that pullover." Betty clucked like a hen. "Beige does absolutely nothing for you."

Erica felt as though she were in a dream. It was all so familiar, yet strange at the same time.

"My God, Betty, let her be," Constance remonstrated. "She just got home. Come into the kitchen, Erica. You'll have a cup of coffee while I make dinner."

They each grabbed an arm and escorted her inside.

The coffee revived her. All through dinner, her aunts babbled and chattered about who had died, gotten divorced, married, or remarried in the three years she was away. Erica told them she'd been working as an editor upstate and was thinking of changing her job. She didn't mention that she was married.

After dessert—Aunt Constance's famous apple pie—Erica got her things from the car and followed her aunts upstairs to her old bedroom.

Standing in the doorway, seeing the familiar desk, the narrow, virginal bed she'd slept in for twenty-two years, she felt the grip of panic.

I'm back. They'll keep me a prisoner here until I die. Don't be ridiculous, she chided herself. *You're only staying for a day or two. Besides, you're a married woman, remember?*

"We left your room exactly as it was," Betty chirped. "We always hoped you'd come home after you grew tired of being away."

Erica entered the room only far enough to drop her suitcase beside the bureau. It was still covered with miniature dolls and snapshots from high school and college.

"If you'll excuse me a moment, I have to make a phone call. It's very important." Damn it, they were making her feel like a child again.

"But, Erica, dear," said Aunt Constance, a whining tone replacing her earlier high spirits. "You just got home. Who do you have to call first thing?"

"Now, now," soothed Betty. "Leave her be, Connie. Erica's all grown up now and has her own life to lead. We don't want to chase her off, do we?" She smiled knowingly at her niece, who blushed with embarrassment and cursed herself for ever coming back to this house.

"Look," Erica blurted. "I have to call Sherman Hartley. It's about...business."

Aunt Constance brightened. "I'm afraid whatever it's about will have to wait. The Hartleys are away now. In England."

"France," Betty corrected her. "England was Christmas vacation."

"All right then, France," Constance conceded ill-naturedly. "What difference does it make? They're always away, hopping from one country to the next. Not that I begrudge them," she added quickly.

"When are they getting back?" Erica asked. "I must speak to Sherman."

"Let's see." Constance sank onto the bed. "They left three weeks ago on a Friday—"

"Tomorrow night!" Betty supplied, as pleased with herself as if she'd answered an important question on a quiz program. "I remember Monica saying they had to cut their trip short because Sherman has to be in court sometime this week."

"Oh, no." Erica sank onto the bed and covered her face with her hands. "I must see him immediately."

Aunt Constance put an arm around her. "Can't it wait until Monday?"

"Is it about your inheritance?" Betty asked softly.

Erica stared at her. It was the first time either of her aunts had ever mentioned her monthly allowance.

"I need a large sum of money." Erica looked from Aunt Betty to Aunt Constance. "That's why I've come here. To see if Sherman can advance it against my allowance. Or lend it to me."

"So that's why you're back! I might have known." Constance sighed mournfully. "Are you in trouble, Erica?"

"How much do you need? I could manage a few hundred dollars," Betty offered, her keen eyes studying her niece's face.

"Thanks, Aunt Betty. I need more than that." Erica's eyes filled with unshed tears. "Much more, in fact. But I appreciate your offer."

"Just how much?"

"Let's let Erica unpack and rest now, Connie," Aunt Betty interrupted, her tone sweet but firm. "I'm sure she'll feel a lot better after a good night's sleep."

Grateful, Erica closed the door behind them. She lay down on the pink quilt. In seconds, she was asleep, her glasses still perched on the bridge of her nose.

She awoke hours later, the pale moon shining through the gauzy curtains. Where was she? Her heart beat wildly, but her knowing fingers located and switched on the bedside lamp.

She found her aunts downstairs in the family room. Constance was watching TV. Betty sat at the card table, grading papers.

"Ah, there you are," Constance greeted her. "We were wondering if you were napping or asleep for the night."

I simply must ignore their comments, Erica told herself. *That's the only way to deal with them. Besides, once they find out I'm a married woman, they'll think twice before they treat me like a child.* And now, she decided impulsively, was as good a time as any to tell them about Terry.

"I'm married."

Astonishment, joy, and alarm flitted across her aunts' faces, each emotion revealing itself so nakedly and in direct conflict with the others that Erica nearly burst out laughing.

"Well, where is he?" Aunt Betty demanded. "When are we going to meet your husband?"

The questions came nonstop, as she'd dreaded they would. She managed to remain vague, telling them that Terry was away on business, that they would be meeting him in a few days. And then she feigned interest in the inane program Aunt Constance had been enjoying before she'd come downstairs.

Here I am, she thought, *perpetuating the same lie that Terry told me. I'll be happy when all this is over.*

When the show ended, Erica yawned, said she was exhausted, and had better turn in. Upstairs, she unpacked and showered, then lay down, welcoming the familiar contours of her old bed. She was about to turn out the light when a huge figure appeared in the doorway, startling her.

"Thought you could use a cup of hot cocoa. You always liked cocoa when you were growing up." Aunt Constance placed the mug on the night table. "Good-night, Erica, dear. See you in the morning."

Erica was touched. *They mean well,* she mused, sipping the hot, sweet liquid. *If I can only manage to shut my ears to their prying questions and provoking comments, I'll sail through the next few days.*

She awoke late on Sunday morning, and was both flustered and pleased when Aunt Constance insisted on fixing her favorite breakfast of pancakes.

"Where's Aunt Betty this morning?" she asked, reaching for her fourth pancake.

Aunt Constance snorted. "Out. Out for the day."

Erica took note of her aunt's disapproval and decided not to press for details. When Constance spoke again, a few minutes later, her tone was almost apologetic. "I hope you won't mind, Erica, but I have to go out later, as well. The Civic Association is running a carnival, and I promised to help out."

"Don't worry about me," Erica assured her before Aunt Constance could suggest she join her. "I'll stay home and read the paper."

As soon as Aunt Constance left, she called Terry's cell phone and their home telephone, and was connected to voice mail. She tried a few more times during the day and got the same results. She held off until nine-thirty that evening, when Aunt Constance was watching TV and Aunt Betty was upstairs showering, to call Mrs. Bressler.

"Is that you, Erica?" her landlady shouted into the phone in response to Erica's tentative hello. "I thought I recognized your voice."

"How are you, Mrs. Bressler? Has Terry come back?"

The older woman chuckled. "Yes, indeedy. He walked through the door not half an hour ago. I reminded him about that phone call, just like you asked me to."

"Thank God." Erica sank onto the flowered seat of the kitchen chair. "And thanks, Mrs. Bressler. Is he upstairs? May I talk to him? Although I suppose I should—"

"Hang on a minute and I'll get him. No need for you to make another call."

Erica was about to tell her not to bother, but Mrs. Bressler was gone. No matter. Nothing mattered! Terry was back. He was safe!

It was minutes before he came to the phone, his voice still groggy with sleep. "Erica, honey, how are you? I only got in a while ago and was trying to get some shut eye, when Mrs. Bressler came pounding on the door."

"Oh, Terry, it's so good to hear your voice! I've been so worried about you. I was beginning to fear I'd never see you again!"

"Come on, babe." He sounded embarrassed as he always did when she became emotional. "Look, I'm sorry about what happened yesterday. Really sorry. I read your note. Sean had no right dragging you into this."

Erica took a deep breath and pulled herself together. "It's better that I know. You should have told me." She stopped herself. Now wasn't the time to get into it. "Right now, I'm just so happy to hear your voice."

"Me, too," Terry mumbled. He spoke so softly she had trouble catching all his words. "I miss you. Can't talk. Mrs. Bressler. Come on home, Erica. You shouldn't have run off like that."

Her heart sang. At least she was certain of one thing—Terry loved her. "I can't," she said. "I'm here to try to raise the money you owe."

"That damn marker." His voice was flat. "All I could borrow was a lousy five hundred and now that's all gone."

She bit her lip. No need to ask how the money had disappeared.

"Look," she forced herself to remain calm, "I'll try to have the money for you tomorrow."

"Erica, stay out of this. You don't know what you're—"

But she was too carried away by her own plans to be stopped. "No, Terry. You listen to me, for once. I'll help you out this time, but then we're going to sit down and have a serious talk about your gambling. I'll call you tomorrow and let you know if I have any success. If I do, it might be better if you come down here. Then you can go meet that...that gangster or whatever he is in the city and pay him back."

"Erica, you've no idea what's involved here." Terry sounded sad. "Come home and I'll explain everything. I should have leveled with you a long time ago."

She paid little attention to his words. She was too busy making sure she'd covered everything.

"The directions to the house are in the envelope. And don't forget to call him. He was very definite about that."

"Yeah, I'll call Sean. In fact, I'll probably be seeing him tonight."

Terry didn't sound frightened, at all. Suddenly, Erica didn't understand. Maybe Terry was right. Maybe she was completely out of her depth.

"Look," he went on. "I appreciate your trying to help me, babe, I really do. And it would be great if you could borrow the money. I'll pay you back. I swear, I will. But I don't want you getting involved. You're like a kid. You don't understand the first thing about gamblers and guys like Sean and Andy."

"I'm not a kid!" she retorted.

"I gotta go. I'll call you tomorrow. You're staying at your aunts' house?"

Her frustration flared. *Damn it, why did everyone see her as a child?* "It's *my* house, not my aunts'!"

Aunt Constance chose that moment to knock on Erica's bedroom door. She was too busy saying good-bye to Terry to notice her aunt's face was stricken with pain caused by the thoughtless remark.

"Talking to someone, dear?"

"To Terry. My husband."

"I certainly hope we'll be meeting him soon."

Erica was too preoccupied to realize her aunt's voice was quivering.

"Maybe tomorrow."

And maybe not. Terry was more unpredictable than ever. She had expected him to welcome her help. Instead, he'd tried to persuade her not to get involved. But that was silly. He needed the money.

And she needed him. Erica was beginning to wonder when she would see her husband again.

Monday morning couldn't come soon enough for Erica. She'd called Sherman Hartley's office at nine, and was told by Miss Fitzroy—Monica's homelier and more efficient replacement—that she could squeeze Erica in at noon. "For ten minutes, no longer," the brisk secretary warned. Erica assured her that was all the time she needed.

She arrived promptly at twelve and was told there'd be a slight delay. She sat for fifteen minutes, then incurred Miss Fitzroy's displeasure by pacing up and down the plush beige carpet.

"Mr. Hartley will see you just as soon as he's free," she told Erica with a sniff. "He's a very busy man, especially today. You're lucky I was able to fit you in on such short notice."

And you're lucky I won't tell you what I think of you, Erica thought. She sat down.

At last, Sherman came out to greet her. "Welcome home, Erica. What a lovely surprise!" He kissed her cheek.

She almost gagged on his overdose of aftershave.

Sherman Hartley tried and failed to conceal the truth about himself—that he was short and pudgy, and nearing sixty. His thinning hair was shoe-polish brown, considerably darker than it had been three years ago. His glasses were nowhere in sight, undoubtedly replaced by trifocal lenses. Today, he wore a three-piece gray suit that failed to hide a Santa Claus paunch. Erica controlled a shudder as he placed a moist palm on her arm and led her into his private office. She'd forgotten what an unappealing man he was.

He beamed at her from across his huge oak desk, his customary unctuous manner intact. "I must say, you're looking beautiful." He studied her carefully, as he would a painting. "More like your mother every day."

"Thank you, Sherman." She stumbled over his name. She had always called him "Uncle Sherman," but had decided this morning she'd outgrown that childish form of address. "The office looks lovely."

"Thank you, my dear. I had it redone last year." The evident pride in his voice equaled that of a father of a newborn infant.

Erica glanced around her. The office did look lovely, if not out of place. The dark paneled walls covered with oil-painted hunting scenes belonged in an English country house rather than in this modern glass and steel building.

"What can I do for you, Erica?" Sherman leaned forward, his fingers forming a steeple.

His intense gaze startled her. Disconcerted, her words came out in a rush. "I came back to Manordale to see you, I suppose. Actually, I didn't want to come here, but I had to." She realized she was babbling, stopped, and took a deep breath. "I need money. A lot of money. Twenty thousand dollars."

Sherman's eyes widened, then he burst out in a guffaw. "You shall have it, my dear. You shall have it!"

"I will?" Erica was stupefied.

"Indeed, you shall. I was just about to track you down via your banking address."

"You were?"

Damn it, he always managed to reduce her to a speechless five-year-old. She watched as he reached into a file cabinet and pulled out a sheaf of papers.

"Erica, dear, come May fifth, two weeks from tomorrow, you become a very wealthy girl—er—woman."

Erica gulped. "I do?"

"Indeed, you do." Sherman riffled through the papers. "Including all assets and investments, less taxes, you're worth something over twenty million dollars."

Erica simply stared at him. She wondered if Sherman could have heard of Terry's trouble and was now playing some kind of cruel game. Then, she realized how ridiculous that was. Sherman was far from her favorite person, but lawyers didn't make jokes about sums like twenty million dollars.

Twenty million dollars! As the reality of the situation began to sink in, a flicker of rage rather than joy stirred her to speak.

"Why didn't you tell me this before?" she demanded. "I knew absolutely nothing about this money. Why didn't my aunts tell me? We could have used it to—"

"Erica, Erica." Sherman held up a ringed, well-manicured hand to stop her flood of words. "Let me try and explain. You know, of course, that your father and I were very close friends."

"Yes."

"I set up the trust for you many years ago, just before your parents were—died."

Erica thought back. While her mother had always dressed well, she'd never owned furs or expensive jewelry. And her parents had always kept their cars for several years.

"But my parents weren't wealthy," she protested, trying to understand. "The house is far from a mansion. My aunts struggle to keep up with expenses. Why, just yesterday, Aunt Constance was saying she wished she could get a part-time job so that—"

"Erica, dear, do listen. Just before the accident, your father made some brilliant business coups." Sherman gave a rueful laugh. "He asked me to go in with him on every one of them, but I was much more conservative then. I refused to take the risks, and so I lost out on the gains." His mind seemed to wander for a moment, but he brought himself back to the subject at hand. "At any rate, your father came out a winner. Unfortunately, he and your mother never had the chance to enjoy their newfound wealth."

"But," she stammered, still unable to comprehend her ignorance of such an important matter for so many years, "my aunts! They never said one word."

"They couldn't. Because of his new financial status, your father drew up a new will, naming Constance and Elizabeth as your guardians, and me as executor of the estate. We were instructed, in no uncertain terms, to keep you uninformed of your financial situation until just before your twenty-fifth birthday, on which day the estate is to be turned over to you." He coughed discreetly. "Of course, I would be happy to continue to advise you, but that decision rests with you."

Her composure regained, she asked, "What would you have done if I hadn't come back to Manordale?"

"As I said before, I would have gotten your address from your bank and written you a letter informing you of your inheritance. If you refused to come back here, I would have forwarded the necessary papers to be signed and witnessed, etcetera."

"That may still be necessary," Erica said. "I have no intention of staying here for two more weeks."

He shrugged. "Whatever you wish, Erica."

"Just be sure to include all financial statements dating back to the year my parents died. I want to go over them."

Sherman pulled himself up so that, short as he was, he seemed to be looking down his nose at her. "Certainly, Erica. That was always my intention."

From his suddenly formal tone, she knew she'd insulted him. Impulsively, she leaned forward.

"Sherman, I'm sorry! It's not that I don't trust you. That goes without saying. It's just that I want to become familiar with every aspect of my estate. I majored in accounting, you know, although I never worked as an accountant."

"I'm afraid understanding the complexities of an estate involves a bit more than knowing how to prepare a tax form," he told her coldly.

She flinched. She hadn't meant to offend him, and now he was making her feel foolish and ignorant. Fortunately, her curiosity overcame her discomfort. She thought about Constance and Betty taking care of her all those years.

"Didn't my father leave my aunts any money?"

"Several thousand dollars each. Also, what he then considered to be a generous monthly allowance to cover the house, your college expenses, and what have you. I needn't tell you how times have changed and what inflation has done to the value of the dollar."

"Couldn't they get more money from the estate if they needed it?"

Sherman slammed down the pen he'd been fingering. "No, they couldn't! Just as, for four years, you've been allotted fifteen hundred dollars each month and no more. Of course, if you were to die before your twenty-fifth birthday, your aunts each stand to inherit half of your estate."

Thoughts eddied about in her head, churning up unpleasant memories. All those years of pinching and saving. Not being allowed to go away to college. But it was no one's fault, she realized. Her parents had done their best for her, and they had succeeded. She'd forged her independence, won her freedom, and now she was rich! Everything was available to her now—to her and Terry.

She smiled. "Thanks, Sherman, for this wonderful news. As I told you, I need twenty thousand dollars. And now you can give it to me! As an advance against my inheritance."

Sherman's eyes narrowed. His manner suddenly became that of the shrewd lawyer facing a skilled opponent. "Twenty thousand dollars? Even in view of your pending inheritance, that's a considerable sum of money, Erica. May I ask why you need to raise twenty thousand dollars on what appears to be very short notice?"

She faltered before those cold, critical blue eyes as she side-stepped his question.

"Can't you advance it? Or lend it to me? I'll pay it back." She swallowed. "With interest, of course."

He leaned across his desk. "Why do you need the money, Erica? As executor of your father's will and a trustee of the estate, it is essential that I ask these questions." His tone softened when he saw her lips purse together. "I'm only looking out for your interests."

"It's for my husband," she blurted out defensively. "He needs it for—business expenses."

"So, you're married, eh?" He rose from his desk, pacing behind her, apparently deep in thought. "This does seem to complicate matters."

Her common sense told her he had no choice but to lend her the money. Yet she could see that he intended to stall and delay, and time was running out.

Finally, Sherman returned to his desk and sank heavily into his chair. "Who did you marry, Erica? I don't suppose it's anyone I know."

"No, he's from upstate New York." Actually, Terry was from Long Island, but she didn't feel like going into all of that.

"I see." He gazed at her. "Can you tell me a little about your husband and why he needs twenty thousand dollars so urgently?"

Pompous old ass, she thought. Just what Jason used to call him. A pompous old ass with a yen for that cow, Monica. Jason! Why hadn't she thought of him earlier? His mother had come from a wealthy family, and she'd left all her money to him when she'd died. Erica could borrow the money a lot quicker and with fewer hassles from her old friend.

"Where's Jason?" she asked abruptly.

"Jason? I suppose he's still out at the cottage in Montauk."

"What's he doing there?"

"Trying to write the great American play, or so he claims." Sherman gave a derisive laugh. "He hasn't written anything since college. Or was it high school?" His eyes narrowed. "You're not thinking of borrowing from Jason, are you?"

"That's my business, isn't it?" She tried to match his icy tone, but her voice cracked.

"Maybe he still has twenty thousand dollars stashed away. Maybe not. My son claims he's penniless. I send him money each month, though God knows there's nothing keeping him from getting a job." Sherman shook his head. "How he squandered all that money away, I'll never know. I offered to help him invest it, but he wouldn't listen."

She stood. There was no time to waste. "Good-bye, Sherman. I may be going out to Montauk to see Jason. I should be back in a day or so. I'll stop by and let you know where you can send me the necessary papers."

She thrust her head high. "One thing is certain. I won't be in Manordale on my birthday."

"Good-bye, Erica, dear." He clasped her unwilling hand between both of his. "I sincerely hope that you and your husband will be able to resolve your financial difficulties."

With no help from you, Erica thought as she stormed past an offended Miss Fitzroy.

She returned home and found Aunt Constance in the living room, supervising the cleaning woman. Her aunt pulled her into the kitchen, amidst the cleansing foams and powders and sprays.

"Did you speak to Sherman? Did he tell you about your inheritance?" Aunt Constance's eyes glowed with excitement. "Now we can finally fix up this house."

"Yes, Aunt Constance. He told me."

Disappointed by Erica's reaction, Constance pressed on. "I thought you would be thrilled. Now you can do whatever you want, go wherever you please. What's wrong, Erica?"

"He told me about my inheritance, all right. But he wouldn't give me the advance I asked for."

Constance nodded thoughtfully. "Maybe he's afraid you'll spend it frivolously."

Erica bristled. "Aunt Constance, I need that money. Immediately."

"All right, Erica. I won't ask why because it's as clear as day you don't intend to tell me. But if you like, I'll call Sherman and see if I can persuade him to change his mind."

Erica shook her head. She didn't want Sherman telling her aunt that she needed the money for Terry. "No, don't call him. I'm going out to Montauk to see Jason. Maybe I can borrow the money from him."

She headed for the staircase, intent on packing a change of clothing.

Her aunt came trudging up behind her. "I wish you luck, dear. Will you be staying overnight?"

"I thought I'd stay at our cottage." She searched for the most tactful way to ask what condition she'd find it in. "Have you or Aunt Betty been out there lately?"

"Betty went out last summer for a few days. Joe Kolowsky still keeps an eye on things. The water's turned off and—"

"No problem. I'll stop at Joe's when I get there."

In her room, Erica threw underwear, a few polos, a sweatshirt, and jeans into her canvas bag.

"Better take along an extra blanket," Aunt Constance advised. "And some fresh linens. Whatever's out there is as old as the hills."

Erica went to the linen closet and pulled out what she needed. "I'll bring some towels, too."

Constance hovered behind her. She wasn't finished. "Of course, the phone's disconnected."

"No matter. I have my cell phone." Impulsively and partly to stifle her aunt, Erica turned and kissed her cheek. "Thanks, Aunt Constance. For everything."

The older woman beamed. "It's nothing, Erica. Nothing at all. You know I have your welfare at heart. I always have."

Terry! In her haste to pack and get moving, Erica had forgotten to call him. Her heart racing, she dialed his cell phone. It went straight to voice mail. She left a message saying she was driving out to Montauk and would probably spend the night. Then she tried Mrs. Bressler.

Her landlady sounded surprised to hear from her. "Terry just left. Didn't he call you? I thought I heard him on the phone. Anyway, he'll see you soon. He told me he was heading for your aunts' house on Long Island."

"Today?"

"I'm not sure."

"But I'm leaving," Erica practically wailed into the phone. "And I probably won't be back here until tomorrow or the following day."

"He seemed upset, Erica. I know he wants to talk to you about something."

Now she was upset. What had happened since she'd spoken to him last? To cover all bases, she gave Mrs. Bressler directions to the cottage. On impulse, she added, "If you speak to Terry, tell him I love him."

She also left written directions with Aunt Constance to give him when he arrived. "I can't imagine why he hasn't called me to say he's on his way," she told her aunt for the third time. "Are you sure he hasn't called the house?"

"I'm positive, child!" was Aunt Constance's exasperated reply. "I'm not senile, Erica."

Erica kissed her cheek and started out for Montauk. Automatically, she made the necessary turns to the expressway as she worried about Terry. Had Sean threatened him when they'd talked last night?

She shivered, suddenly overcome by a desperate need to see Terry.

Come to the cottage tonight, she told him silently. *You'll be safe out there with me.*

CHAPTER THREE

The East End traffic was light, not the slow-moving snake that crept along each weekend from late May through mid-September. After spending the first hour of her trip convincing herself that everything would turn out just fine, Erica let herself be swept up in the euphoria brought about by her sudden good fortune.

"I'm rich!" she shouted out the window as she drove through Bridgehampton. "I'm a multi-millionaire!"

The words sent her into a paroxysm of giggles. Her image of a woman of enormous wealth had always been a tall, elegant, middle-aged woman who wore silk dresses, antique jewels, and spoke in a clipped British accent. Certainly no one remotely resembling her. She couldn't wait to tell Terry the good news. Now they could do whatever they liked. Travel to Europe or China or anywhere in the world.

In view of her new status, getting hold of twenty thousand dollars was a mere inconvenience. A piddling concern. Surely, Jason would lend it to her. It would only be for a few weeks, and she'd be more than happy to pay him the interest he'd be losing, plus a few hundred dollars for his trouble. She chuckled with glee. Tossing large sums of money around, even in her mind, was a novelty after stinting and saving most of her life.

How had her aunts managed to keep her inheritance a secret from her all these years? They were always strapped for money, counting every penny they'd spent on her college education and the house. Their tendency to complain about every unexpected expense made their restraint at not dropping so much as a hint even more astounding. But there must have been slip-ups, innuendoes.

Even engrossed as she was trying to recall past conversations and retorts made in anger, she couldn't help but notice the blue car filling her rearview window. It wove drunkenly from one side of the two-lane road to the other.

Suddenly, it came bearing down on her, inches from her tail. *Dummy*, she thought. *He has plenty of room to pass me. No one's coming from the opposite direction.*

She sighed with relief when the driver finally moved into the next lane. Still, he made no move to pass her. Obligingly, Erica hugged the shoulder of the road to give the moron more room. This was farm country. Large fields flanked both sides of the road, interspersed by an occasional house or restaurant. There wasn't another car in sight except for the one still hanging on her tail.

Instead of zooming ahead as she expected, the idiot remained on the wrong side of the road, close behind. And now he was veering toward her!

Erica swung the Honda onto the narrow shoulder. Her mouth opened in a silent scream as she saw the clump of evergreens coming up. If he pushed her any farther, she would crash into the trees!

The blue car drew abreast. The sun glittered on shiny, new paint. Desperately, Erica's hand hit the horn, blaring her fear and outrage.

Someone! her mind screamed. *Someone come and help me!*

She glanced at the driver. Was he deaf? Drunk? For a moment, she doubted her own sanity. His window was down and a hysterical giggle rose in her throat when she saw the Darth Vader mask covering the man's face. At least she assumed it was a man. What woman would—?

Erica cast another terrified glance to her left, and her gaze fixed on the small gun that appeared in the driver's gloved hand.

"No!" she screamed. "What are you doing?"

Painfully, her hands gripped the wheel. The car began to buck as her right wheels ran off the shoulder. She braked and fell behind her assailant. She was so terrified, she couldn't be sure if she heard a shot ring through the countryside or in her worst imaginings.

"Thank God," she whispered as the blue car continued to move ahead.

But she wasn't to escape so easily. Now it was slowing down. She knew if she stopped, as she desperately longed to do, and if there had been a shot, there was no chance he'd miss a second time.

Panting with fear, she stepped on the accelerator and forged past the blue car.

She was just beyond the clump of trees when she saw it—a narrow road, little more than a path, running through the overgrown fields.

The blue car was pressing on her tail again.

She braked, spun the steering wheel to the right, then corrected her overzealous gesture. The car shuddered. The tires squealed, but they held the dirt road. She heard the scream of the other car's brakes, but it couldn't slow down in time, and drove past the turnoff.

Clinging to the wheel, praying that she wouldn't hear the roar of the other engine behind her, Erica continued down the road. It did not go very far, but swung sharply to the left before ending abruptly in front of a weather-beaten house only slightly bigger than a shack. A thin young woman in a shapeless dress was hanging up laundry on a rope stretched between two trees. At her feet, a curly-haired toddler dug with a twig in the earth. The woman observed Erica, then continued hanging up her clothes.

"Sorry," Erica gasped.

He couldn't hurt her now, not with a witness there.

She shut off the ignition. The full impact of the shock hit her, and she began to tremble. Someone had tried to kill her! Her head fell against the steering wheel. She stayed there with her eyes closed.

After a minute or two passed, she looked up. The young woman had stopped her work to stare at her. Erica took a deep breath to calm herself.

"Do you mind if I rest here a minute? Someone just tried to run me off the road."

"Suit yourself," the woman told her, returning to her wash.

Was running people off the road a usual occurrence around here?

The woman finished her basket of clothes, then gathered up the child and disappeared inside the house. She returned with a glass of water.

"Thanks." Erica gulped down the cold spring water.

The simple acts of sipping and swallowing did much to soothe her. As did the realization that too much time had passed for the man to have followed her. There was always the danger that he was waiting for her at the start of the road, but she couldn't stay here forever.

She handed back the glass, thanked the woman again, and started the car.

At the sharp bend in the road, Erica stopped and peered out, ready to reverse back to the house and scream for help, but the blue car was nowhere in sight. Minutes later, she ventured onto the main road and situated the Honda between a station wagon and a dusty pickup truck, a position she maintained all the way to East Hampton.

It was nearly three o'clock when she stopped in East Hampton to get a bite to eat. The two main streets were far from crowded, but there were enough people walking about, children riding bicycles or licking ice cream cones, to give her a feeling of safety. Her knees almost buckled under her as she stepped out of the car.

"It's only because I'm light-headed from not eating since breakfast," she told herself.

She was hungry and in desperate need of a break. Her neck ached from stretching it in all directions as she'd tried to steer clear of all blue vehicles. Blue, she was beginning to notice, was a very popular color for cars.

She found a cozy, near-empty restaurant and settled into a corner table. As she was finishing her shrimp salad sandwich, suddenly everything became clear. It must be that Sean or one of his cronies who had half-frightened her to death on the road. *How dare they*, she thought angrily. And why?

When the answer dawned on her, Erica burst out laughing, drawing a glare of disapproval from an elderly woman at a nearby table. They were using scare tactics! A Darth Vader mask. A gun shooting blanks. It had to be. No one in his right mind would put on that get-up and risk the chance of really shooting someone on a main road in broad daylight. And all in the service of forcing Terry to pay up.

Erica's fear evaporated in light of the obvious. She decided to celebrate.

"I'll have a piece of seven-layer cake," she told the waitress, and ate every crumb of it.

Her own woman again, Erica stopped at the gourmet food shop up the street. Her wire basket was quickly filled with coffee, black bread, cheddar cheese, and milk. She spotted other favorites: English tea biscuits, apricot preserves, enormous strawberries—Terry loved strawberries—and something for dinner. She decided on two stuffed squabs, a cold pasta salad, and a freshly baked pecan pie. She noticed a few more items and bought them all. *No need to watch my budget any longer*, she reminded herself.

She hummed as she drove on her way. Aside from the unpleasant task of having to ask Jason to lend her the money, she felt as though she were on her way to a party.

Not that Jason was the party-going type. He was pretty much a loner, as was she. How she'd clung to him after her parents died and Missy was sent away! Jason had been the only person left she could talk to. His sharp insights had helped her make the best of an intolerable situation.

Too bad he couldn't do the same for himself. His mother's death had changed him, left him bitter and full of self-pity. Regina Hartley had adored her son. She had appreciated his quick intelligence and sensitive nature. For eighteen years, she'd been his gentle but secure buttress against a rougher, coarser world and a critical, sardonic father.

But, Erica thought as she approached Montauk, it was Sherman's callous neglect and sudden marriage to Monica that had sent Jason over the edge. Made him lose interest in school and start popping pills. She'd never forget the night he'd almost overdosed. He'd come to the house and thrown pebbles at her window to get her attention.

"Are you crazy?" she'd called down, annoyed to have been awakened from a deep sleep. "It's three o'clock."

"Come down, Ricky. Come down and play."

She hadn't liked the way his words slurred together, or his eerie, high-pitched giggle. She'd thrown on a bathrobe and raced downstairs.

Erica had been grateful both her aunts slept like the dead, or Jason might have joined the dead that night. Walking him around the kitchen was almost impossible. Jason was six foot, three, a foot taller than her. Somehow, she managed to get four cups of coffee down his throat, and hadn't minded cleaning up the vomit.

She'd practically had to drag him out to his car and drive him home—the two hundred year old house which Sherman and Monica had purchased soon after their wedding—and drive herself back in his car. She remembered sleeping until noon that day, waking to learn Jason had come earlier for his car. He'd avoided her for weeks after that. When he finally had come to visit her, just before going back to college, he didn't mention that evening. He never had, in fact.

Nor did they ever speak about that other night when...

Erica shook her head vehemently. She didn't want to think about *that*.

Though Montauk had been spruced up since her last visit, to Erica, it was still a fisherman's town with none of the Hamptons' chic elegance. She liked it that way. She drove past the strip of motels fronting the ocean, the array of stores and shops. A few more miles, and she'd arrived.

The cottage stood on high ground, two blocks from the ocean. She never cared that she couldn't see the water from her bedroom window because she could hear the waves breaking against the shore, a continuous, comforting sound that lulled her to sleep at night. The cottage was old and weather-beaten. Although the living/dining area was spacious and airy, the bedrooms were just large enough to hold a bed and a bureau with a tiny night table.

She had spent her childhood summers out here, digging in the sand, jumping in the surf, eating large, meaty lobsters that her father bought live, then boiled in a huge cauldron. The witch's cauldron, she used to call it. How she loved the cottage when she was young. Sunny days were perfect and even rainy days were fine, as long as she had a good supply of comic books and Jason for company.

She parked on the gravel driveway, overgrown with crab grass. Scraggly bushes grew around the cottage. Wooden shutters, now gray and peeling, covered every window. Erica reached behind the old lilac bush, and scratched at the hard soil until she felt the metal box. With quivering fingers, she opened it and removed the key to the front door.

But the door was ajar!

She peered around the cottage. Parked behind the bedrooms and completely hidden from the road was a blue car.

She froze. *Jason! I must get Jason. He'll help me!* But the little path that led to the Hartley place was in full view of the front door. *Maybe the person inside didn't hear me drive up,* she thought. *Maybe I can manage to....*

She turned the corner as the front door flew open.

"'Lo, Erica. Thought I heard you pull up."

It was Joe Kolowsky, the fisherman-carpenter who had looked after the cottage for as long as she could remember.

"Joe." She breathed rather than spoke his name. "How did you—I mean—who told you to come?"

"Sorry if I frightened you," Joe drawled, pushing back the fisherman's cap he wore summer and winter. He was a pale man with washed-out blue eyes. His khaki shirt and chinos did nothing to brighten him up. "Jason Hartley called me. Told me you'd be comin' out, so I'm here to turn on the water and take down the shutters."

Jason knew she was coming. There went her advantage of surprise.

Joe went to the back of the house and started removing the shutters. Erica tagged after him.

"Who told him I was coming out?" she asked.

"Beats me. He just said you'd be staying over a day or so."

She felt a flush of annoyance. It must have been Sherman. But why? Had he told Jason her reason for coming, as well?

She carried the groceries inside. Damp, salty air filled her nostrils, stirring up old memories. She had dreamed so often about the cottage these past three years, her actual presence here seemed surreal. She wandered from room to room, looking, touching, reclaiming as she went.

Everything was clean and in order, if a bit shabby. The fabric on the living room couch was wearing thin in spots. The yellowing cotton bedspreads with their little pompoms were from another era. She put away the food and gave a silent prayer of thanks that she hadn't found dead mice in the cupboard.

The house grew lighter as Joe removed the shutters and allowed sunlight to stream inside. Now it looked exactly as she remembered it—homey, bright, and cozy.

"I'm finished," Joe announced when he was done. "Let the water run some. It's been sitting in the pipes all these months."

"Thanks, Joe. I appreciate your doing this."

He turned to leave.

She was suddenly uncomfortable. She didn't know if she should be paying him or not.

"Er—Joe? What do I owe you?"

He dismissed her offer with a wave of his hand. "Don't worry your head about it. Your Aunt Betty will be sending me money, beginning' of May."

She felt a rush of gratitude toward her aunts. Neither of them liked the cottage or visited it very often. They probably considered Joe's caretaking an unnecessary and unwanted expense. As though reading her thoughts, he turned back again.

"Listen, Erica," he poked his thumb above, "she'll be needin' a new roof. I told your Aunt Betty so more than once, but she looks at me like I'm an old worrywart. Too many shingles are beginnin' to go. Once it starts leakin', you're in bad shape. See what you can do to convince her."

"I will," Erica said fervently. "I'll take care of it."

"Thought you would," he said calmly, and was gone.

Erica raced around, flinging open every window and door to rid the cottage of its stagnant air. No sign of the blue car, so it must have been Joe's. Her heart thumped as she remembered the other blue car chasing her, threatening her. She took deep breaths and told herself she couldn't think of it now. She needed to keep her wits about her to plan her next move.

She made herself a cup of coffee and carried it into the living room. She gazed out the window while she considered the best way to approach Jason. Should she ask him for the money straight out, assuming he already knew why she was here, or try to win his sympathy? She really had no idea what his financial situation was. If Sherman was giving him money as he claimed—

"Guess who." Thin, bony fingers covered her glasses.

She jumped to her feet, fists flying.

"Hey!" Jason complained.

"Sorry. I just . . ." Annoyance and pleasure mingled as she hugged his long, reedy body.

"Thought I'd give you time to settle in, then come over, neighborly-like, bearing Scotch and ice."

"That was kind of you."

They went into the kitchen. Erica rinsed out some glasses, then watched him pour. Jason's hair had darkened to a burnished auburn and was thinning at the crown. Perhaps to make up for the missing hair, he had grown a beard. The beard and his prominent nose gave him a Lincolnesque appearance. He had on well-worn jeans and a plaid shirt, the sleeves rolled up to the elbows.

"What a wonderful surprise it is to see you!" Jason sounded cheerful. "I was sitting at my computer, facing a blank screen, when your Aunt Constance called and asked me to call Joe."

"Aunt Constance?" She was surprised. "I thought it was your father who called."

"My father?" His tone went sour. "Why the hell would he be calling? I'm not due for his charity check and lecture for another two weeks." He followed her back to the living room.

As soon as they sat down, Erica jumped up. "I almost forgot. I have biscuits and cheese. I'll put them out and we'll have a party."

She returned a few minutes later with a plateful of snacks. Her face was probably glowing. "It's wonderful being out here. I'm just beginning to realize how much I've missed this place."

"Have you missed me, too?" He looked at her, vulnerable, the way he used to look at his mother.

"Of course, I missed you," she reassured him. "You're very dear to me."

But instead of gaining solace from her remark, he huddled over his drink and seemed to shrink in size. "I was just about to give up on this writing bit, tell myself, 'well, kiddo, you've failed again,' when your aunt called."

She ignored his self-pity. "What are you working on?"

"A play. A damn good play, I thought. I had it all worked out in my head, so I decided to bring my new laptop out to Montauk and get it all down."

"And?" she prompted.

He ran his fingers through his beard. "The first ten pages came easily. Then, a major problem cropped up. Every time I sit down and try to figure out how to handle it, I get distracted. I feel restless and nervous, and before I know it, I'm in the car heading for one of the Hamptons." He gave her a rueful smile. "I've seen the inside of almost every bar from here to Hampton Bays."

"Do you see friends?" she asked. "Anyone would go bananas, living out here alone."

"I drive into the city on weekends, but I guess you're right. I'm thinking of packing up and leaving in a day or so. Staying out here wasn't such a bright idea, after all. Mistake number 583."

The new beard didn't hide the grimace that accompanied his litany of self-disparagement. She knew Jason was begging her to contradict everything he'd just said. He wanted her to reassure him, to insist that he was bright and talented and capable of writing his play. Though she felt sympathy for her old friend, she had neither the time nor the patience just then to resume her role of supportive counselor. She took the plunge.

"I'm married, Jason."

"Really?" Her news was startling enough to command his full attention. "What else have you been doing these past three years? I've often wondered where you were, abandoning me so cruelly and abruptly." He gulped most of his drink.

For a moment, exasperation diverted her from the urgency that had brought her to Montauk. "I abandoned you? When I left Manordale, you were living in California with Gigi. Or was it Fifi? Besides, your father knew where I was. I had to tell him the name of my bank so he could send me my monthly allowance."

"I asked him once, but he refused to tell me. Claimed it was privileged information. Privileged, my ass. The old prig! He's only interested in his cow Monica, who's getting fatter by the day. And his latest craze, collecting art. Can you imagine? That old philistine, who doesn't have a cultured bone in his body, is suddenly spending thousands on art work. Says it's a good investment. Hah!"

He stood suddenly and let out an embarrassed laugh. "Sorry, Erica. Didn't mean to give it to you with both barrels. Let me make it up to you. Come for dinner. Around six. Steaks and salad, and Portuguese vinho verde. I went to the market as soon as I heard you were coming." He smiled, his face aglow with the innocent charm of his boyhood. "You'll tell me all about your new life and your husband. I promise not to rant and rage about my father."

She thought a moment. There wasn't much chance that Terry, even if he was speeding as usual, would arrive before nine. And she could leave a note for him on the kitchen table telling him where she was.

"Fine, Jason. I'll bring a pecan pie for dessert." She swallowed her disappointment as she stood on her toes to kiss his bearded cheek. She would have to wait until after dinner to ask for the loan.

The Hartley cottage wasn't really a cottage, but a suburban ranch with wall-to-wall carpeting and every conceivable appliance.

Jason was in good spirits as he swept Erica inside later. From his high coloring, she knew he'd already started on the wine. Still, he kept up a steady chatter as he turned the steaks, tossed the salad, poured the wine. Her old friend had the potential to be happy—and would be happy—if only he'd had a different father.

"Delicious," she said after tasting her steak.

"Thanks. Steak and salad are two things I manage to get right."

They ate in comfortable silence.

Jason cleared the dishes, then downed two slices of her pecan pie. Over coffee, Erica told him about her life upstate and how she'd met Terry.

"What's he like?" Jason wanted to know. They were sitting across from each other on nubby white love seats.

"Tall, dark, and handsome. He rides a motorcycle. And he's a gambler, it turns out."

There was a mocking tone to his laughter. "Not exactly the kind of fellow I would have thought you'd marry."

Hurt, she asked, "What kind of husband did you have in mind for me?"

"Oh." He scratched his beard as he thought. "Maybe an accountant. Or an engineer."

"Someone safe and steady. That's what I would have imagined." She took a deep breath, thinking it was now or never. "Jason, I need money. A lot of money, and I need it right away."

"Well, don't look at me, Erica," Jason said, aggrieved. "I'm virtually living off of good ole Sherman."

"What about the money your mother left you?" she persisted. "You can't tell me it's all gone."

A cunning expression crossed his face. "No, for once I did something smart. After my business went bust in California, I worked something out with my father. He takes care of me as long as I behave. No scenes, no turning up at the office. And a few other arrangements I refrain from mentioning."

"How much is left of your inheritance? Ten thousand? Twenty?"

He eyed her suspiciously. "Maybe. But I can't lend you ten or twenty thousand dollars, Erica. You know that. Besides, what do you need all that money for?"

"It's for Terry. A gambling debt."

He sprung to his feet. "No! Absolutely not! I know those debts. They grow bigger and bigger. They never end."

She stood, glaring at him as the emotional assaults she'd suffered in the past few days took their toll.

"I need that money, Jason. Saturday, two goons came to tell me Terry had better get the money together or else. I don't know what they plan to do if they don't get paid, and I don't want to find out. Today, they tried to scare me by driving me off the road. They even shot at me."

It sounded ominous to her own ears. And melodramatic.

He laughed in disbelief. "Come off it, Erica. They wouldn't come after you."

"Oh, wouldn't they? Terry gave them the impression I have money. I tell you, they're trying to scare me!" She reached up and gripped him by the shoulders. "And you're my last hope, Jason. My only hope. Your father was no help."

"What's so surprising about that?"

"Plenty, considering he knows I come into a large inheritance on my birthday. We're talking about over twenty million dollars."

His eyes practically bugged out of his head. "Come on. You don't have to make up stories to me."

"Go call your father if you think I'm making it up. I can pay you back in less than three weeks with a few hundred dollars interest. Please, Jason, you're the only person who can help me."

"Is that so?" He spit out the words as he threw himself down on the sofa. "After not hearing from you in three years, suddenly you've tracked me down to ask me to lend you twenty thou. It's too much to expect of anyone."

She was frantic. She'd never considered the possibility that Jason wouldn't want to help her.

"But you sure as hell expected plenty from me," she said wildly. "And I'm not even talking about the time I saved your life. I mean, when you came running to me after you hit that woman on the turnpike. Or did you forget?"

His face turned white. "I sent her money," he mumbled.

"Sure, you did," she jeered. "After I threatened to tell your father if you didn't."

"But she's all right," he said petulantly. "You know I called the hospital every day, said I was her nephew. She was out in days. Good as new."

"Lucky for her. And lucky for you, there were no witnesses." She paused, hating herself for what she was about to say. "I wonder what your father would do if he found out you nearly killed someone while you were stoned."

"Erica! You wouldn't!" His voice quivered with self-pity.

"I don't know what I'll do or how far I'll go if I have to. I only know I need that money. I'll pay you back. I swear, I will, and give you five hundred dollars besides."

"All right, all right. It's yours. I'll take care of it tomorrow." He kept his eyes averted. "Only, for God's sake, don't say anything to my father. He'll cut me off without a cent."

She rummaged through her pocketbook for her cell phone and Sean's card. Her heart was thumping.

"I need to call someone." She went into the kitchen for privacy. A woman answered on the third ring. "Hello. I'd like to speak to Sean, please."

The woman laughed, sounding amused. "You would, would you? Who is this?"

"Erica Parker," she said, feeling foolish. "Is he there?"

"Nope."

"I need to leave a message."

"Be my guest, hon."

"Tell him I have the money."

"You have the money," the woman repeated, making it sound like a joke.

Erica bridled at the woman's flippancy. "The money my husband Terry owes. Tell him I'll have it tomorrow."

"Sure, hon." She hung up before Erica could say anything else.

Erica returned to the living room. "I better go. Terry may come out to the cottage tonight. He'll worry if he sees the car and I'm not there."

"Want me to come over and keep you company for a while?" Jason's tone had swung full circle, to that of a puppy who'd just soiled the carpet and would do anything to get back into his mistress's good graces.

"No thanks, Jason. I'm really tired after the trip and the news, and that incident on the road. See you in the morning."

She left the outside light on, and hoped Terry would be able to find the cottage in the dark. She felt a sudden stab of longing for her husband. She yearned to hold him close. Breathe in his familiar scent. Make love with him.

She climbed into bed, intending to read and wait up for him, but her eyes refused to stay open. She fell asleep with a smile on her lips, imagining Terry's expression of delight when she told him she'd raised the money as she'd promised.

For once, everything was working out fine.

CHAPTER FOUR

Erica awoke the next morning, shivering with cold. Outside, a gray sky released a slow and steady rain. Her low spirits were consonant with the dismal weather.

Where was Terry? Why wasn't he here by now? She slipped into jeans and a polo, and prepared her breakfast. But she barely touched the black bread and cheddar cheese she'd purchased so joyfully the day before. Sipping her coffee, she mulled over her situation. She should be happy. After all, she'd managed to raise the twenty thousand dollars. But it felt like a hollow victory without Terry here to share the good news.

Around eleven-thirty, Jason appeared, check in hand.

"Here you are," he said none too graciously as he tossed it on the kitchen table. "Speaking as an old friend, you're going to have to do something about your husband's gambling." His tone was cutting. "Unless you plan to let him run through your money. He's made a great start."

She already knew that. "Oh, shut up. It's none of your business."

"Don't bite my head off." His tone was milder. "I'm only telling you like it is. It's time you faced facts, and you know it."

"Sorry, Jason. You're right. And thanks for getting me the money so quickly. I'm just worried about Terry. I hope nothing's happened to him. He should have gotten here by now."

"It is pouring out." He stared at the rain beating against the windowpane. "Not a pleasant trip on a motorcycle. He probably stopped somewhere."

"Why didn't he come last night? It wasn't raining then."

She rose from her chair, and he followed her into the living room.

She sat cross-legged on the couch. "I would think he'd set out for Montauk as soon as Aunt Constance told him where I was. We haven't seen each other in nine days. It seems like a year."

Jason looked like he was about to make another sarcastic comment, but had thought better of it. "Want to run over to East Hampton for the day?" he asked instead. "We could have lunch, browse around. They expect it to clear up later on."

"Thanks, Jase, but I want to be here when Terry comes."

She watched him drive off, but her heart skipped a beat. Jason's car was blue!

So what? she asked herself as she poured another cup of coffee. *I know it wasn't Jason on the road yesterday.*

Soon, she was pacing about the cottage, sorry she hadn't gone with Jason. The ride alone would have done her good. Staying here by herself was a bad idea. She grew gloomier and gloomier, and felt a flash of irritation with her husband. He could have called or texted. It would serve Terry right if he got here and found a note saying she was out.

The bookshelves in the living room were filled with old paperbacks, but she was too restless to settle down and read. Instead, she worked halfheartedly on a crossword puzzle book, its corners brown and crumbling with age. Her eyes kept straying to the front door.

When the rain stopped at three-thirty, she grabbed her sweater and walked down to the beach, bypassing the puddles that had formed in the recesses of the uneven road. The sand, strewn with seaweed and debris, was too wet for walking. Disappointed, she stood back and watched the waves break against the shore, the seagulls scavenge for food.

She met no one, only a golden retriever who sniffed at her then ambled on his way back to his master. The sun rose to its full glory, reflecting itself brilliantly in the quickly drying puddles. Her dark mood lifted. Her optimism returned.

Terry had to come to the cottage today! There was no reason why he shouldn't.

She drove into town, laughing aloud as she remembered how he had burst into her life and changed it forever. He'd run into her as she was leaving her office one evening, and nearly knocked her to the ground.

"Jeez, I'm sorry!"

The handsome stranger reached out both arms to steady her.

Erica's head was reeling—whether from the collision or his closeness, she couldn't be sure. She felt a pang of disappointment when he'd released her in order to pick up her pocketbook and tote bag from the sidewalk.

"Here you go." His dark eyes probed hers, studied her face. "Hey, are you okay? Do you want to sit down someplace to catch your breath?"

"No, I...I'm fine," she stammered, dazzled by the attention and his marvelous good looks.

His expression of concern lightened into a grin. "In that case, I insist you let me make it up to you. Have dinner with me tonight."

It was an order, not a request, which she—who was usually so cautious—didn't consider refusing.

"And I haven't regretted it since," she said aloud.

In town, she browsed in a few shops then returned to the cottage, her spirits buoyant, her appetite renewed.

She was singing along with the radio as she cleared her dinner dishes when the front door opened. She stiffened. Her hand went to her heart. Was the man in the blue car...?

"Erica, honey. It's me."

Terry! He was finally here.

She dropped the plate in the sink and ran to her husband. He swooped her up in his arms, kissed her lips, and pressed her against his hard, lean body.

"My God, Erica, it's so good to see you." He took off his leather jacket and threw it, and his helmet, on a chair.

"I was so worried about you. I didn't know what had happened." She reached up and covered his face with kisses. Then, to her horror and his dismay, she began to cry.

"Hey, cut that out." He sat her down on the couch and patted her back, but the sobbing continued. "Take it easy, babe. It's all right. I'm here now. That's what matters."

He stood awkwardly, seeming uncertain of what he should do. Then, he grinned, sure of himself once again.

"I'll get you some tissues. Where are they?"

She took off her tear-drenched glasses. "In the small bedroom to the right. On the night table."

"I meant to call last night to let you know when I'd be here," he said as she blew her nose, "only things took longer than I thought they would, and I didn't want to wake you."

Where were you? she wanted to ask. *Where have you been these past nine days and nights while I've been worried sick over you?* But she didn't. She knew how he reacted to her questions. Besides, it no longer mattered. Terry was with her again. She could hold him, lay her head against his chest, and be soothed by his beating heart.

"I've been so worried. About those men and everything they told me." She leaned back to gaze into his dark eyes. "But I have the money. I borrowed it from Jason. That's why I came out here. He was our last hope."

Triumphantly, she reached for the check and handed it to Terry. He stared down at it before putting it into his wallet.

When he spoke, his voice was thick was emotion. "Thanks, Erica. I'll never forget this. You'll get every penny of it back, if it's the last thing I do."

She sighed, finally content. After all her efforts, the scene she had envisioned, yearned for, had come true. She threw her arms around her husband.

"Oh, Terry. I love you so."

The kiss, long and passionate, stirred them both. She took his hand and led him into the bedroom. She sat down on the narrow bed from her childhood and watched her husband undress. Even after nine months of intimacy, she remained entranced by his every gesture.

He moved with the natural grace of a cat. His habits were something else. The long-sleeved polo, the frayed jeans and underwear, landed helter-skelter on the floor.

"Aren't you getting undressed?" he teased her. "Or are you just here for the show?"

Normally neat, this time she couldn't be bothered. She tossed her clothes on top of his.

They made love leisurely and thoroughly. She enjoyed herself completely. He had always been able to arouse her, and by now, he could play her body like a well-tuned instrument. Engulfed in a dreamlike, sensuous lassitude, she followed his erotic lead—now tender, now forceful.

She'd had very little sexual experience, had been a virgin, in fact, when she and Terry had met. It pleased her she'd never had the least bit of difficulty reaching a climax, as some magazine articles led her to believe she might. From the beginning, she was drawn by his strong sexual charisma and little-boy charm that, at the same time, put her totally at ease in this, her first and only involvement with a man.

How lucky she was to have "caught" Terry! There were many girls around much prettier and sexier than her.

Afterward, they lay side by side under the covers—she on her back, him facedown, his arm flung across her body. She could feel the restlessness he was trying to suppress. His nerves were still taut. Was something else bothering him?

She sighed, exasperated. Well, she wouldn't be the one to spoil the mood.

He sat up abruptly and reached into the pile of clothing for his cigarettes. He lit up and smoked in silence. She nuzzled against his chest. At first, he let her, tousling her hair. Then, he pulled away and moved farther back until he was leaning against the wall.

She couldn't bear it any longer. "Terry, what is it? What's wrong?"

He let out a deep sigh. "I didn't mean to tell you today. I wrote you a letter, Erica. Everything I want you to know is in that letter. You'll have it in a couple of days."

She tried to meet his eyes, but he was gazing off into space. "What letter? What are you trying to tell me?" Suddenly, she was frantic. "Don't tell me you owe more money. I can't believe this." Her voice shook with disbelief and anger.

Jason was right. It would never stop.

"It's nothing as simple as that." His laugh was rough and without humor. "No, babe, this is about you and me."

His words sent a shiver through her body. She switched on the little bedside lamp and studied her husband's handsome profile. He seemed so distant now, almost a stranger. Still, she watched him, like a rabbit fascinated by the oncoming headlights of a speeding car. In dread, she waited to hear what Terry was about to say.

He glanced at her briefly. "First of all, I lied to you about my past." He ignored her sharp intake of breath. "That story about going to college in the Midwest, then quitting because I got sick was all a pack of lies. I've never seen the inside of no college. I quit school at sixteen." He paused to inhale deeply, to gather his thoughts. "I've been on my own these last eight years, and sometimes I needed money real bad. Sometimes, I had to do things."

He caught a glimpse of her shocked expression and chortled. "Don't worry. Nothing like armed robbery or murder. But I've done all kinds of jobs you wouldn't like to know about, so I won't go into it." He drew on the last of his cigarette.

She hurried into the living room for an ashtray, glad to escape his words for the moment.

He grounded out his cigarette and continued in a gentler tone. "I was on drugs for a while and did some pretty stupid things. The cops pulled me in a few times, but they couldn't prove anything, so they had to let me go."

"How did you get off drugs?" she asked.

"Well, somebody helped me out. It doesn't matter who and that's how... Anyway, I got hooked on a new addiction—gambling." He swallowed. "That's why I'm splitting."

"Splitting?" She grabbed him by the shoulders and forced him to look at her. "You mean, you want to leave me? After all this? I thought you loved me."

"Erica, baby, I do love you. That's why I'm doing it. We're not right together. We're too different. I thought I could... I'll probably keep right on gambling, and who knows what else. Believe me, it's better that I leave."

She perched on her knees, desperate. "But I have money," she said quickly. "I never got the chance to tell you. I'm rich, Terry!

On my birthday, I inherit twenty million dollars! We can travel, live anywhere we like."

He stroked her cheek and appeared to be memorizing her face.

She stared back, willing him not to go.

He shook his head.

"It can't work, babe. Believe me. Not the way I lead my life. When we first met, I didn't know... I didn't realize what would happen. I never thought it would be so hard."

"What didn't you think would be so hard? Terry, you're not making any sense."

"Just remember that I love you, Erica." He buried his face against her naked shoulder. Hot tears spilled down his face and onto her breast.

"Then don't go. Don't leave me. I need you, Terry. You're the only person—"

Abruptly, he pushed himself from her and started getting dressed. "I have to go. Now." He had on his underwear and grabbed his polo. "I'll write to you. And I'll pay you back, I swear." He laughed mirthlessly as he dressed. "Who'd ever guess that leaving you would be the best thing I ever did in my entire life?"

She tried to wrap her arms around his waist, but he shook her off. "I told you. That's it. Let me go."

Hurt, confused, she huddled into herself as he pulled on his boots and left the bedroom.

But at the sound of the motorcycle starting, she grabbed her glasses and her robe, and raced to the front door.

"Terry, come back here!" she shouted after him as he drove down the driveway and onto the road. "You can't leave like this! We have to talk."

But she knew he couldn't hear her above the noise. And even if he did, he wouldn't stop. He was set on leaving. But why? He loved her. He said he did, and she knew that to be true. She held onto this one glowing fact, ignoring all the other nasty details he'd let fall. She'd cope with them later when she wasn't feeling so upset and vulnerable.

Suddenly, she had an idea. She'd never gotten to tell him about the attempt to scare her.

She threw on her clothes, ran to the Honda, and started after Terry. She raced along the highway well above the speed limit, passing the few cars going west. There was no sign of Terry's motorcycle. She drove even faster, got as far as Amagansett before she turned around. Silly to chase him all the way to New York City or...

It startled her to realize she had no idea where he was going. Probably to pay Sean's boss, wherever he might be.

And then what? She didn't know any of his friends, or whether he still had relatives living on Long Island. He had told her his parents were dead. Maybe that was a lie, too.

Tears streamed down her cheeks. Nothing was right. Nothing was happening the way it was supposed to.

Back at the cottage, she brewed coffee. Then, still crying, poured half of it on the counter instead of in her cup. She cleaned it up and sipped from her mug.

The coffee revived her. Suddenly, she was famished. She opened the refrigerator and pulled out everything she could find—the remaining squab and pasta salad, the strawberries. In minutes, it was all gone.

What should she do now? Sated and feeling better, she almost chuckled at her predicament. Here she was, alone on the tip of Long Island and abandoned by her husband, to whom she'd just handed over twenty thousand dollars—money that wasn't even hers.

Abandoned after telling him she was about to become extremely rich.

Terry had to be the only gambler in the world to turn up his nose at *that*.

Her temporary good humor dissolved into tears. She lay face down on the living room couch and pounded away. Damn it, Terry had no right to decide their marriage wouldn't work. It would work perfectly well if he managed to control his gambling. He could go for help. The important thing was she loved him and he loved her. He *did* love her. Only a man in love would run away from twenty million dollars, if he believed that staying would hurt the woman he loved.

She sat up and dried her eyes. The life she'd made for herself these last three years had fallen into shambles in a matter of days. After everything that happened, she had no desire to return to her job upstate or to her apartment in Mrs. Bressler's house. It would be too painful. She'd call Mrs. Bressler and ask her to send her things to Manordale.

But where would she live? Definitely not in the house on Chestnut Drive. That would be a disaster. She'd stay there until her birthday, no longer. And then what? What was she going to do with the rest of her life? The rest of her life without Terry. The tears started flowing again.

The hours slid by in dumb misery. She sat huddled on the living room couch, letting sad, morbid thoughts fill her mind and crush her heart. The night seemed to go on forever.

At some point after midnight, she tried to go to sleep. Fresh tears filled her eyes as she remembered their lovemaking only hours earlier. She thrashed about in her bed, wondering about Terry. It frightened her to think she'd lived with a man for almost a year, totally unaware that he had committed crimes, taken drugs. Aunt Constance would have a field day if she knew. "That's our Erica," she'd say. "Never stops to think, to find out what she's getting involved in."

Thank God, Aunt Constance need never find out.

Sleep didn't come until the birds started chirping at the first light of dawn. It seemed she had just drifted off when someone knocked at the door.

Maybe Terry was back, regretting leaving. She bolted out of bed, hopeful. She put on her robe and glasses, then glanced at her watch. It was close to eleven.

The knocking began again.

"Just a minute. I'm coming!" she called eagerly.

She flung open the door. Jason was standing there with two policemen, their faces grave.

"Sorry to disturb you, ma'am," the larger, burlier officer said, "but are you Mrs. Terry Parker?"

When she nodded, he said, "Name's Donnelly." With his chin, he indicated his taller, younger companion. "This is Officer Finney. Suffolk Police."

"I told you who she is, officer," Jason said petulantly.

Both policemen ignored him. Their eyes were fixed on Erica.

"Y...yes?" she stammered. "What's wrong?" Had Terry committed a crime in the hours since he'd left her?

"We'd like to come in and speak to you, Mrs. Parker."

The three men followed her into the living room. They remained standing.

"Sit down," Erica offered and sank onto the couch. "Is it Terry? Is he okay? I mean, he didn't do anything..." She stopped, embarrassed.

Jason sat beside her. He tried to put his arms around her, but she shrugged out of his embrace. "Erica. Dear, sweet, Erica. I'm so sorry."

"Mr. Hartley!" Donnelly admonished him. "We'll handle this, if you don't mind."

Erica gasped. "Sorry?" she whispered. Her eyes widened.

Donnelly stood looking down at her, his eyes brimming with sympathy. "Your husband has been in an accident. On his motorcycle."

"Is he badly hurt?" She started to get to her feet, but the officer put out a hand, telling all.

"He was killed, Mrs. Parker. The doctor said it happened instantly. He didn't suffer."

She fell back against the cushions. A keening sound escaped from her throat. She swayed back and forth, hugging herself. "Terry's dead, Terry's dead," she whispered.

Officer Donnelly eyed Jason. "See if she has some brandy."

Jason dashed into the kitchen.

Dazed, she heard him yank open cupboards. He flew out of the cottage and returned, panting, minutes later, a glass in his hand. "Here, drink this, Erica. You'll feel better."

She swallowed, too distraught to refuse. On her empty stomach, the brandy made her nauseous and dizzy, but it did manage to steady her. Numb, she let Jason take the empty tumbler from her hand.

"When did it happen?"

"Difficult to say, Mrs. Parker. The doctor thinks some time between ten and two this morning. The motorcycle and the deceased—your husband—were thrown into bushes along the road. It was a desolate spot, so nobody noticed anything until six this morning. Was he coming from here?"

"Yes, he was," she said softly. "Is he...does he look okay?" She shuddered to think of that beautiful face ruined.

"His face was untouched," Officer Donnelly said tactfully. "I'm going to have to ask you to go to the morgue and identify your husband, seeing as you're next of kin."

"But, I can't," Erica protested. "I won't be able to." The tears started again.

"Is there someone else who can? A brother? His father?"

She shook her head. "I don't... Terry has no family."

Officer Donnelly looked at his partner, then sighed. "We'll make it as easy as we can, ma'am, but he has to be identified by a relative. It's the law."

He stared at Jason meaningfully.

"I'll drive you there," Jason told her. "It's a long way to Hauppauge."

She nodded, tears streaming from her eyes.

One of the policemen cleared his throat.

She drew a shaky breath and wiped her face. *Enough!* she told herself. She'd been crying ever since Terry had left her. Crying didn't help. She had to pull herself together. Regain control of her life.

"What caused the accident?" she asked, urged on by a twinge of guilt as well as her need to know. Was she in part responsible for the accident because Terry had left the cottage upset? Because she'd tried to hold onto him when he wanted to go? "Didn't anyone see something?"

"No," Officer Finney answered. "As we said, it's a desolate stretch of road. Someone hit him. The motorcycle was badly damaged. It had blue paint on it."

"Blue paint?" She sat up, alert. "From the car that hit it?"

"Looks that way, ma'am," Finney said. "It rained yesterday and again last night. The road was pretty slippery. Maybe someone was going fast, skidded into him. But so far, no one's come forward."

"It's him! I mean, it's them," she said frantically.

"Who, ma'am?" Finney leaned closer. He held a notebook in one hand, and a pen poised in the other.

She glanced at the older policeman, but Donnelly's face was blank. Should she tell them of her suspicions about Sean? But he wouldn't kill Terry! He only wanted the money Terry owed his boss. Unless Terry had been in worse trouble than she knew.

Suddenly, she was confused. All those blue cars. Joe Kolowsky had a blue car. So did Jason. And Sean. And Aunt Betty.

"I don't really know," she finally said. "A blue car almost ran me off the road yesterday as I was driving out here."

Donnelly's eyebrows shot up. The next moment, he was expressionless once again, but she decided not to mention the gunshot.

"I think it must be the same person, don't you?"

"Can you identify the car, Mrs. Parker?" Finney asked. He was writing furiously on his notepad.

"No. The driver was wearing a mask."

"What kind of mask?" Donnelly asked.

"A Darth Vader mask," she said, aware of how foolish she sounded. "It covered his entire face."

Donnelly's eyes bore into hers. *Did he think she was making this up?*

"Why didn't you report this yesterday? Do you know of anyone who's out to harm you or your husband?"

Tell them about Sean and Andy's scare tactics. Let the police handle it, she ordered herself. *But they're gangsters. What good will it do to tell the police? They'll only come after me*, she decided.

She drew back her shoulders. "My husband owed somebody—I don't know who—a large sum of money."

"Is that why he was carrying a check made out for twenty thousand dollars?"

She gave a start. "You found the check?"

"It was in your husband's wallet. We called Mr. Hartley's bank first thing this morning and they told us where we could find him." Donnelly allowed himself a thin smile. "He, of course, led us to you. An easy bit of detective work for a change."

She stood. "I'll go and get dressed. Jason, why don't you make some coffee? We all could use a cup. And I need a moment to myself."

"Spunky lady," she heard Finney say as she left the room. It helped keep her from crying as she showered and put on jeans with a clean polo so she could go to the morgue to identify Terry's body.

She'd never been to a morgue, but imagined it to be a cold, sterile place like the ones in the TV shows she sometimes watched.

The realization that Terry was dead brought fresh tears and remorse. If only he hadn't run off like that, angry and upset. Maybe it was an accident. Sometimes—no, usually—Terry drove recklessly fast. He loved speeding down long stretches of empty road, forcing the Harley to its utmost.

She shook her head. Much as she preferred the idea of an accident, she couldn't deceive herself. She was through with self-deception. Terry had been killed. Maybe he'd still be alive if she hadn't gotten involved. But that was silly. His death wasn't her fault. Or was it?

She brushed aside the tormenting thoughts flooding her mind and followed the aroma of freshly brewed coffee. The men's voices faded away as she entered the kitchen. They stirred and sipped, no one saying very much.

When they got up to leave, Erica brought up the subject uppermost in all their minds.

"Do you think you'll be able to catch the man who murdered Terry?"

Officer Donnelly held open the screen door for the others. He waited until Officer Finney and Jason were halfway down the path before he answered her. "Let's not jump to conclusions, Mrs. Parker. We don't know your husband was murdered. It looks like a hit and run. Remember, it was pouring last night, and the road was slicked over."

"Shall I call your aunts?" Jason asked. "Have them meet us there?"

"No!"

He looked at her in surprise.

"I want to do this alone. I'll call them after." *After she knew for certain that Terry was gone.*

Erica started to follow him when Officer Donnelly touched her shoulder. She looked into his deep brown eyes that gave nothing away.

"What was the twenty thousand dollars for, Mrs. Parker? The money you obviously borrowed from Mr. Hartley to give to your husband?"

"It was for a gambling debt."

"A pretty big debt, I'd say. Was Mr. Parker involved in any illegal activities?"

When she hesitated, Donnelly sighed wearily. "It's best if you tell us now. We'll find it all out sooner or later."

"I only knew about this one debt," she said. "Terry never told me anything."

Donnelly made no comment, although she felt his eyes on her as she hurried after Jason.

Erica didn't remember much about the two-hour drive to the morgue or even entering the building. A kindly woman led her to a viewing window.

She swallowed a few times, then forced herself to peer into the room beyond. Only Terry's face was visible. His eyes were shut, and he looked peaceful. Thank God his beautiful face wasn't marred.

"Is that your husband, Mrs. Parker?" the woman asked.

Erica nodded, and stumbled as Jason led her away.

They went to an office where someone asked her a few questions, handed her Terry's wallet and ring, then let her go. Outside, she blinked at the sun's brilliance. She resented the leafy trees, the green grass, all oblivious to her sorrow. Her young husband was dead and nobody except her gave a damn.

When they were seated in Jason's car once again, he turned over the motor and looked at her. "Are you hungry?"

"No."

"Still, you have to eat something. We're going to a diner."

"Okay." She had no appetite, but she didn't have the strength to argue with Jason.

She drifted into sleep, vaguely aware of Jason making calls on his cell phone. Some minutes later, the car stopped, and she opened her eyes. They were in the parking lot of a diner.

"We've arrived," Jason said. "Your Aunt Betty and my father are meeting us here. She'll drive you home."

She had a moment of panic. *Where was she?*

It all came back in a flash. Terry was dead. She was a widow.

"But my car's in Montauk."

"My father's coming back with me. He'll drive your car home."

"That's kind of him."

"Isn't it?" Jason said sarcastically. "Ready?"

Erica stepped out of the car. Her legs were wobbly, and she was grateful when Jason took her hand and held it as they walked to the back door of the diner. Inside, she sank into a booth and stared at the unopened menu.

"How about a tuna fish sandwich and some coffee?" Jason asked.

She nodded. But when her order arrived, she stared at it.

"Take a bite of your sandwich," Jason said. "You'll feel better. You haven't eaten anything all day."

She looked at him blankly, then forced herself to speak. "Thanks, Jase. Thanks for going to the morgue with me. I never could have done it alone."

"Go on, eat. You're fading away to nothing." He lifted the sandwich to her mouth as if she were a child. "It looks delicious."

She bit into the sandwich. It *was* delicious, and she was hungry. She chewed and swallowed. Greedily, she took another bite.

He grinned at her. "I told you it was good."

She tried for a smile. Today, Jason was her old and caring friend.

She finished the sandwich and sipped her coffee. He'd ordered a cheese Danish, and Erica ate that, too. Suddenly, she was very tired. She could hardly move her limbs.

"Relax," Jason told her. "Your aunt and my father will be here soon."

She dozed, and awakened to the sound of familiar voices. Aunt Betty slid in beside her and held her in her arms.

"Oh, my poor darling!" Betty was crying herself, a rare occurrence. She clasped her niece to her bosom. "I'm so sorry, Erica, dear. So very, very sorry."

Erica returned her aunt's warm embrace. She had never been so happy to see her. Both sniffing, they sat with their arms around each other. Aunt Betty made an effort to regain her composure.

"Such a terrible, terrible tragedy, Erica, but you're young. You have your whole life ahead of you. I'm sure you'll fall in love again."

Erica stiffened. Even at a time like this, Aunt Betty felt compelled to assume her Pollyanna air. "Can we leave now?"

"Of course, baby," Betty babbled. "We're going home. Constance and I will look after you. We'll take care of everything. You needn't worry about a thing."

Home? Erica wondered as she followed her aunt to the parking lot. *I have no home.*

CHAPTER FIVE

The next few days ran into one another like bleeding colors. When Erica tried to sort them out later on, they remained shrouded under a haze of grief and confusion. Ensconced once again in her childhood home, she felt all will and determination slip away, and she gave herself over to her aunts' fussing and care. She allowed Aunt Constance to administer tranquilizers to help see her through "this sad and trying occasion," as her aunt put it. Erica, who hated taking even an aspirin, dutifully swallowed the little pills every four hours. Welcomed them, in fact. They dulled her senses and induced her to sleep.

She was grateful to Aunt Betty and Sherman Hartley for handling the funeral arrangements. Sherman demurred a bit when Erica said she wanted Terry buried in her family plot, but gave in immediately when he caught sight of the determined look on her face. *Good*, Erica told herself smugly. *Let that pompous ass know I'm someone to be reckoned with.* But her show of spirit was momentary, and she sank back into her mournful lethargy.

Friday, the day of the funeral, was a perfect spring day. Erica broke out in hives as they left for the funeral home, which didn't subside until she was home again. Besides Erica and her aunts, the only people who attended were Sherman and Monica

Hartley, and Jason, who had returned to Manordale with his father. At the grave site, Erica couldn't help but notice the chirping birds, the trees in new green splendor, the colorful flowers adorning some of the graves.

And the blue car.

A brand-new blue car was parked near the freshly dug grave. Seeing it, she reeled and nearly fainted. The murderer was here. At Terry's funeral.

Jason caught her, preventing her from falling. For a moment, she allowed herself the luxury of leaning against him, but it was a false comfort. She was alone even amidst family and old friends. While they cared for her, they understood nothing about her or her life with Terry. Her breath caught in a strangled sob. She missed him so.

As the sermon drew to a close, she thought about Doug Remsen, and realized he'd been hovering in the back of her mind. He was the only friend of Terry's whom she'd met, and he'd been very kind to her the day that Sean and Andy had come by on their boss's errand. Unless he happened to read about it in the newspaper or saw it on TV, he wouldn't know that Terry was dead.

Remembering her encounter with Sean and Andy made her tremble with fear and outrage. She'd made every attempt to help Terry pay off his debt, but they killed him anyway. Why? Terry was worth more to their boss alive than dead. And why hadn't they taken the check? Probably because they wouldn't have had time to cash it before the murder was discovered. Or else they didn't want the check traced to them.

But they wanted their money, didn't they? That had been the whole point.

She was baffled. She shook her head as the most recent pill Aunt Constance had given her started clouding her mind. She knew so little about Terry's nefarious activities. Maybe she'd never find out what really had happened.

The funeral was over, the casket covered with earth. Erica let her aunts lead her back to the waiting limousine.

"Erica, sweetie, let's go." Aunt Betty urged her to step into the vehicle.

She was about to obey when she felt a hand on her bare arm.

It was Monica Hartley, her rouged face streaked with tears. "Erica, I'm sorry. So very sorry."

Erica suffered herself to be engulfed by this large, voluptuous woman. Today, Monica wore an expensive beige suit and a silk flowered blouse. She reeked, as usual, of perfume. The diamonds on her fingers, ears, and neck were truly spectacular as they glittered in the sunlight.

"I know what a terrible loss this is for you, but in time, you'll smile and find life wonderful again."

Who invited her? Erica wondered. She certainly hadn't. She had always avoided Sherman's second wife, partly out of distaste, partly out of allegiance to Regina and Jason.

"You're young. You'll marry again," Monica droned on, "and this terrible tragedy will seem like a bad dream."

"Come along, Monica. Time to go." Sherman pried his wife from Erica and patted Erica's shoulder in one skilled maneuver. "Take care of yourself, my dear," he said as he led Monica away.

Erica slumped against the soft cushions of the car, too drained even to cry. Constance and Betty entered the limousine, flanking her on both sides. At least they had the good sense to remain silent.

At home, Erica went to her bedroom, undressed, and fell into a long, dreamless sleep.

When she awoke, it was Saturday afternoon. She felt clear-headed for the first time in days. Now that she'd slept off all effects of the drugs, she was filled with resentment. Terry was dead and she'd been deprived of the first depth of her grief by her aunts' everlasting desire to help and protect her. No more sedatives! She had a right to her feelings, even if they tore her apart.

But at the moment, she was not wracked with sorrow. She felt calm, if a bit weak, as though she'd just recovered from a serious illness. The copious tears she had shed the day Terry died and at the funeral had succeeded in separating her from her husband. They also helped her realize that he was gone, irrevocably and forever.

Her clock said five o'clock. She peered out the window and noted it was light out. At first, she couldn't determine if it was morning or afternoon. Afternoon, she decided. She tiptoed down the stairs, not wishing to attract her aunts' attention. She had an overpowering need to be alone. And to eat something! She was ravenous.

On her way to the kitchen, she was careful not to make a sound as she passed the family room where her aunts were conversing in low tones. She rummaged through the refrigerator, pulling out cold chicken, mayonnaise, a tomato, and bread. They must have heard her because immediately they were upon her, a false smile plastered on each wrinkled face.

"Look, our Erica is up," cooed Betty. "Fresh and rested after a pleasant sleep, I hope."

"Let me fix that for you," Constance offered, reaching for the knife in Erica's hand.

She shook her head and held on to the knife. "No thanks, I'll do it," she said too loudly. "It will give me something to do."

"Before I forget," Betty said, claiming Erica's attention, "you got two phone calls."

Her heart raced. She put down the knife. "Who called?"

"Officer Finney, for one." She gave a coy laugh. "He said he would be stopping by to ask you a few more questions. Just routine, he assured me. Such a polite man."

Erica stifled a sigh of exasperation. Aunt Betty still acted like a silly teenager whenever she had to deal with a man. *Any* man. "And the other call?"

"Someone named Doug Remsen. He said he was a friend of Terry's. He tried calling you on your cell phone, but couldn't get through."

That was because she'd turned off her phone. But how did Doug get the house number? Her pulse quickened as she figured out Terry must have given it to him. Which meant they'd spoken recently. Doug was her only link to Terry. She might never find out the truth about her husband's death, but it wouldn't be for lack of trying. She'd contact Doug immediately and make him tell her everything he knew about Terry. Since he also knew Sean and Andy, there was a good chance that Doug, too, was a gambler. But that wasn't important. What mattered now was that he could tell her whether or not he thought Sean and Andy had something to do with Terry's so-called accident.

She forced herself to remain calm. It would do no good to upset her aunts by letting them know she considered Terry's death a homicide. They had looked askance upon learning he had been killed while riding a motorcycle. But to give them credit, they had refrained from making any sarcastic comments. And had been nothing but supportive these bleak few days.

"Did Doug—Mr. Remsen—leave any message?"

"Ask me. I spoke to him," Aunt Constance said. When she had Erica's attention, she gave a smug smile and continued. "He said he'd call back this evening. Don't bother trying to call him because he's not home." She turned away to fuss with something on the counter.

In the midst of her contained excitement, Erica almost missed it. Aunt Constance was surreptitiously opening a pharmacy vial of pills. Her pills, that the doctor had prescribed over the telephone.

"You'll be wanting a cup of cocoa, I suppose," her aunt was saying. "Shall I warm it?"

Why was Aunt Constance hiding the fact that she was taking out a sedative? Erica wondered, though she pretended not to notice. It only meant she'd have to dispose of whatever drink Aunt Constance put it in. That was easier than arguing. And it had its advantages. If her aunts thought she was groggy, they wouldn't be at her to "talk out her grief" or wonder why she was so quiet.

"I'd rather have some milk," Erica said. "It's too warm today for cocoa."

Both aunts gave her a doting smile. Aunt Betty finished preparing her sandwich.

All this attention was making Erica uncomfortable. When the doorbell rang, she leaped to her feet, welcoming the excuse to leave their presence, if only temporarily.

"I'll get that," Betty offered. "You stay here and eat."

Constance put the glass of milk on the table. It had more bubbles than usual, as if it had been shaken or stirred. Erica had just taken a bite from the sandwich when Betty reappeared with Officer Finney at her heels.

"Sorry to disturb you, Mrs. Parker," he said stiffly, obviously flustered by the open scrutiny of the two older women, "but I'd like to ask you a few more questions."

"Of course. Come with me."

Erica picked up her sandwich and milk and led him to the living room. This had been the most elegant room in the house when her parents were alive. Now its brocade furniture was shabby and worn.

Her aunts followed behind, intent on joining them.

"I would like to speak with Mrs. Parker in private, if you don't mind," Officer Finney said with obvious difficulty.

"Certainly, officer," Betty simpered. "We quite understand."

Erica sighed with relief. She switched on the lamps on either end of the sofa and sat down.

Finney hesitated, then pulled over a straight-backed chair and sat facing her.

"Have you learned something new?" she asked. "I mean, about the blue car."

"Nothing really. Except that the car was either new or recently painted."

He sat on the edge of the chair, his pen and notepad in hand. "We did find out something about your husband. He spent some time in juvenile detention when he was in his teens. Did you know that?"

"No! No, I didn't."

"Seems he was mixed up with drugs. Both using and selling."

She bit her tongue to keep from speaking.

Finney waited a bit, then asked, "Do you know any of his associates? Anyone he'd been in contact with recently?"

"Not really." The only people she could lie to successfully were her aunts. "Terry only told me about his past the night he was killed."

Finney picked up on the hesitancy in her voice. "What else did he tell you?"

"That...that he was leaving me."

"Why?"

She sighed. "He said it was because of his gambling, and I believed him."

"What did you do when he left?"

"After a few minutes, I went after him."

"Why the delay?"

Again, blood rose to her face. "I wasn't dressed."

"Were you both drinking before your husband left the cottage?"

"No!" Her eyes widened in astonishment. "Did they think Terry was drunk when he died?"

"There was a good deal of liquor found in the—in your husband's system."

"That's odd," she mused. "Terry hardly ever drank."

"Maybe he was upset. About leaving you and all."

"He was upset, I'm sure of it!" Her voice shook with emotion. She recalled the tears he had shed. They were genuine, she knew. "Terry could have stopped at a bar along the way."

Finney stood abruptly. "Thank you, Mrs. Parker. You've been most helpful and cooperative, but we may have to talk to you again. I'm sorry. I know this has been painful for you."

When she stood, his dark eyes fixed on hers. "Please call us if you remember anything. A name, an address, anything at all. It could prove important."

Her heart beat faster. "Are you considering Terry's death a homicide?"

Officer Finney nodded. "We have good reason to think so. We'll know for certain very soon."

She walked him to the door, compressing her lips together so she wouldn't blurt out Doug Remsen's name. *Finney knows I'm holding something back*, she thought. *Why don't I tell him my suspicions? Who do I think I am, checking out Soprano-type goons by myself? The police are equipped to deal with people like that.* But the only words she spoke were those bidding Officer Finney a good afternoon.

She returned to the living room and finished her sandwich. Then, she carried the glass of milk into the kitchen and poured it down the drain. Just in time! Aunt Constance was coming.

This is ridiculous, Erica thought. *I'll have to tell them I don't need their little pills anymore.*

"I hope there's nothing wrong, dear," Aunt Constance said, sounding concerned.

"Nothing wrong," Erica said smoothly. "Officer Finney stopped by to tell me that they're looking for the car that hit Terry. They haven't found anything so far."

"That's a pity." Constance's voice turned rough with anger. "When they catch who did it, he should be tarred and feathered! Killing an innocent boy, then driving off like that."

She caught Erica's expression and clamped her hand over her mouth, but it was too late. "Oh, I'm so sorry, Erica, dear. Me and my big mouth."

Erica burst into tears. Aunt Betty came into the kitchen, and Erica found herself caught between her aunts, who patted and stroked her arms and back in the mistaken belief that they were helping her to feel better.

The phone rang, saving Erica from further commiseration. Betty rushed to answer it.

"It's Jason," she reported. "He wants to talk to you."

Erica took the receiver, barely concealing her disappointment. "Hello, Jason."

"Would you like me to come over? You sound kind of down."

"Thanks, Jase, but I'd rather be alone just now."

"I understand," he said, but he sounded hurt. "I only want to cheer you up."

She felt a prick of conscience. He had been a good friend these past few days, supportive and comforting the way he used to be. "Maybe next week. I'll be better company then."

Heartened, he suggested they have dinner out. "How's Monday night?"

"Monday's fine," she agreed, feeling strangely defeated.

She had just buried Terry and already demands were being placed upon her. Perhaps she should go off and be by herself. She grimaced. She had gone off impetuously in all directions, and that certainly hadn't improved her life one iota. Maybe if she hadn't run home to Manordale, then out to Montauk, Terry might still be alive.

She shuddered and pushed that thought away. No, she was better off staying where she was. For the time being, anyway.

Aunt Constance's loud voice boomed through the kitchen. "Come in here and sit a while, Erica. You shouldn't be alone."

Gritting her teeth, Erica went into the family room. She reminded herself she was grateful for her aunts' support these past few days. She would simply have to put up with their intrusive ways.

Constance patted the sofa cushion next to her.

Erica sat down as she was bidden.

Betty was crocheting in her corner chair, squinting at her work in the lamplight.

"How nice that Jason called," she cooed. When Erica made no response, she went on. "Such a nice boy. He's been wonderful to you ever since that horrible accident."

Piqued, Erica asked, "Since when do you like Jason? You used to tell me he should be spending his free time outdoors playing sports."

Undaunted, Betty answered smoothly. "Did I? I suppose we didn't accept sensitivity in boys and men too readily years ago. I think Jason's a very kind person and a good friend to you."

"Yes, he is a good friend." Erica stood. They were driving her crazy. She had to leave the room before she said something unkind.

The phone rang again. This time, Erica reached it first.

"Hello, Erica."

It was Doug, sounding warm and friendly.

"Y...yes?" She pretended not to recognize his voice. Her pulse raced. Her mouth went dry. Probably because he might know Terry's killer. Certainly not because she was glad to hear from him.

"This is Doug Remsen, Erica. I hope you remember who I am."

"Yes, you were a friend of Terry's."

"I was very sorry to hear about his death."

"How did you find out?"

There was the slightest of pauses, then, "It was in the papers and on TV."

"I see." Her words had come out harsher than she'd meant. But his hesitation had made her wonder if Doug had his own business connection to Sean, Andy, and their boss, Mr. B.

He cleared his throat. "Actually, I saw Terry Monday night. He was supposed to stop by the following evening. When he didn't, well, I got word of what happened."

So, he hadn't found out about Terry's death through the media. Erica's mind started racing. The best thing would be to get Doug to meet her so she could pump him for information. But how?

"Where did you see Terry Monday night?"

"In a bar in the city. A place where some of us often get together."

Some of us? Some gang bangers? Gamblers? "He had the money he owed. He was going to pay it back."

"I know." Doug sounded sheepish. "He told me Tuesday night when he called."

"You mean you spoke to him after he left me at Montauk?" She suddenly felt vulnerable. Exposed. What if Terry had told Doug that he'd left her? Her face grew warm with humiliation.

"Erica, Terry called to remind me to give you something he left with me. A letter."

"The letter," she echoed. Doug had the letter Terry had mentioned. "Why didn't he mail it to me? Or hand it to me before he left?"

"There are things we have to talk about, and I don't mean over the phone. Besides, there's something else. Something Terry wanted me to explain."

"He did?" This was too much. Even from the grave, Terry was confounding her, making her realize how little she knew about him.

Doug interrupted her swirling thoughts. "I'm sorry I missed his funeral."

"Thank you."

"Could I stop by your house tomorrow evening?" Doug asked. "We could talk then."

"No," she answered quickly. She didn't want Doug Remsen anywhere near her house. She didn't want her aunts finding out what kind of life Terry had led. "I think it would be best if I met you somewhere."

"Oh," he said, sounding surprised. "Where would you like to meet?"

He was glad he was letting her choose the place, although nothing came to mind. She hadn't been to a restaurant or a bar in the area for close to three years. How could she know if the same places were still in business? Then she recalled a small restaurant in the next town that served wonderful continental food. It had a small, cozy bar where they could talk undisturbed.

"I've just thought of a place. Let me check to see if it's still in business."

She reached for her cell phone, found Fiorello's Facebook page, then gave Doug the name and address of the restaurant. They arranged to meet there at eight the following evening for a drink.

She was surprisingly lighthearted when she returned to her aunts in the family room.

"Who was that?" Aunt Constance asked before Erica sat down.

"Terry's friend, Doug Remsen. I'll be meeting him tomorrow night to discuss a few matters regarding Terry's estate." She marveled at the way her words skimmed the truth, sounding totally believable.

Her aunts looked at each other in consternation. Before they could express their anxiety, Erica spoke. "I'm going out for a drive now. Just to get some air."

"But Erica," Aunt Constance protested loudly. "You can't."

"Don't worry, Aunt Constance. I didn't drink the milk. And please don't give me any more tranquilizers. As you can see, I don't need them any longer."

Her aunt's mouth fell open in surprise.

Erica was out of the room before either Constance or Betty could think of a reply.

CHAPTER SIX

Erica was on her way to the bathroom the next morning when she heard the front door open.

Puzzled, because it was only eight-thirty, she peered out the window. Aunt Betty was getting into her blue Camry. How curious. She hadn't said anything last night about having early morning plans. Where could she be off to, and in her very best suit?

At breakfast, Erica was about to ask Aunt Constance, when she remembered her aunt's disapproval regarding the very same subject last Sunday. It was wiser not to say anything that might rake up unpleasantness, she decided.

She felt more like herself for the first time in weeks. The major thrust of her grief had spent itself and she'd found temporary peace. The warm, balmy weather helped restore her basically sunny nature. Looking back, she admitted that Terry's secrets and lies had impacted their married life, making it somehow seem unreal. As if she'd been dreaming and had finally awakened.

Aunt Constance was supposed to spend the day working at a bazaar for one of her organizations, but she was reluctant to leave Erica alone. Erica urged her aunt to keep her plans, telling her repeatedly that she'd be perfectly fine, and finally, Aunt Constance left.

Erica was delighted to have the house to herself. She lolled around the entire day, reading the Sunday papers and sunning herself on the worn chaise longue she'd dragged out of the shed.

We must do something about this lawn, she thought. *And buy some new outdoor furniture. The table's all rusted, the cushions are ripping.* Then she remembered she was only staying until her birthday. She'd be happy to give her aunts whatever money they needed to fix up the house, but the details were theirs to decide.

Aunt Betty came home around six and found Erica watching the news in the family room. "How are you feeling, dear?"

"Fine, Aunt Betty. I sat outside for a while."

She squinted as she scrutinized Erica's face. "So you did. You look better with some color in your face, though next time, remember to wear sunscreen. Your nose got all red."

She then disappeared inside her room.

Aunt Constance arrived home fifteen minutes later, exhilarated with the bazaar's financial success. She bustled off into the kitchen and started preparing dinner.

"Don't bother making anything for me," Erica said. She suddenly got butterflies in her stomach at the thought of seeing Doug in two hours.

Aunt Constance gave a grim nod in response to Erica's news. She went to stand, hands on hips, at the foot of the stairs. "Elizabeth," she boomed, "are you having dinner with me?" There was no missing the irritation in her voice.

"No thanks, Connie," Aunt Betty called down. "I had a big lunch this afternoon."

"Humph!" Constance muttered. "Big lunch. Big deal."

Erica dashed upstairs to shower and dress. She knew what she was wearing, had known ever since she'd put down the phone last night. Her new flowered dress would be perfect. She'd bought it on impulse just before Terry had disappeared, and never had the occasion to wear it.

She hummed as the water cascaded over her body.

This wasn't a date, she reminded herself as she toweled herself dry. No need for extra fuss. She was meeting Doug Remsen to find out more about her dead husband's life, and to finally get the letter Terry had told her about. Doug might be kind, but he wasn't the type of man she should think about considering.

Why had those thoughts come into her head? She wasn't planning to start a new relationship any time soon. Terry had just died. Though part of her *was* angry with him for having deceived her with lies, she had cared for him deeply and completely.

She slipped into her high-heeled sandals, and returned to the bathroom to put on her makeup and blow-dry her hair. When she was done, she studied herself in the mirror. Her nose was red, but her cheeks looked rosy, and the blue-gray shadow heightened her eyes behind her glasses.

"I need a haircut," she said aloud, surprised to find her bangs were brushing against the tops of her glasses. Weeks must have passed since she'd last taken notice of her appearance.

No matter. She grinned at herself. Even to her own critical eyes, she looked fine.

Aunt Constance was clearing her dinner dishes. Her gloomy expression changed to one of astonishment when she saw her niece.

"Goodness me, Erica, you look lovely. Like you were going to a party."

Erica smiled. "I'm only going out for a drink. To discuss some business, remember?"

Her aunt's expression grew somber. "Drive carefully now. You don't want to get into an accident."

"Don't worry, Aunt Constance. I will." *Nothing bad can happen. I'm meeting Doug in a public place.* On impulse, she planted a kiss on her aunt's cheek.

Taken aback, Constance scolded her. "What about your dinner? You didn't eat anything."

"I'll eat something later." Erica sailed out the door.

It felt good getting away from the overly solicitous household and into the cool evening air, but she suddenly began to worry. How smart was it to be meeting with a total stranger who was possibly a gangster? No one knew where she was going. Doug could do away with her—she snapped her fingers—like that!

Nonsense! She brushed the possibility from her mind. Doug was going to give her Terry's letter and explain things to her. That's what he'd told her and that's what she intended to believe. Besides, she needed more information before she dared make any more assumptions.

She drove along the turnpike to the next town. It was nearly eight o'clock. The last light of day had faded into darkness. It could have been noon or midnight for all she cared. She—a person grounded in following schedules and the routines of daily life—had lost all sense of time.

The blue BMW was parked in the half-filled parking lot behind the restaurant, but there was no sign of Doug. Erica pulled in next to it and climbed out of her car. She found herself examining the front fenders. She stooped to get a closer look for possible dents, scraped paint, or any sign that it had been in a collision.

Nothing.

"Checking for damage?" Doug asked from behind her.

She rose and stumbled backward into his muscular chest.

Flustered, she turned to face him. "You scared the living daylights out of me."

He grinned. "If you're playing detective, you shouldn't be so obvious."

She was too embarrassed to think of a reply.

"I drive a blue car, but you can't believe that I ran Terry off the road." He gently took her elbow, and escorted her into the restaurant.

"Of course not. Except..." She was annoyed with herself for having been caught doing something stupid. Doug was Terry's friend. Besides he wouldn't have driven a battered car for her to see. "How did you know about the blue paint anyway?"

"The police paid me a visit and happened to mention that small detail." There was a glint of amusement in his eyes, but underneath it, she detected a flash of anger.

"I didn't send them," she said defensively.

"You didn't? Hmm. They must have found my number among Terry's papers." He studied her intently in the dim light as they waited to be seated.

The maître d', a middle-aged paunchy man, smiled as he approached them. "Two for dinner?"

"How about it, Erica? Care for some dinner? I seemed to have skipped that meal entirely."

"I guess I have, too," she admitted, wondering why her heart was fluttering like a trapped bird.

The maître d' led them through the candlelit room to a corner table. The ambience was seductive, intimate. Near the bar, a pianist was playing romantic songs on a white grand piano.

Erica bit her lip. This certainly wasn't the Fiorello's she remembered. What must Doug be thinking of her choice of restaurants?

He didn't appear to notice her embarrassment. "Seems nice enough," he said as she slid onto the well-padded banquette. He sat in the chair facing her.

Behind her enormous menu, she drew a deep breath. She felt vibrant with anticipation, as though she were about to embark on a wild adventure. *My husband's just been killed, and I'm out having dinner with another man*, she chided herself. *Only to talk about Terry*, she rebutted. And remained unchastened as she ordered a vodka martini and shrimp scampi.

"How does it feel to be a widow?" Doug asked unexpectedly.

She looked at him sharply, but there was no trace of mockery in his voice. Nor in his eyes, which she realized had been scrutinizing her since they'd met in the parking lot.

"I'm not sure," she admitted. "At first, it was a nightmare, but my aunts kept me so doped up, I only came out of it yesterday. I'm feeling better today, but I'm terribly confused. My whole life's gone haywire since those two gangsters followed me into the Sweet Shoppe." She gave him a rueful smile. "I'm back at the one place I swore I'd never return—home with my exasperating aunts."

He said nothing, but she felt his total attention, which encouraged her to go on.

"And every minute of the day, no matter what I'm doing, I think about Terry. More truthfully, I scrutinize everything I've recently learned about him—from you, the police, and Terry himself. I'm angry because he lied to me, and I'm angry at myself for having been so trusting and naive. The complete fool." She shook her head. "Was there anything real about our marriage? What did we really share besides sex?"

"Erica, don't do this to yourself. Terry loved you. I know that for a fact." Doug's suntanned hand covered hers, adding strength to his words.

She blinked furiously, but couldn't stop the tears from rolling down her cheeks. He handed her his handkerchief. She dabbed at her face without a trace of self-consciousness. When she could, she continued speaking.

"Today I took a long, objective view of our relationship. We had fun. We enjoyed being together, but we didn't have much of a marriage. I hardly knew Terry. We hadn't known each other long, and he was away a lot. All those activities he was involved in. I don't even know what they are, except I know they're as alien to me as skydiving."

"Like gambling?" His voice was soft.

"Gambling, and worse."

Their salads arrived, and they ate without speaking, but there was no awkwardness in their silence.

"I understand you're about to become a wealthy woman," Doug said, changing the tone and the subject.

She gave a wry smile. "You'd think Terry would have stayed with me for the money. He should have! Then he wouldn't have gone off in the middle of the night and gotten himself killed." This time, she managed to blink back her tears.

"Perhaps. We'll never know." He circled the rim of his water glass with his finger before going on. "Terry and I had a rather personal conversation Monday night."

"I can only hope it wasn't too personal."

"Not personal that way," he said, obviously wanting to assuage her hurt pride. "And I don't mean to give you the impression that I knew your husband all that well. Actually, it wasn't until Monday night that I realized he was all right."

"What do you mean?"

"To tell the truth, I always figured him to be a punk. Someone who'd weasel out of any deal if he thought he could get away with it. But I had him all wrong."

Their entrees arrived, and they said little except to comment on the excellence of their dishes.

A while later, as they sat leisurely over coffee and slices of Italian cheesecake, Doug said, "Terry called me as soon as he found out you were trying to raise the money." He shook his head. "He was furious when I told him Sean and Andy had frightened you half to death as well as spilling the beans about his gambling debt. I told him he was kidding himself if he thought he could keep his gambling a secret from you."

He stopped to give her a hard look. Remembering the part she'd played in keeping herself ignorant of Terry's unexplained absences, her face grew hot with a blush.

He dropped his gaze. "Anyway, Monday night, he stopped by Smithy's Bar, and we got to talking." He paused. "He told me about his childhood, about the miserable foster home he lived in until he ran away and lived on the streets."

"Lived on the streets? I never knew. I wish he had told me."

It pained her to think Terry had never told her details about his unhappy childhood. But she couldn't blame him for confiding in Doug. Here she was, doing the very same thing herself. Doug seemed to be one of those rare people who actually listened. He drew people out. Got them to reveal their most intimate thoughts and deepest secrets.

She sighed. "Terry told me he'd lived with an aunt. She died when he was eighteen."

"He lived with her for a while when he got out of juvenile detention."

"Officer Finney told me about that."

Doug shook his head. "Don't be so hard on Terry—or yourself. He didn't want you to know the worst because he was afraid it would drive you away."

She smiled sadly. "It wouldn't have made any difference to me. At least, not after I got to know him. But I suppose he couldn't have known that."

"Anyway," he sounded faintly regretful, "It's time I handed over his letter."

The plain white envelope had *Erica Parker* written in pencil. She opened it with trembling fingers. Inside were two sheets of lined paper. All four sides were covered with Terry's scrawling script.

"Go on, read it," Doug urged. He reached inside his pocket and took out a pencil-thin flashlight. "Here." He placed the flashlight on the table. "Now you can see."

There was very little in the letter she hadn't recently learned—his involvement in criminal activities when he was a minor, his gambling, and that he was leaving her because he loved her. When she'd finished, she folded the pages into the envelope, and slipped it into her pocketbook.

"There's one more thing," he said carefully. "Terry didn't want to put this in writing. He didn't want to scare you, in case it wasn't necessary. But I think it is. Very necessary, Erica."

"What more can there be?" She was weeping again. "He obviously knew he was going to leave me when he came out to Montauk. He was planning it all along."

Her sobs grew louder. Tears streamed down her face, and she took off her glasses. Without thinking, she held out her hand for Doug's handkerchief. He handed it to her. She wiped her face, then her glasses.

"Hey, you'll smear them," he warned.

"How do you know?" she asked. "You don't wear glasses."

"Right, but my sister does. She's always washing them and wiping the damn things off."

He had a sister! It was the first personal thing he'd told her about himself. It made her smile.

"This is serious, Erica," he persisted. "Terry thought there was a good chance someone—someone you know—doesn't wish you well."

"What does that mean, doesn't wish me well?"

He cleared his throat. For the first time since she'd met him, he looked uneasy. "Terry seemed to think someone might try to harm you."

"But why? Certainly not for my inheritance!" It sounded so preposterous, so absurd, she covered her mouth as soon as she spoke.

"Could be."

She gave a start. How did Doug know about her inheritance? She hadn't wondered about it earlier when he'd alluded to it, but now it raised all kinds of questions. "Who told you about that?"

He hesitated, then said, "Terry did. Monday night."

That was a lie. Terry hadn't learned about her inheritance until he came to see her at the cottage on Tuesday. But were she to point this out to Doug, he might suddenly remember that Terry told him about her inheritance on Tuesday night.

Distressed, she bit her lip. He was in control here. She'd know as much as he wanted her to know, and nothing more. She met his steady gaze and drew a deep breath. She should be terrified of him, but she wasn't. He had a calming, hypnotic effect on her.

"Erica, Terry didn't say the money was the reason you're in danger, but I believe it is."

She shuddered, suddenly frightened. "Someone tried to run me down a few days ago. And took a shot at me. He was wearing a black Darth Vader mask. I thought it was Sean or Andy."

"One of those guys caught wearing a Darth Vader mask? You have to be joking." He burst out laughing, then stopped abruptly when he caught her terrified expression.

"How do you know them so well? Do you work for Mr. B, too?" she all but shouted.

The sound of raised voices in the near-empty restaurant brought their waiter scurrying to their table. "Can I get you anything else?" he asked, obviously wishing they would leave.

Doug asked for more coffee and the check. When the man left, he turned back to Erica. "Let's say I help look after Mr. B's investments."

My God! What had she done—getting involved with a gangster as bad as the two who had frightened her? And Doug's car was blue. "Maybe you were the one who shot at me that day."

"Me?" He sounded genuinely perplexed. "Why on earth would I put on a Darth Vader mask and try to kill you?"

"I don't know. Maybe to scare me, so I'd get the money Terry owed *your* Mr. B. Or maybe..." Her eyes widened with shock as a new possibility occurred to her. "Well, Terry told you I was getting money every month. Maybe you thought..." She couldn't finish the sentence.

His lips twisted into a grimace. "You mean you thought I'd knock you off so Terry would inherit, and we could collect? Come on, Erica. There are easier ways to make people pay up."

That was true. She felt silly, even ashamed, for having entertained such a thought. "If you still want me to pay off Terry's debt, I'll do it. But you'll have to wait until I receive my inheritance. I can't ask Jason for another loan."

"We'll talk about that some other time. Right now, I want you to tell me who you think was after you the other day. Besides me, Sean, and Andy."

He grinned, and she had to stop herself from punching his arm. Instead, she tried to imagine who had been wearing the Darth Vader mask.

"I don't know," she finally said. "Probably the same person who killed Terry, since it was a blue car in both cases. I suppose the police told you about finding blue paint on the motorcycle."

"They questioned me the next day." His jaw clenched in anger. "Good thing there were five people who could swear they'd been with me all of Tuesday evening."

Were any of them women? she wondered, and felt her ears burn with embarrassment. She'd just lost her husband, and here she sat, curious over another man—a gangster, no less—who was merely showing her some kindness.

With a pang, she realized dinner was over.

Doug reached for his wallet. He handed money and the check to the waiter, who bowed obsequiously and wished them a good evening. Doug nodded perfunctorily and turned to Erica.

"I'm going out of town for a few days," he said, eyeing her carefully. "If I can do anything or if you feel you want to talk, call me at the number I gave you. I'll get the message."

"Thank you." The lot was almost empty as they exited the bar. She glanced up at his profile as he walked her to her car. It was a good profile, with strong, even features. "Why are you being so nice to me?"

He drew in breath, and started to say something, then obviously thought better of it. He took the car key from her hand and unlocked the door. "Let's say I'm doing it for Terry's sake."

She slid behind the wheel, and he leaned over to kiss her cheek. His action startled her so much, she almost missed his parting words.

"Be careful. Don't be too trusting of anyone. Especially of anyone you think you know well."

"Be careful. Don't be too trusting of anyone. Especially of anyone you think you know well."

CHAPTER SEVEN

In spite of the gray skies threatening rain, it was a happier Erica who traipsed down the stairs late Monday morning. She found Aunt Constance in the kitchen, pouring herself a cup of coffee to go with a generous piece of cake on her plate. Her mood seemed matched the weather.

"You came in late enough last night," she grumbled.

"Around eleven." Erica took the container of orange juice from the refrigerator. She forced herself to speak calmly. "You're going to have to stop sitting up for me. I'm almost twenty-five."

"And a widow already," Constance said gloomily. "We never even got to meet Terry. Or his family."

A good thing, too, Erica mused as she drank her orange juice, then busied herself with toasting an English muffin. She regained her equilibrium. Once again, she could think clearly and logically.

A residue of sadness remained, but in the deepest recesses of her heart, she wondered if she wasn't relieved that Terry was gone. Not glad that he was dead, of course, but that he was no longer part of her ongoing life. In spite of what she'd told Doug,

Terry's past mattered. His lifestyle was so different from hers, she doubted she could have stayed with him, regardless of the love they'd had for each other. He'd put her in danger, and lied. She could only imagine what other criminal activities he'd been into. The gambling was bad enough.

Reflecting back on their whirlwind courtship, she remembered how Terry had brought up the subject of marriage only days after they'd met.

"Let's do it, babe," he'd murmured as he nuzzled her neck, making her dizzy with desire. "Let's make it legal."

She'd bolted upright on her old sofa. "You mean, get married?" she asked, both stunned and flattered.

"Of course, get married," Terry said, grinning. "When two people feel the way we do, they want to keep it forever."

Now she wondered why he'd been so keen on getting married, given his chaotic life, the frequent gambling trips. And her? Blood rushed to her face, recalling how needy she'd been when Terry had entered her life. In retrospect, he was the type most girls would have an affair with, not marry.

"Did you discuss your husband's business last night?"

"Hmm?" Lost in her thoughts, Erica had missed part of her aunt's words.

"Did the fellow you saw last night help you put Terry's business affairs in order?"

"Er...yes. He gave me information I absolutely needed." The last part, at least, was true, although so far, she'd avoided considering the implications of Doug's warning.

Constance took a forkful of her cake. "Call Sherman if you need any advice. He's been wonderful to Betty and me, helping us with legal and business advice, and not charging us a cent." She sighed deeply. "I can tell you now, keeping up this house all these years hasn't been easy."

"I'm sure," Erica mumbled absentmindedly. She was not in the mood to discuss money matters.

Neither was Aunt Constance, it seemed. She finally got back to what was really on her mind. "And I don't mind telling you, I was restless all evening while you were out with a perfect stranger, God knows where."

Erica bit back the retort she was about to let fly. It was a waste of energy to lash out at her aunts each time they aired their thoughts.

Constance went on. "You're an heiress. A woman of substance. You can't just run off, helter skelter, with some man who claims he knew your husband."

"I know him, Aunt Constance," Erica said, an edge to her voice.

But Constance was gazing ruefully at her now empty plate. "I shouldn't have eaten that. Dr. Harris wants me to watch my weight and my cholesterol." Before Erica could comment, she changed subjects again. "You'll soon be rich and important, and don't you forget it."

She laughed. "Important? Come on, Aunt Constance. I'm still the same old Erica."

"Same old Erica, eh?" Constance echoed her words. Then she brightened, a smile softening her broad, creased face. "Would you do me a favor?"

"What is it?" She was leery. Aunt Constance was capable of the most outlandish requests.

"I have a doctor's appointment in the city on Wednesday. Just a routine examination. Monica Hartley offered to take me in, but to tell you the truth, she drives like a maniac. And I hate to ask Betty to take off from school again."

Her mouth pursed in unspoken anger, but Erica was too disturbed by her aunt's request to notice. A thousand times, a million perhaps, Erica had wished her aunt would vanish into thin air. But not now. Life wouldn't be the same without booming, bossy Constance. Her aunt might drive her mad, but Erica couldn't bear the thought of losing her.

"What's wrong, Aunt Constance? Is it your heart?"

Aunt Constance patted the spot above her ample bosom. "My heart's about the same it's always been. I told you," she said, sounding impatient, "it's a routine visit, nothing more."

Erica knew she'd get no more information from her. "I'd love to drive you in," she offered. "It would be my pleasure."

"You mean that?" Constance seemed surprised, then bestowed a glowing smile on her niece. "I didn't want to bother you, with Terry's death and all, but I'd rather go with you." Her voice faltered. "I've been noticing something lately I want to discuss with you. Never mind, we'll talk about it on the drive into the city."

Erica caught the determined look in her aunt's eye and kept her curiosity to herself. "A trip to Manhattan would do me good. I haven't been there in years." She sipped the last of her coffee, then stood and started clearing the table.

"Leave everything," Constance ordered. "I'll take care of it. Go and enjoy yourself."

Erica kissed her and went upstairs to get dressed—torn, as usual, between feeling affection and exasperation for her aunt.

Around noon, the rest of Erica's clothes arrived. She was touched by Mrs. Bressler's immediate response to Aunt Betty's call. Mrs. Bressler had included a sympathy note and a request that Erica stay in touch. Erica reached for her checkbook to reimburse her former landlady, then stopped. Mrs. Bressler would be hurt if she sent her money. Instead, Erica wrote her a note thanking her for all her kindness, and made a mental note to send her a gift later on in the week.

She laid out her clothes on the bed and grimaced. Dull, dull, dull. Everything—blouses, skirts, pants, and sweaters—were shapeless and lacking in style. She'd never realized what a penchant she had for drab colors that did nothing for her. Aunt Betty was right. A woman's wardrobe was a reflection of who she was and deserved considerable attention.

"It's time for a change," she declared aloud. "I need sexy, stylish clothing in colors with pizzazz."

She spun herself around until she fell, dizzy and laughing, onto her bed. "And I refuse to think about anything unpleasant for the rest of the day."

She decided to spend the afternoon in town, shopping in the new boutiques on Main Street. They would have just the kind of clothes she was looking for. Hopefully, she'd find something for tonight when she went out for dinner with Jason. She didn't want to wear the flowered dress she'd worn last night with Doug.

Doug. While she enjoyed basking in the rosy segments of their brief time together, now she pushed him quite deliberately from her thoughts. Doug was a gangster. The strong-arm man of his mysterious Mr. B. Sure, he was handsome and easy to talk to, but his life was the underworld—crime, extortion, and worse. Hadn't she learned her lesson?

She shuddered to imagine what evil deeds Doug might have committed, but they weren't her concern. She and Doug had no connection. Dinner last night had been an act of kindness on his part. She sighed as she drove through the development. Most likely, she'd never see Doug Remsen again.

The few blocks that made up the little town were bustling with traffic and pedestrians. Every parking spot on the street was taken. Business must be booming in Manordale, she thought as she turned into the municipal lot a few blocks from a boutique called Lulu's. The skies, which had been threatening rain all day, now opened up. Drops fell on her face. She wished she'd thought to bring along an umbrella. Or had worn her raincoat as

Aunt Constance had called after her to do. But since when did she listen to her aunt, no matter how practical her suggestions might be?

In spite of the shower, she enjoyed strolling down Main Street, delighting in the red, white, and yellow tulips blooming around the curbside trees. And the shops themselves seemed to have been given a recent facelift. Some municipal committee or bigwig was certainly making an effort to beautify the town.

She crossed the street and glanced at the three-story building that housed Sherman's office. Thank goodness she didn't have to go there today. But she'd call tomorrow and make an appointment to see him very soon. It was time she became knowledgeable about her holdings and investments.

When she was a block from Lulu's, she found herself in front of a beauty salon. She stopped and fingered the ends of her hair, which now reached down the back of her neck. She definitely needed a cut.

On impulse, she stepped inside. A small, slender man wearing jeans, cowboy boots, and a wildly colorful shirt was snipping away at a customer's hair. When he saw her, he put down the shears, and went to stand behind the counter.

"Howdy, miss. I'm Jack, the owner of this here spread," he said, grinning broadly. "How can I help you?"

"I need a haircut."

He eyed her professionally. "Indeed, you do."

Jack explained that his receptionist and another operator were out sick, but he would be downright happy to style her hair if she could wait just a tick, as he had to run to the bank as soon as he finished with this customer.

She agreed to wait. She leafed through a magazine, stared at the stark-white stucco walls, and wished she could throw something at the stereo system blasting hard rock music into her ears.

I must call Aunt Constance, she suddenly remembered, *and tell her I won't be having dinner at home.* She reached inside her pocketbook for her phone.

"Where are you, in some bar?" Aunt Constance demanded the minute she heard Erica's voice.

"Of course not. I'm waiting to have my hair cut."

"That's nice," Aunt Constance said before Erica could explain why she was calling. "I just got off the phone with Jason. He'll pick you up at seven."

"Too bad," Erica said. "I was hoping he'd forgotten."

"Erica!" Aunt Constance sounded shocked. "He's your good friend."

"Of course, he is," she said contritely. "It's just...oh, never mind." If she said she wasn't in the mood to go out for dinner so soon after Terry's death, her aunt would only remind her that she'd been out the night before. "'Bye. I'll be home around five."

She sat down again, not fully understanding why she was now reluctant to see Jason that evening. Ever since Terry's death, he'd been thoughtful and understanding. Still, something bothered her, something she couldn't put into words or explain, even to herself.

Ten minutes later, Jack left for the bank, promising to be back pronto. Time passed slowly. She was about to leave when he returned, apologizing profusely.

The results were well worth the wait. Jack was a genius. His styling gave Erica a knowing, gamin look. Each hair fell perfectly into place. She smiled at herself in the mirror and cheerfully paid the exorbitant bill.

Outside on the street, she found herself looking in store windows to catch a glance of her new look. She startled when someone called her name.

"Hello," she said to the tall, balding man who appeared to be her aunts' age. Was he a neighbor? He looked somewhat familiar, but she didn't know from where.

The man laughed. "You don't recognize me. Ron Jennings. I'm the principal of the school where your Aunt Betty teaches."

"Of course. Nice to see you, Mr. Jennings," she said, wondering how he recognized her after all these years.

"I heard you were back in town."

Aunt Betty must have mentioned it. "Just for a visit."

"I was sorry to hear about your husband's accident. My condolences."

"Thank you." She turned to continue on her way. She didn't want talk about Terry.

Mr. Jennings got her message. "It was lovely running into you, Erica. Be well."

Shopping in Lulu's proved to be the perfect diversion she'd needed. The boutique was larger than she'd first realized, and carried everything from shorts to gowns. The ideal place to start her new wardrobe.

She darted from rack to rack, halting whenever an item caught her eye. With a pang, she realized she hadn't enjoyed shopping since her mother's death. After that, buying clothes with Aunt Betty had turned into a chore. Now she felt the excitement she used to when she'd accompany her mother on one of her rare shopping binges.

The thin, gray-haired woman in the shop, who introduced herself as Martha, met Erica's eagerness with an indulgent smile. "Shall with start with clothes for work?" she asked. "Do you wear suits or less formal attire?"

This inspired a burst of laughter from Erica. "I'm in between jobs," she explained so that Martha wouldn't think she was laughing at her. "In between lifestyles, you might say."

"In that case, let's look at sportswear," was the suggestion.

Erica nodded. It seemed as good a place as any to start. She dove into the experience and lost all sense of time, trying on everything that appealed to her, no matter how outlandish, how faddish, how expensive. Martha proved to be an experienced lady-in-waiting, making gentle suggestions of what went well together, what suited Erica best. Best of all, she carried away Erica's rejects without a comment.

Finally, she decided on three pairs of capris, a jeans jacket, several tunics and tops, a colorful peasant skirt, a bathing suit, and two shorts outfits.

"It's five-thirty," she overheard Martha telling another saleswoman when asked the time.

Erica gave a start. It was later than she'd imagined. If she hoped to find something to wear this evening, she'd better concentrate on that and fast.

She picked out a long navy dress with large chartreuse flowers and a khaki pants outfit. Back in the dressing room, she thought about the evening that lay before her and grimaced. How could she have forgotten? Dinner with Jason meant eating a hamburger in some diner while he whined about his unhappy life or—to be fair—commiserated with her about Terry's death.

The point was, she didn't want to spend the evening with Jason. She was going out of a sense of duty. Was that what her life was to be about from now on, duty and obligations? Seeing people she had no desire to see so as not to hurt their feelings, wound their pride? Her life was reverting to how things had been when she'd left Manordale three years ago. It was *why* she'd left Manordale, and here she was again.

Her good mood plummeted to something close to despair. Automatically, she tried on the dress. She took no joy in seeing that it fit perfectly, and put on the khaki outfit. She was about to slip out of it when Martha peered in.

"How lovely! It suits you, my dear. It will go perfectly with the khaki and yellow silk blouse you chose earlier."

"I suppose," Erica said dully.

"If you prefer something more cheerful, try on the navy dress."

"I did."

The saleswoman frowned, clearly puzzled by the change in Erica's demeanor. "If you're undecided, why don't you come back tomorrow? We're closing now anyway."

"No, I'll take this." She fingered the lapel of the jacket she had on. One outfit was as good as another.

She used her credit card to pay for her purchases, and was shocked at the cost. She had spent more money that afternoon than she usually did in a month. *Forget it*, she chided herself. *Money is no longer a concern*. But she grew restless when she noticed the time. It was past six o'clock.

The sky was dark with clouds, although the rain had stopped, leaving the sidewalk wet and riddled with puddles. Main Street bustled with activity as working people and late shoppers headed for home. Cars, their headlights gleaming, filled the streets.

She heaved her heavy shopping bags, one in each hand, and hurried off in the direction of her car. As she approached the corner of Main and Second, the light turned red. Damn! Just her luck.

What a time to be running late! She'd barely have enough time to shower and dress. And Aunt Betty was sure to insist on scrutinizing every item of clothing that she'd bought.

Erica teetered on the edge of the curb. Six or seven people joined her in her wait to cross the street. She tapped her foot impatiently at the Second Street traffic zipping by. She sighed. Such a long light.

A hand pressed hard against her back. Or was it two? All she knew was that, one minute, she was waiting restlessly to cross, and the next, she was sprawled in the street, dreading the oncoming car that would hit her any second. Foolishly, she noticed one package had landed safely beside a tree at the curb.

Angry brakes skidded to a stop, the car only inches from her face. *Her face.* She shuddered to think what might have happened as strong arms lifted her from where she lay. Her knees were so weak, she couldn't stand alone. Her glasses had miraculously remained unbroken.

"Is she all right?" different voices asked.

"Are you all right?" the kindly man attached to the arms holding her asked.

"I think so." It took great effort to get the words out. Her heart was still pounding, her knees and palms sore and scraped. Her right cheek was bleeding.

"What the hell's the matter with you?" The driver strode over to where Erica stood, supported by her rescuer on one side, a middle-aged woman on the other. "In a real big hurry or are you all tanked up?"

"Are you crazy?" she managed to sputter in indignation. "I'm not drunk. I was waiting for the light to change. Somebody pushed me."

She looked around. A small crowd was milling about. Someone had been thoughtful enough to retrieve her packages for her.

"Nobody pushed you, dearie," a shocked woman's voice came from behind. "What a terrible thing to say."

"I was standing next to her," Erica's rescuer told the driver. "She must have slipped off the edge of the curb."

"That's right," the woman still holding Erica's arm agreed. "It's very slippery from the rain. And she was standing at the very edge. It was an accident."

The word "accident" echoed through the crowd.

Erica was growing sick of that word. Lately, there were too damn many accidents in her life. She was grateful when people started moving on. In their preoccupation with averted catastrophe, they seemed to have forgotten her. Horns blared, urging the car that had almost hit Erica to move.

Mollified, the driver patted Erica's arm and returned to his vehicle.

Only the man who had saved her hovered close by. "Can you make it home or would you like me to drive you?"

Erica was touched by his kindness, but she wanted to put the whole incident behind her. "I'm all right. My car's in the municipal lot." She pointed.

"I'll walk you there."

She demurred, claiming it wasn't necessary, that he'd done enough, but he ignored her protestations. She was grateful that he had. She discovered she was still shaky. She drove home slowly and cautiously, wondering what would befall her next.

Should she call the police? Did someone push her? Now she wasn't sure. After all, people had been crowding around her. She could have been shoved by accident.

Accident. There was that word again. The word she was growing to detest.

"You look absolutely stunning tonight," Jason told her, grinning across the restaurant table. "And your hair is terribly chic."

"New haircut, new dress," was Erica's flippant answer. She forced herself to smile.

She was tired, drained by her ordeal, and aching from her fall. At the moment, she regretted she hadn't listened to Aunt Constance and called the evening off. But since she'd made light of the incident, claiming she'd merely slipped and scraped her face, she didn't want to spend the evening at home, forced to suffer her aunts' ministrations. Her only concession to her jangled nerves had been to call Jason and ask him to come for her at eight instead of seven.

To get her mind off herself, she glanced around the exquisitely decorated Indian restaurant. She took in the painted tapestries and intricate wooden screens, let herself be soothed by the soft sitar music playing in the background.

"A new Erica," he said appreciatively. "I don't remember you ever looking this lovely." He had commented earlier on her bruised cheek, and had accepted her explanation of how she had fallen.

"Thank you, but stop that, Jason," she lightly reprimanded him to hide her discomfort. "It's me, remember? You've never noticed how I looked all these years, and I much prefer it that way."

"I should have paid more attention. Now I know what I've been missing."

She frowned. Why was he acting this way? True, her hair looked better than it ever had, and her new clothes gave her a stylish, up-to-the-minute kind of elegance. Yet, Jason was her childhood friend, not some date coming on to her.

In fact, if anyone's appearance was startling this evening, it was his. He had shaven off his beard, and was wearing brown slacks with a subdued print shirt under a well-cut, beige sports jacket. She was surprised he owned a sports jacket. It was the first time she'd ever seen him in something other than jeans.

She said nothing, and was glad their waiter was serving their samosas. The truth was, ever since they'd returned to

Manordale, Jason had been acting as attentive as a—as a beau. She laughed out loud as the old-fashioned word crossed her mind.

"What's so funny?" he asked, always sensitive to ridicule. "Can't an old friend see you in a different light?"

"I suppose," she answered cautiously. Then, to change the subject, she asked, "How long are you planning to stay in Manordale? It must be pretty dull for a vagabond like you."

He smiled. "I'm thinking of staying. Settling down and getting a decent job."

"Really?" She made no attempt to hide her astonishment. "I thought you considered Manordale the most boring spot on earth."

He laughed, embarrassed. "I'm starting to look at things differently, Erica. Manordale's as good a place as any. It's forty minutes from Manhattan and, hell, why not put Dad's connections to work and come up with a cushy job?"

"And live with him and Monica?" she asked, incredulous, remembering the history of bad feelings between Jason and Sherman. And would he have the nerve to stay in Monica's house after all the scathing things he'd said about her, sometimes to her face? But that was Jason all over. Anything that made life easier was the way to go.

"Don't be ridiculous," he replied indignantly. "I plan to get my own place soon enough. Maybe one of those apartments they're putting up near the mall. But Dad and Monica are all right. In fact, they've been pretty damn nice to me lately."

She gave him a scornful look. "Going respectable, are you? It sounds like you're doing everything you swore you'd never do, or don't you remember?"

"Well, we all have to grow up some time." He reached over to cover her hand with his.

She delicately pulled her hand away, ignored his meaningful smile, and concentrated on her food.

Her discomfort grew as the dinner progressed. He was acting out of character. Tonight, he seemed to be adopting his father's unctuous manner. He appeared intent on impressing her as a man might impress the woman he adored.

But why, she wondered again? In all the years she had known him, Jason had never found her especially attractive. He had never gone for petite blonde girls who wore glasses. He preferred them tall and buxom, with long, flowing brunette hair. So, why this sudden turnabout? Why was he turning this dinner into a date?

He asked her question after question. What did she plan to do after she received her money? Where would she live? Did she think she'd be receptive to another relationship soon?

During the main course of curried chicken and vegetables, and later over coffee, Erica hedged each question. She had no idea how she'd be spending the rest of her life or how she felt about getting involved with another man, but she certainly didn't want to share her bewilderment with Jason. They soon ran out of things to talk about. She sighed with relief when he finally asked for the check.

"How about a ride down to the beach?" he suggested as they walked toward his car. The wind was blowing, and she shivered inside her trench coat.

"In this weather? It's too cold." All she could think of was getting home and going to sleep.

"It's only fifteen minutes from here. We could just drive by and see if it's changed since we were kids." He started up the motor.

"I'm sure it hasn't. Look, Jason," she began, choosing her words carefully, "I'd rather go straight home, if you don't mind. It's only been a few days since Terry's funeral and—"

"Sure," was his quick retort. "But it was perfectly all right for you to run out to dinner last night with your new boyfriend."

How do you know? she felt like screaming. *And what business is it of yours?* But she forced herself to remain silent. It hadn't been a date. She wasn't up to a quarrel, and it was just possible Jason was truly concerned about her welfare. He did have her best interests at heart when they were younger. And as for last night, maybe one of her aunts might have mentioned it to him when he'd called.

The silence in the car was as thick as Hollandaise sauce. She knew he was sulking. He always sulked when he didn't get what he wanted, which was why she used to let him win at games when they were little, do almost anything to put him in a better mood. They were older now, she told herself. She wasn't going to let him get his way by sulking any longer.

Still, as they turned into her development, she found herself responding to old patterns.

"I'm sorry, Jason. Terry died less than a week ago and I'm still not myself. We can go to the beach some other time."

"Forget it, Erica. I shouldn't have insisted," he said magnanimously now that she'd apologized. His face lost its clenched hardness and she knew he was finished brooding. He went on, excitement in his voice. "We'll go out on my father's new boat just as soon as it gets warm enough. You'll love it, Erica! I just know you will."

He parked in front of her house.

She hardly noticed the car pulling out of the driveway, the familiar figure entering the house. She was too busy shuddering at the image of being trapped aboard a boat with the three Hartleys. Of Sherman running the boat aground as Monica pranced around in too-tight shorts offering drinks.

"I didn't know your father had a—"

Jason's arms wrapped around her. His lips pressed against her mouth. Despite her shock and outrage, it registered somewhere in her brain that his kiss was devoid of any passion. She jabbed her elbows and shoved him away.

"Jason! What the hell are you doing?"

"Sorry, Erica, I got carried away." But his lips belied his words. They were curled in a triumphant smile.

"Keep away from me!" she shouted, slamming the door behind her. She raced up the walk, searching furiously in her pocketbook for her key.

She found it just as Aunt Betty opened the door. "Have a good time, dear?"

She sounded breathless. She still wore her leather jacket.

"Not especially," Erica grumbled, wondering where Aunt Betty had been. And with whom.

Aunt Constance came into the hall in time to hear their exchange. "That's too bad," she boomed. She stared pointedly at Aunt Betty. "But you had the time of your life, didn't you, Elizabeth?"

To Erica's amazement, her birdlike aunt became as flustered as a child caught in a lie. "I...I," she sputtered, then hurried upstairs to her room.

Aunt Constance placed a hand on Erica's shoulder, who was just as eager as Aunt Betty to reach the privacy of her own bedroom. "Monica was just telling me today that Jason's finally settling down," she told her unwilling listener. "And he and Sherman are getting along. Imagine that, after all these years." She shook her head, a meaningful look in her eye. "I suppose he'll soon be looking for a wife."

"Well, he sure won't find one here," Erica said firmly. "Good night, Aunt Constance. I'm going to sleep."

Erica awoke the next morning with the clear understanding she had to get away from Manordale, her aunts, and the Hartleys, if only for the day.

She decided to call Lindy Jamison, a good friend from her college days. Lindy's mother mentioned she was married, the mother of an infant girl, and living in Connecticut now. Erica was thrilled at the idea of seeing her old friend that very afternoon. She jotted down instructions to her house and promised to be there in less than two hours.

She left a note for Aunt Constance, then suddenly thought of Sherman Hartley, and frowned. She needed to arrange a meeting with him and get a complete list of her holdings. Miss Fitzroy told Erica that she was indeed very fortunate because Mr. Hartley's ten o'clock appointment on Friday had just canceled. Erica expressed appreciation she didn't feel, then raced out of the house before Aunt Constance woke up.

It was a cool, end-of-April day, perfect for a short car trip that held none of the tension and anxiety of her more recent treks.

Lindy looked the same—large, sensible, and capable of taking on the world—although now all her attention was focused on her crawling nine-month-old, as she cooed over every movement and sound the baby made.

Ordinarily, such a scene would have bored Erica to yawns, but in the midst of her own tragedy and upheaval, she took delight in the simple domesticity of it all. She lay back in Lindy's one comfortable lounge chair and let her friend extol the joys of marriage, motherhood, and owning a home. Erica smiled and nodded without offering any information about her own life, other than that she'd been living upstate for three years.

"I'm sure you'll settle down one day," Lindy finished, a trifle superior because she obviously assumed Erica was still single.

"I'd like that," she admitted. "It all seems so very peaceful."

"Peaceful?" Lindy was puzzled and a bit offended. "Taking care of a baby and a large house is far from peaceful. You never have one moment to yourself."

Erica smiled to herself as her friend enumerated all of her responsibilities and chores. Would her own life ever again be mundane and routine after the last two weeks she'd been through? She certainly hoped so.

At three-thirty, feeling calm and restored, Erica started for home. She paid close attention to the several blue cars that she passed on the road. Maybe one day, she mused, she'd marry again like her friend. Perhaps she'd even have children.

But not for a very long time.

CHAPTER EIGHT

As much as Erica had enjoyed the drive to Connecticut, the trip into Manhattan the following morning proved to be a harrowing experience. Constance was a most anxious passenger. She jerked and started at passing vehicles as though fearing for her life. Erica didn't remember her aunt being this nervous in a car. Maybe she'd been in a recent accident. The thought reminded Erica of the unpleasant incident on the drive to Montauk. Thank goodness it hadn't made her nervous about driving.

They encountered road work and slowdowns every few miles. Finally, she sped through the Midtown Tunnel and into Manhattan. She headed westbound, crossing a few avenues, until Constance told her to pull into a garage a block from her doctor's office.

Erica stepped out of the Honda, happy to leave the car to the garage attendant. "We'll be an hour or two," she told him.

"More like three hours," Constance advised.

"Three hours?" she asked, surprised.

Aunt Constance gave an emphatic nod. They crossed the street and entered the brick corner building.

"Just you watch," she told Erica as she led the way through the lobby to Dr. Harris's ground floor office. "There'll be a dozen people in the waiting room. You'll have plenty of time to do some shopping if you'd like. I can call you when I'm done."

"Well, all right," Erica said reluctantly, "but I'd rather stay and keep you company." She still wasn't convinced the visit was routine, although Aunt Constance kept insisting it was.

In the office, they waited at the reception area for someone to take her name.

"I'm sorry, Mrs. Harding," a middle-aged nurse told Aunt Constance, "but the doctor is running behind schedule. We're backed up about forty-five minutes."

Constance eyed the eight people already seated. "She means an hour and a half," she boomed, ignoring the dirty look the nurse sent her way. She settled her large body into a padded vinyl seat. "Go on, Erica. No need to stay here. I've brought a book to read."

Erica hesitated. Obviously, her aunt wanted her to leave. She wasn't sure if that was because Aunt Constance was afraid she'd be bored or because she didn't want Erica to speak to the doctor. Perhaps she *should* speak to Dr. Harris.

Erica opened her mouth to say she'd stay, then realized she'd be interfering, which she hated when Constance did it to her. Her aunt had a right to privacy.

"Fine. I'll come back at twelve-thirty."

She took her aunt's suggestion, strolled over to Fifth Avenue, and stopped at Saks. She browsed and tried on clothes at her leisure. She was pleased to discover she was developing a sense of what looked good on her. She bought a blouse and a pair of sandals.

Delighted with her purchases, she returned to the doctor's office, hoping Aunt Constance was finished and they could go someplace for lunch.

"Still here," Aunt Constance said cheerfully, an I-told-you-so note in her voice. She was sitting in the same chair she had claimed hours earlier. The surrounding seats were filled with a new set of waiting patients. "You must be hungry, Erica."

"A little," she admitted.

"There's a nice coffee shop around the corner. Go and have lunch. Please bring me back a turkey sandwich and a cup of tea."

The crowded coffee shop was manned by a harried but experienced waitstaff. After a brief wait, Erica was led to the inner room and seated at a small table against the wall. Her waitress took her order and returned a minute later with a smile, a cup of coffee, and the promise that Erica's tuna fish sandwich would be arriving momentarily.

Erica believed her. No one could touch a Manhattan waitress when it came to speedy service.

Having nothing else to do, she glanced around the coffee shop to observe her fellow diners. She amused herself by picking out the businessmen and women on their lunch break, the shoppers, the occasional tourist. Her gaze wandered across the narrow room to the far corner, and stopped at the sight of a familiar masculine head set above broad shoulders in a tan jacket.

She blinked, blinked again, then told herself she must be wrong.

But she wasn't. There sat Doug, not twenty feet away. She gasped, causing the young couple at the next table to stare at her in consternation. She watched him toss back his head as he laughed. He was talking to a small, weasel-faced man who wasn't laughing. A minute later, Doug wasn't, either.

"Doug!" she called, heedless of the young couple gaping at her. Her voice barely rose above the lunch hour roar. "Doug," she tried again, before caution stopped her.

What on earth was she doing? Who knew what business he was transacting with that ratty-looking fellow?

Too late. Doug turned to glare at her. Even from that distance, there was no mistaking the blazing anger in his eyes.

Unfortunately, she'd caught the waitress's eye as well. She came rushing over. "Can I getcha something?"

Erica shook her head, and the waitress took off in a huff. She sipped her coffee as she glanced furtively in Doug's direction.

His scowling companion got up and left.

Doug scribbled something on a napkin. Then he walked toward her table. Her lips formed a smile, until she noticed his face was still set in grim lines and he had no intention of stopping. He merely flicked his wrist and deposited the crumpled napkin next to her mug.

Before she could retrieve it, however, the waitress came and plunked down Erica's sandwich. She scooped up the crumpled napkin and mumbled something about bringing more napkins.

Erica held out her hand. "Can I please have that?"

The waitress gave her a strange look. "Sure, honey. Whatever you say." She dropped the crumpled napkin on the table and left.

Erica's fingers were trembling as she smoothed open the napkin. "You don't know me," was what he had written.

You don't know me? She could have screamed with frustration. Was that all he had to say to her after their lovely dinner Sunday night? She eyed her sandwich with distaste. Doug's reproach had taken away her appetite. And he'd looked so handsome, too, striding toward her in his tan cashmere jacket.

She shouldn't have called out like that. It had been a stupid thing to do.

And it would be stupid to skip lunch.

She forced herself to eat. She asked for more coffee and wondered why Doug didn't want Weasel Face to know they knew one another. Her heart started to pound as all sorts of possibilities flooded her mind. No doubt, Weasel Face was a criminal. Had he known Terry? Did he work for the person Terry inferred might want to harm her?

In her preoccupation, she left the coffee shop without Constance's lunch, and only remembered it as she was about to enter the doctor's office. She returned to the coffee shop, more alarmed with every step she took. Seeing Doug with Weasel Face reminded her Doug's boss was a loan shark, and probably expected her to pay off Terry's debt. Maybe Doug had been wrong when he'd told her not to concern herself with the money Terry owed. Maybe they'd come after her now!

No. She refused to paralyze herself with lurid speculations and maybes. She took deep breaths and managed to calm herself as she walked back to the doctor's office.

A nurse, one she hadn't seen before, told her Mrs. Harding was in with the doctor. Erica sat down to wait.

Although she'd succeeded in quelling her apprehensions, she couldn't stop herself from thinking about Doug. He had been more than kind to her. He'd told her he was going out of town. Now, she wondered if he'd actually gone, or if he'd only said that so she wouldn't bother him.

Then why did he tell her to call if she needed him?

She sighed with exasperation. It was silly to try to figure out Doug's intentions when she knew nothing about him, nothing about his life. She was making the same mistake all over again—getting emotionally interested with a man as elusive and as unsuitable as Terry. A man who consorted with criminals, even if he wasn't one himself.

Most likely, his show of compassionate concern Sunday evening had nothing to do with his regard for her as a woman. Undoubtedly, Doug took plenty of women to dinner. Slept with plenty of them, too. This last thought was surprisingly painful, and she wasn't sure why. Erica forced her mind back to her aunt's state of health. But a minute later, she was thinking about Doug again.

When Constance finally came out, Erica asked her how everything had gone.

"Fine, just fine," Constance boomed. "Dr. Harris gave me a new prescription to fill. For angina."

Erica was relieved. It was only a checkup, after all.

As they walked to the garage, Aunt Constance was unusually silent. A thought that had been niggling at Erica's mind suddenly pushed itself front and center. All the time she'd been back in Manordale, she now realized, Aunt Constance had never once driven her car. Any car. Whenever she went out, someone came and picked her up.

"I'm curious, Aunt Constance. Why didn't you drive in today? Is there something wrong with your car?"

"Car?" Constance echoed, as if she'd never heard the word before. "I...I haven't had a car for quite some time now."

She stared at her aunt. Constance avoided Erica's eyes. Her face seemed a little redder than usual. But she could have sworn she'd seen Constance's car parked in its usual place when she'd driven down from Upstate.

Before she could pursue this, the attendant brought the Honda to a roaring standstill.

As soon as they were inside the car, Constance said, "Erica, there's something I must discuss with you."

She pulled out of the garage and headed for the Midtown Tunnel. She was so taken aback by her aunt's tone and statement, she put aside her concern regarding Constance's driving for the moment. She had never used this tone of voice with her. Only with Aunt Betty, and it meant she wanted to discuss a sensitive issue of vital importance.

"What is it, Aunt Constance?"

Her aunt cleared her throat. "I feel awkward broaching this subject with you, because it concerns your Aunt Betty."

Erica waited.

A minute later, Constance continued. "I needn't tell you this is strictly between you and me."

"Of course."

"I'm only telling you because it's been weighing on my mind, and frankly, I don't know what to do." Half-apologizing, she added, "You're a grown woman now, Erica, and a widow, to b oot."

"Yes, Aunt Constance." She contained her impatience as she approached the entrance to the tunnel. Something was bothering her aunt, and prodding her would only add to her upset.

"I don't know how to put it, but Betty's been going out at night."

Relieved, Erica laughed. "And why shouldn't she? She has plenty of friends to visit. Or maybe she goes shopping."

"She says she has all these meetings to attend because she's on some committee."

"Well, maybe she is." They were entering the tunnel now. The sudden darkness gave Erica a spooky feeling, which vanished as soon as she saw the lights on both sides.

"She isn't on any committee! Her chairman, Dr. Bryce, called one evening and asked to speak to Betty. He sounded surprised when I told him about the committee meeting. Clearly, those so-called meetings have nothing to do with school." Constance let out a sigh. "For a week or two, whenever the phone rang, she rushed to answer it. The few times I picked up, the caller hung up as soon as I said hello. This past week, she's been using her cell phone more often, and those calls have stopped."

"Hmmm," Erica mused, not sure what to make of what her aunt was telling her.

"She's taken to disappearing on Sundays, Erica. For the entire day. You must have noticed."

"I admit, I haven't. When did all this start?"

"A few weeks ago. I didn't want to bother you with all the trouble you've been through, but I had to get it off my chest and tell you today."

"Why don't you ask Aunt Betty what's going on?"

Constance snorted. "That Elizabeth is a stubborn woman. I did ask her, and she denied everything. Even about going out late at night and coming in at all hours. Oops." She covered her mouth with her hand. "I wasn't going to mention that part. But you can see how it has me worried."

"I don't blame you for worrying, Aunt Constance. That's not at all like her." She was puzzled. Aunt Betty wasn't secretive by nature. "I don't know what to say. I didn't realize..." She stopped as she remembered Aunt Betty coming home only minutes before she had on Monday night.

"Ah-ha! You saw it for yourself! Now the question is, what should we do about it?"

Erica blinked as they drove out of the tunnel and into bright sunlight. "What can we do?" she asked, trying to keep the worry out of her voice. "After all, Aunt Betty is a grown woman. She has a right to her own life."

"I suppose so, Erica, but it's all very strange just the same." Constance paused to think. "Betty keeps telling me to leave you be and let you handle your own life. Maybe now, I'm doing the same thing to her, at least in my mind." She hesitated, then added, "Only, I'm concerned for good reason. She hasn't always acted wisely in the past."

"What do you mean?"

But Constance, a hand propped under her chin, didn't answer. In minutes, the relief of having shared her burden along with the lull of the moving car had put her to sleep.

Now Erica had something else to worry about. She remembered what Doug had told her—that somebody close to her might try to harm her. But not Aunt Betty! She loved her. Besides, she was harmless. Aunt Betty wouldn't hurt a fly.

There was no doubt about it. Aunt Betty wasn't herself. No animated chirping emerged during dinner that evening. She ate sparingly, and kept her eyes downcast. A few times, Erica noticed, she was on the verge of speaking, but clamped her lips shut instead.

Aunt Constance, on the other hand, appeared to be in good spirits. She chatted on about the trip to the city and the upcoming antiques bazaar sponsored by one of her organizations. She seemed oblivious to Betty's withdrawal. But the second time Betty failed to answer her question and say whether or not she'd be stopping at the cleaners tomorrow, Constance pounced.

"I see it's no use talking to you, Elizabeth, dear. You have more important things on your mind."

Betty turned crimson and mumbled an apology.

Erica was astounded by her aunt's guilt-stricken response. Come to think of it, Aunt Betty had been acting almost furtive these past few days. Could it have anything to do with Erica and the crude attempts on her life?

No. Of course not! Aunt Betty, Erica decided, was simply having difficulties of her own. Difficulties which she obviously didn't care to discuss with Aunt Constance.

An uncomfortable silence descended over the rest of the meal. With a grunt, Constance heaved her heavy body from her chair and started clearing the table. As usual, she refused Erica's offer to help.

Erica headed for the stairs, glad to escape the tense atmosphere.

But escape was not to be. Aunt Betty's claw-like hand gripped her arm. She steered Erica down the hall and into the darkened living room.

"What did the doctor say?" she whispered.

Erica wondered at her wide-eyed stare, the urgency in her voice. She knew Aunt Constance couldn't hear them. She was running water and rattling dishes at the other end of the house.

"I didn't get to speak to Dr. Harris. He gave her a new prescription, though."

"Oh, my God!" Betty clutched her scrawny chest. "Her heart condition! It must be worse."

Erica's own heart started racing. For all her fluttering and chirping, Aunt Betty was a sensible woman. It wasn't like her to make a situation seem graver than it was. Could Aunt Constance be sicker than she'd let on? Had her heart condition grown worse? She'd seemed the same as she'd always been—running the house, doing the cooking, straightening up. She didn't complain of pain or dizziness, at least not to Erica. But that didn't mean very much. She was beginning to realize both her aunts had worries of their own, worries they did their utmost to keep to themselves.

Still, she refused to let her imagination run wild. "Aunt Constance says she has angina, nothing else."

"Angina." Betty sank onto the couch. "If only that were all. Then I wouldn't hesitate to—"

"Erica, honey! Are you sure you don't want some cake before I put it away? You didn't eat much of a dinner."

Erica and Betty stared out at the hall as Constance's heavy footsteps sounded closer.

"So, there you are!" she boomed triumphantly, as though finding them together in that rarely used room confirmed her worst suspicions. "Just what I expected. The two of you whispering behind my back." She glared at Betty. "And just what nonsense are you saying about me?"

"Don't be silly, Connie," Betty said, her voice shaky. "Erica and I were merely talking—"

"Or are you after a handful of Erica's inheritance? Is that it? You bring it up often enough!" Constance's eyes gleamed with a wild and dangerous light.

"Constance!" Aunt Betty was shocked. "Is that what you think? My God, I was only asking Erica what the doctor said today, as you don't seem to think it's any of my business."

"Hoping I don't have much more time to live?"

Erica was thunderstruck and unable to utter a sound. Her aunts never quarreled like this.

Aunt Betty threw back her shoulders and spoke with the dignified authority of a teacher disciplining a delinquent student. "That's a terrible thing to say, Constance, and I've done nothing to deserve it."

Constance sniffed, the winds gone out of her sails. "A lot you care. You couldn't take me to the doctor today or on a Saturday, and those were the only appointments I could get for months." Her voice dropped. "You know I feel better when you take me."

So that's what this was about! Aunt Constance's hurt feelings. Well, Erica's feelings were hurt, as well. She'd believed Aunt Constance when she'd said she wanted Erica's company today.

"I...I couldn't," Betty said, her eyes on her folded hands. "I'm sorry, Connie, but I wasn't free to take you either day."

"More secrets, eh? Like Monday night? And all those other nights you went out and thought I didn't know? Do you take me for a fool?" Aunt Constance pounded her massive chest. "After all these years together, Elizabeth Madsen, and suddenly you and I have secrets from each other."

Constance stomped out of the room, stomped up the steps, then slammed her bedroom door.

Erica was too embarrassed to meet Aunt Betty's eye. She had just been an unwilling witness to probably the worst fight her aunts have had in years.

They'd had an awful argument when she was in third grade. Aunt Constance had been so mad at Aunt Betty that she'd refused to visit at the same time Betty was there. Erica's mother wouldn't say what was wrong, so Erica had asked Missy.

The housekeeper had thrown back her head and laughed. "It's woman's stuff, baby. I'll tell you about it when you're older."

But Missy never got the chance, and Erica never found out. Her aunts became good friends again. Certainly, they bickered and occasionally exchanged barbed retorts, but that was their way. It allowed them to vent their differences, their feelings, and opinions, yet remain on an equal footing in a home that neither of them owned. Now, something was happening that shook the foundation of their friendship. Aunt Constance considered herself the injured party, and Aunt Betty had a secret.

Betty sank onto the couch and sobbed silently into her hands. She looked so forlorn, huddled into herself, that Erica suppressed the desire to dash upstairs to her room. Instead, she sat beside her aunt with her arms around her. She was as bony as an undernourished sparrow.

"Don't cry, Aunt Betty. It can't be that bad. I know you must have a reason for what you're doing."

The sobbing continued, and Erica stumbled on as best she could. "Why don't you go up and talk to Aunt Constance? Explain to her—"

"That's just the trouble. I can't," Betty wailed, her sobbing growing louder and more emotional.

"You can tell me what's bothering you." The words had come from nowhere. Erica certainly hadn't planned to say that.

Blindly, Betty clutched for her niece's hand. "Such a wonderful girl you turned out to be."

She reached in her pocket for her handkerchief and dabbed at her face. Her weeping subsided. "I'm so sorry you had to see this. There was sadness in her voice. "Connie and I hardly ever argue. Not like this. I know she's hurt, terribly hurt, but I don't know what to do. And that's what's making it worse."

Erica was afraid her aunt would start crying again, but Betty held herself erect and sniffed.

"I understand you have an appointment to see Sherman on Friday."

"Who told you?" Erica asked, unnerved. She hadn't mentioned it to anyone.

"Constance or Monica," her aunt said vaguely. "I forget who. Anyway, I was thinking of taking a personal day from school on Friday. Would you like me to go with you to Sherman's office? We could have coffee together afterwards. I won't be able to make lunch," she quickly added. "I'm meeting someone at twelve-thirty." A red flush covered her ears.

She considered her aunt's proposal. It might be a good idea to have Aunt Betty present when Sherman explained about her stocks and bonds and other holdings. Aunt Betty taught business classes and probably knew a great deal about such matters. Erica was determined to come across as knowledgeable and savvy when she met with Sherman Hartley.

"Sure, Aunt Betty, I'd appreciate your coming along."

Her aunt's response of deep gratitude astonished Erica. "Bless you," she murmured, her small hands gripping Erica's. "There's something I want to discuss with you over coffee." Then she spoke so softly, Erica barely caught her words. "There's no one else I can talk to about this." She gave a thin smile, and patted her niece's hand. "A week ago, I'd have said you were the last person I would have chosen, but you've been through so much yourself. Maybe you'll understand. As much as anyone can."

She sighed deeply, then rose to her feet. "I'm going out now. Why don't you take a nice cup of tea up to your Aunt Constance? With plenty of sugar. She likes that when she's upset." Betty put an arm around Erica and kissed her cheek. "And tell her I'm sorry I upset her. I didn't mean to."

She tried to follow Aunt Betty's advice, but met with no success. When she knocked on Aunt Constance's bedroom door, which was her parents' old room, her aunt refused to answer. Erica turned the doorknob. It was locked for the first time since Erica could remember. Her heart twisted when she caught the muffled sounds within. Aunt Constance was sobbing her heart out. While Aunt Betty's tears had stunned and embarrassed her, Erica felt a stab of deep pity for this aunt who had irritated and exasperated her all of her life. It pained Erica to know Aunt Constance was so unhappy.

Her stomach clenched with apprehension. What if Aunt Constance was as sick as Aunt Betty had inferred? Her crying and carrying on this way could be harmful to her health. What if she had a coronary? Betty shouldn't have left her alone in this potentially dangerous situation.

Erica took a deep breath and forced herself to think rationally. No need to be melodramatic and imagine the worst. Aunt Constance seemed well enough this evening, preparing dinner and cleaning up afterward. She still ran the household as vigorously as ever, although she no longer had a car. Erica made a mental note to find out why.

Calmer now, she decided to take Aunt Constance's word regarding her health—at least, for the present—and leave her in peace. Though she'd keep one ear open for trouble.

Erica was finishing her breakfast the next morning when Constance came downstairs, red-faced and puffy-eyed.

"Good morning, Aunt Constance." She rose from the table. Her aunt probably wanted to be left on her own.

"Sit down, Erica, and stay with me a while." Constance sank heavily into her chair. Her salt and pepper hair, always neatly in place, was disheveled, giving her a wild look. "Is there any coffee left?"

"A little. I'll make some more."

Erica went to the sink to rinse out the carafe and start a fresh pot of coffee. For once, her aunt made no attempt to take over. "Like some toast, too?"

Constance nodded. Erica remembered her aunt's medicine—the new tablets the pharmacy had delivered late yesterday. Should she remind her aunt to take a pill? For that matter, should Constance be drinking coffee? Shouldn't she be watching her diet?

Erica suddenly felt protective of her, as if their roles had been reversed. Although Aunt Constance had made it clear that she didn't want to discuss her health, if she were sick, Erica was obliged to see that she got the proper care, regardless of what her aunt wanted. Lost in her thoughts, Erica didn't hear her aunt's question.

"Sorry. What did you say?"

Constance let out a *humph* of exasperation. "You're getting just like your Aunt Betty. I asked if you knew what you were going to do with the house."

"Do with the house? I don't know. Nothing, I guess. I haven't thought about it."

She brought Constance her toast along with some marmalade, then held her breath to see if her aunt would eat it instead of the butter she was always spreading on thick. Constance seemed satisfied with the marmalade, and smeared it on her toast.

"It's high time you decided about the house, Erica. I didn't want to mention it sooner, with Terry's death and all, but you have to deal with it."

"Deal with what?" Had something happened she didn't know about?

Constance slurped her coffee. "To start with, we need a new oil burner. And a new oven. The thermostat's one hundred degrees off, and two of the burners don't work. And the roof needs mending, not to mention a long overdue painting, both inside and out." She clucked her tongue. "I know you and Elizabeth think it's not my place to tell you what to do, but I've been living in this house for nearly fourteen years, and no one knows it better than me." She puffed out her chest. "And I've put a pretty penny into this house myself. From money your Uncle Leonard left me."

Money, Erica thought. *It always comes back to money.*

"I'm sorry you had to spend your own money, Aunt Constance—"

"Even Betty gave up her trip to Europe one summer so we could buy some decent furniture for the family room."

And why shouldn't they put money into the house? Erica thought angrily. Both of them were living rent and tax free in a home that wasn't theirs. They may have helped to raise her, but still.

Constance was eyeing her slyly. "Unless you're thinking of selling it."

"Selling what? The furniture?"

"Don't act wise, Erica Diamond! I'm talking about the house. *This* house!" Constance leaned forward and stared intently into Erica's eyes. "Are you planning on selling the house, now that you're rich?"

She was taken aback by the force of her aunt's emotions. "I haven't made any decisions about anything," she said defensively. "I haven't had time to."

"Well, miss, you'd better start thinking about it. Now that you're back here and a grown woman, the house is your responsibility."

Stunned, Erica put her hand to her face as if her aunt had slapped her. "I'm grateful you and Aunt Betty have kept up the house these past few years, but frankly, it's the last thing on my mind."

Aunt Constance pushed herself away from the table. "Well, be sure to let me know when you put it up for sale, so I'll have enough time to find myself a place to live."

"I said nothing, *nothing*, about selling this house!" She shouted at her aunt's receding back. "Where did you get that idea?"

Constance trudged halfway up the stairs, then threw her parting shot. "You haven't changed, Erica. You still go around in a fog, not planning or knowing what you do. You don't see the facts of life, smack in front of your eyes."

Erica stared up at her, mouth agape. Her aunt's words rankled. It was true that in the past she had often worn blinders, especially where Terry was concerned. But now she was trying her damnedest to see things as they really were—no easy task, considering the lies and secrets swarming about.

And now, Aunt Constance was carrying on about the house. She had no right to badger her this way!

Erica ran outside, slamming the door behind her. One thing was certain. Aunt Constance hadn't changed. She was the same bossy, hotheaded, trouble-making buttinsky as always.

CHAPTER NINE

Sherman was as unctuous as ever, Erica thought, peering at him across his massive desk as he shuffled papers regarding her estate, and spouting empty platitudes. Still, he'd not uttered one condescending comment in the few minutes she'd been in his office, probably because Aunt Betty was at her side.

She smiled at her aunt, grateful for her company. There was no sign of the distraught woman she'd comforted a few evenings ago. Today, Aunt Betty seemed resolute, as though she'd come to some major decision. She asked Sherman several questions—about mutual funds, yields, and tax shelters—which he was only too eager to answer.

He handed Erica several folders of records. "Look these over, if you will. It's a listing of your investments and real estate holdings—what they're worth today, and what they've earned over the last fourteen years since I became executor and trustee of your estate."

Erica opened a folder and thumbed through pages filled with columns of numbers. In truth, she understood very little of what she saw.

Sherman caught her expression of confusion and laughed. "Don't worry. Next week, we'll go over every item in detail. You'll understand it thoroughly by the time we're done."

"What does it add up to?" Erica asked, regaining her aplomb.

"Twenty million, fifty-six thousand dollars. More or less. All yours when you turn twenty-five."

"Unless something happens to me."

"Hmm. If you should die before your twenty-fifth birthday, the estate, according to your father's will, is bequeathed to your two aunts, to be divided equally. Ten million twenty-eight thousand dollars each."

There was silence.

"Over ten million dollars," Betty said reverently. "I've never been this close to that much money."

Shocked, Erica glared at her aunt. "Aunt Betty! You only get it if I die."

Her aunt put an arm around Erica's shoulders. "Don't upset yourself. You know I want you to be well and happy. I'm simply astounded by all that wealth!"

"Of course, nothing will happen to our Erica," Sherman interjected smoothly. "She's destined to lead a long and happy life."

Erica looked at him solemnly. "How do I know it's all there?"

"Erica!" Betty gasped, her turn to be shocked. "What a question! Sherman's been executor of your estate for all these years. Your father trusted him implicitly."

Sherman raised his hands in a conciliatory manner, displaying his star sapphire cufflinks. But her question had obviously unsettled him.

Erica was glad, for once, she'd gotten past his armor.

"A perfectly reasonable question, Betty, from someone not familiar with trusts and estates. And it does show Erica is willing to undertake the responsibility of her inheritance." His tone had turned condescending.

Touché, Erica thought. *I suppose I deserved that.*

He turned to her. "You see, there are all sorts of checks and protections, my dear. Laws that protect an heir. I could explain them now in detail, if you care to hear me out."

Erica shook her head, her ears burning with embarrassment. "Not necessary," she mumbled. For all his faults, she had no reason to consider Sherman anything but scrupulously honest. Her father had trusted him, so she would, too. "I trust you, Sherman."

"I'm certainly glad to hear that." He rubbed his hands together. "Shall we proceed?"

"What if I want to turn it all into cash?" Erica asked.

She could have kicked herself. Why was she being perverse, asking these provocative questions? To irritate Sherman? To let him know she was an adult and a person to be reckoned with? If so, this was one hell of a way of proving it.

He chose to answer her question. "Of course, your holdings can be liquidated into cash. But why do something that foolish?" He seemed hurt by the suggestion. "You'll lose money if you sell your bonds before they come due. Study the papers I'm giving you. They explain how your investments make money. You can live very nicely off the interest and dividends."

"I was merely asking. I should familiarize myself with every aspect of my portfolio. Don't you agree?"

"Absolutely."

A sense of power surged through her body. For the first time in her life, she was in control. And she couldn't resist wielding her power over Sherman Hartley who, so often in the past, had made her feel she went through life with a smudge of dirt on her face.

"I plan to make a study of investments," she continued, as though this were a decision she'd come to some time ago instead of at that very moment, "so I can manage my portfolio."

"I advise you not to do anything rash, my dear. We are talking about a great deal of money." He leaned over to pat her arm. "I'd be more than happy to assist you in any way I can. Your father always valued my counsel when it came to finances."

"That was several years ago."

"Erica!" Aunt Betty chimed.

But, to Erica's surprise, Sherman burst out laughing—a deep, belly guffaw, unlike any sound she'd ever heard him make. It filled the office.

"I do believe our Erica is feeling her oats. This calls for a celebration." He pushed the intercom. "Miss Fitzroy, bring in a bottle of sherry and three glasses, please."

Waterford, Erica was pleased to notice, when the tray was set before them.

Sherman poured and proposed a toast. She sipped her sherry, and observed the change that overtook their little group. Client, relative, and attorney were transformed into three longstanding friends. The matter of Erica's inheritance was dropped for the time being, with the understanding that she would return to th e office on Tuesday to sign the necessary papers and spend some time familiarizing herself with the accounts.

"Oh, my goodness, I almost forgot! Monica will have my head if I fail to relay her message." He held his pudgy hands to his face in mock terror.

They waited for him to explain.

"You're both invited—and Constance, of course—to dinner tomorrow night in celebration of Erica's birthday." He sent Erica a penetrating look. "Unless you have other plans."

"No, I haven't," she said after a stunned pause. "Not with Terry's death and all. To tell you the truth, I haven't given any thought to my birthday."

And before she could explain that she'd rather not make a big to-do about her twenty-fifth birthday, Sherman was rubbing his hands together and beaming.

"That's settled then," he said, taking her hesitancy for acceptance. "We're delighted you can come. Jason will be there, of course. He tells us you enjoyed your Monday evening together."

Erica glared at him, but Sherman didn't notice, as he'd chosen that moment to pour more sherry into everyone's glass. "Erica, is there anyone else you'd care to have us include? Monica said to be sure to tell you the more the merrier."

She would use such a trite expression, Erica thought unkindly. She was annoyed with Monica for having extended the invitation, annoyed with herself for not coming up with a refusal in time. Was there anyone to invite? Doug immediately came to mind, and she shook her head vehemently to rid herself of his image.

"There's no one I can think of."

Aunt Betty stood and clasped Sherman's hands between her own. "A birthday dinner for Erica! How kind of you and Monica. Sherman, I don't know what we would have done without your help all these years."

Dutifully, Erica kissed his cologne-scented cheek. "Thanks, Sherman, and thanks for all your help."

He beamed at each of them. "It's been my pleasure to look after your interests. After all, you're like family to us." He cleared his throat. "Then we'll be six for dinner. Shall we say eight o'clock?"

"Eight o'clock," Aunt Betty echoed.

They sipped their sherry. How very civilized, Erica thought.

She glanced at the hunting pictures on the wall and suppressed a giggle. It was like being trapped inside a comedy of manners where everyone went by the rules, including herself. Then she caught Aunt Betty eyeing her watch, and she glanced down at her own. It was eleven-thirty.

They'd spent most of the morning discussing her inheritance. Soon, she'd have enough money to live the rest of her life in comfort. She could travel. Buy a house in another state. Buy houses in several states. She wished she had a burning ambition, or a particular career she wanted to pursue, but nothing came to mind.

Sherman ushered them to the outer office, and kissed them goodbye. He's a happy man, Erica realized. He enjoys his work, adores his wife, and now he gets along with Jason.

"Jason?" Erica was astonished to see his long, lanky frame leaning over Miss Fitzroy's desk. From the sound of things, he'd reduced his father's grim secretary—who, until this moment, Erica would have sworn lacked the necessary facial muscles to smile—to the state of a silly teenager.

Jason straightened as they approached. "Hello, Erica, Miss Madsen." He doffed an imaginary cap. "Imagine finding you here."

"I understand we'll be seeing you tomorrow night," Aunt Betty gushed.

"I'm looking forward to helping Erica celebrate her birthday."

Jason's wink set Erica's teeth on edge. Monday night's "date" was only too clear in his mind. She felt like kicking herself for not rejecting Sherman's invitation outright. She could have said she was busy. Though she couldn't have counted on Aunt Betty not to show surprise about any imaginary plans. And Sherman would simply have changed the date of Monica's dinner.

Erica sighed. She was going to this dinner party, so she might as well make the best of it.

"Monica spent all of last night deciding on the menu," Jason went on. "And she's hired someone to serve."

"It's very kind of her to want to do this for me," she said stiffly, confused.

Why would Monica assume she and her aunts would be free tomorrow evening?

Of course! Either Constance or Betty had told her.

"Kind enough, once I came up with the idea," Jason bragged. "But I have to hand it to Monica. She's going all out to make this a gala celebration. I promise you, Erica, you won't be disappointed."

So, Jason was behind it all! *Damn it! The sooner I leave Manordale, the better off I'll be.* She was sick and tired of people planning her life as though she were a rag doll with no will of her own. Somebody always seemed to want something from her, something she wasn't prepared to give. Draining her of the precious time and energy she needed to figure out what she wanted from life.

She was fed up with being manipulated, first by her aunts, now by Jason. But no one was going to keep her in that office one minute longer.

"'Bye, Jason. We have to go." She sailed out, almost slamming the door on Aunt Betty.

"You weren't very kind to poor Jason," her aunt accused as they stepped into the elevator.

"Poor, Jason, my eye."

They walked down the block to the Main Street Diner and were seated immediately, their orders taken.

"Now, Erica, dear, I have less than an hour," Aunt Betty said as she glanced at her watch, then around the half-empty diner.

"I only hope it's enough time to explain everything, so you can understand and...and not think too badly of me."

Erica nodded, her mouth too full of her tuna fish sandwich to speak. Aunt Betty might have a luncheon date, but she didn't. And she was ravenous after that session with Sherman.

Aunt Betty made a few more false starts. Her eyes darted about the room, looking anywhere but at Erica. She was as fidgety as a soon-to-be father pacing a maternity waiting room.

"I don't know exactly where to begin," her aunt said for the third time. She stared into her untouched coffee as though she hoped the answer might rise up from the milky brown liquid.

Erica resisted the impulse to grab her aunt by the shoulders and insist she spit out what she wanted to say. Instead, she started on the second half of her sandwich.

"But before I begin, there is one thing I must ask of you." Aunt Betty's fluttering hand reached across the table and landed on Erica's arm. "Please," she said in a voice so low it was barely audible, "not a word of this to anyone, Erica. And that especially means your Aunt Constance."

After the scene the other evening, Erica was not surprised by this request. "You can trust me, Aunt Betty."

"Of course, I'll tell Connie just as soon as I'm able to. But not yet. Not now." Betty took a deep breath. Her words emerged like a gust of wind. "Erica, I'm going to be married. Very, very soon, I hope."

"Oh, Aunt Betty! I'm delighted! I'm thrilled!" Erica jumped out of her seat to hug her aunt.

Betty said nothing, but her eyes were shiny with unshed tears.

"I'm very happy," her aunt said quietly. "I really am, but there are many...complications."

"Who is he? Where did you meet him?" Erica could barely contain her curiosity. This news was out of the blue.

"He's someone I've known for a very long time. In fact, you've met him once or twice."

"I have?" Erica was puzzled.

Aunt Betty's voice fell to a whisper. "It's Ron Jennings."

She gasped. "Mr. Jennings?" Her voice betrayed her shock and disbelief. Mr. Jennings was the principal of the high school where Aunt Betty had been teaching for the past eighteen years. And, as far as Erica knew, he was married.

"Shh," Aunt Betty admonished. "Keep your voice down."

"But Mr. Jennings," Erica said in a stage whisper. "I just can't believe it. I mean, he's—"

"Erica, be still and let me explain." Aunt Betty sat up straight in her chair and sighed. When her emotions were seemingly under control, she began.

"Ron and I became—er—friends many years ago, just before his wife fell ill. I know it sounds callous, trite even, but they never got along. They were sleeping in separate bedrooms even before we got involved. Sylvia's one of those passive, clinging women whose strength lies in her tenacity," Aunt Betty said bitterly.

"Anyway, just as Ron was about to ask her for a divorce, they learned that Sylvia had a debilitating disease and would need constant care as long as she lived. Decent man that he is, Ron couldn't bring himself to leave her."

She stared at her aunt in astonishment. "When did all this happen?"

"Seventeen years ago."

"My God! Seventeen years ago!"

She was too taken aback to do more than gape at her aunt. She had always thought of Aunt Betty as sexless. Virginal. Didn't she always titter like a silly girl when she spoke to a man? It was a shock to discover she'd been involved with someone all these years. And with her principal!

Did they go to motels or did they do it in his office? The image of Aunt Betty in this improbable situation made her giggle. She had to turn away and cover her mouth.

But Aunt Betty was chuckling herself. "Don't worry, Erica. We haven't been skulking around town all these years like we are now. Quite the opposite. After Ron made the decision to stay and care for Sylvia, we agreed not to see each other. It was too painful."

"But you saw him in school," she said softly.

Aunt Betty nodded. "Every day. We simply did our best to avoid one another. I still cared, even though I tried to put Ron out of my mind. I succeeded for short periods at a time."

Erica shook her head. "How awful for you. But wasn't there anyone you could talk to about this?"

A smile lit Aunt Betty's face. "Your mother. My sister Helen knew all about Ron. She was the only person I could share this with, the one person who understood what I was going through. How I felt. She didn't feel compelled to tell me I was a fool to get involved with a married man." The smile disappeared. "Then, somehow, Connie found out. She was so appalled, she avoided me for months."

So, that was why her aunts had been estranged all those years ago! At least some ancient mysteries were getting cleared up. Erica watched her aunt sip her coffee. In spite of her natural sympathy for Aunt Betty, she was intrigued, as well. Who would have imagined that her chattering, scrawny aunt had been experiencing a lifelong passionate love affair? And right under her very nose!

"How did you and Ron get together again?" she asked.

"One day, this past fall, we found ourselves alone in the parking lot. We started talking, went out for a drink, and after several meetings, decided we wanted to spend what was left of our lives together. Regardless of Sylvia." Aunt Betty's mouth set in a grim line.

"When did he ask his wife for a divorce?"

"About three months ago. And a stronger housebound woman you've yet to meet. She's putting up one fierce fight. Doing her best to bleed him dry. She insists on round-the-clock nurses, which she doesn't really need. Along with the house, the furniture, and his car, although she hasn't driven in years. And he still has one son to put through college."

"Is that why you meet him late at night?"

Aunt Betty nodded. "Sylvia knows he's involved with someone, but she doesn't know with whom." Her face turned crimson. "We think she's hired a private detective so she can make as big a scandal of the situation as possible. Poor Ron. He meets with his lawyer at least twice a week to discuss her mounting demands. It's been very hard on both of us."

Poor Aunt Betty. She took her aunt's small hands into her own. "I never realized how much you were going through."

"Then, of course, there are other problems. Your Aunt Constance, for example. I feel terrible about leaving her. At times, I feel as though I can't do it, but then I get angry and remind myself she's been married. She's had her own life." Betty fixed her eyes on Erica's. "I'm fifty-four years old, Erica. I'm entitled to some happiness, too."

"Of course, you are," Erica readily agreed. "Is that why you're so worried about Aunt Constance's health?"

"Partly. She won't admit it, but her heart condition's gotten worse. That's why she sold her car this winter. Not because of that small accident she had—the one she claims shook her up so badly."

So, Erica *hadn't* seen Aunt Constance's car parked in front of the house when she'd returned from upstate New York. Whose was it?

Aunt Betty went on. "Connie insists on pretending that nothing's changed. That she can still handle the house and the cooking and all her organizations. But sometimes I come home and find her napping. And she's breathless after climbing the stairs."

Erica recalled Aunt Constance's bursts of anger against Aunt Betty, against herself, and it suddenly all made sense. Aunt Constance wasn't angry as much as she was terrified. She knew she was sick, and she was afraid of losing the only home she'd had for fourteen years. She couldn't share her worries with her best friend and companion because that friend and companion was keeping secrets from her.

There was one thing Erica could do. At the first opportunity, she'd let Aunt Constance know she was welcome to stay in the house on Chestnut Drive as long as she lived. Still, that didn't deal with the problem of Aunt Constance's poor health.

"What should we do, Aunt Betty? To make sure she gets proper care."

"I don't know what I can do, Erica. I suppose you can stay with Connie. Keep an eye on her."

"Me?" Erica's eyes widened with panic. She gasped for breath. Her worst fear was coming true! She was doomed to be trapped in her childhood home forever.

Aunt Betty patted her hand reassuringly. "Erica, honey, don't worry. You needn't stay with her if you don't want to. It's just that we have to think of something. It will take planning and money." She eyed Erica intently. "All I'm trying to say is, you're old enough to know the true situation so you can help me make the necessary decisions, and it doesn't all fall on my shoulders."

Aunt Betty's words were sensible enough, but something about her tone and the calculating gleam in her eye made Erica squirm.

"Which brings me to another matter." Aunt Betty's stare was riveting, as though all the force of her small body were concentrated in her eyes, which gripped Erica in their hold. She knew that look too well. Her aunt rarely used it, but when she did, it never failed. "Because Sylvia's being so greedy, Ron and I are starting our married life strapped for money. I happened to tell him about your inheritance. Naturally, it came up in conversation."

"I don't see why," Erica sputtered. Her short hairs bristled with indignation.

Aunt Betty loosened her mesmerizing hold on her and smiled—a saccharine, artificial smile. "And we were wondering—that is, I was wondering—if you could see fit to make us a modest wedding gift of, let's say, fifty thousand dollars?" Her smile widened, multiplying the number of wrinkles already crossing her face. "Or more. But that's certainly up to you."

Erica winced. The winsome veneer her aunt had hoped to present was no more than a grotesque mask that did nothing to disguise her brazen request.

"I'll have to think about it," she said coldly. "I'm very appreciative of everything you've done for me, but ever since I've come home, I find everyone's trying to tell me how to lead my life and spend my money."

"Why, Erica, whatever are you talking about?" Betty was obviously offended. "I've not interfered with you since you've come back. And I've done my darnedest to see that Constance doesn't nag you. As for the wedding gift, it was only a suggestion."

"I suppose so," Erica said reluctantly. It was true. Nobody could make her live with Aunt Constance or order her to give Aunt Betty money. But life wasn't that simple. Even though her aunts weren't as interfering as they used to be, they still managed to invade her life. As did the Hartleys. Maybe Betty was too wrapped up in her own problems to realize that, lately, Erica's life had become very difficult and complicated.

"I'm really happy for you, Aunt Betty. I hope everything works out the way you want it to." Erica forced herself to smile. The blatant request for money had taken the joy from her good wishes.

Aunt Betty pushed back her chair. "I'd better leave now if I'm to meet Ron on time." She reached for the check.

"I'll get it," Erica said, taking it from her.

Betty made no sign of protest. She kissed Erica's cheek, but when she spoke, her voice was matter-of-fact. "Thank you, Erica. And please give some thought to what I've told you. Ron and I could use your support."

"I'll think about it," she replied, not hiding her displeasure at this second request for money. Aunt Betty had no right to make her feel as though her future happiness depended on Erica's generosity.

CHAPTER TEN

Erica paid the check and left the diner. What a relief it was to be alone! She breathed in the sweet-smelling air, relished the sun's warmth on her bare arms. It was the first of May. Four more days to her birthday.

The beautiful weather made her think of Montauk, and she was overtaken by a powerful yearning to return to the cottage. If only she could be there now, jogging along the beach in the early morning, eating fresh berries and yogurt for breakfast, then basking in the sun.

"I'll go there as soon as I can," she promised herself. "And try to figure out what to do with the rest of my life."

She gave a start when she realized she'd spoken aloud. Someone might have heard and wondered if she was mentally unbalanced.

Let them wonder. She didn't care!

As she walked toward her car, her thoughts turned to Terry. She was glad they'd made love at the cottage. Although it still hurt when she remembered how he'd hid the dark side of his life from her, their last time together was a memory she could return to, a memory that bridged her old life with the present.

The truth was, Terry and their unusual marriage were fading into her past. Now, Erica was beginning to doubt that she'd really been in love with him. Loved, maybe, but not *in* love. Sure, she was wild about his looks and the fact that he wanted to be married to her. But he had so many secrets, she never really knew him. They'd shared a passion, but that was bound to die out eventually, and would never have been replaced by a steadfast, compassionate love.

So many new developments and revelations were occurring every day, keeping her in a constant state of flux. She was changing. Maturing. Though her life was full of uncertainty, she was certain of one thing. Terry turned out not to be the person with whom she wanted to share the rest of her life. Whatever the future brought, she was determined to meet each situation with her eyes wide open.

She stopped short when she realized she was standing on the same corner where, a few days earlier, a car had almost struck her. She had never called the police to tell them about this second attempt on her life, partly because she'd been rushing to go out with Jason that evening, partly because she couldn't swear she hadn't been jostled, or had merely slipped and fallen. She would have mentioned it to Officer Finney had he called or stopped by again, but it was another officer who had called yesterday to ask her something about Terry's motorcycle. Still, maybe she should—

"Going somewhere?"

The resonant voice sent a tremor through her body even before she felt his hand on her shoulder. Doug! He stood before her, grinning like a happy lunatic.

"Doug Remsen! What are you doing here?"

"I've come to see you. Why else would I be in Manordale?" Today, in jeans and a short-sleeved shirt, he looked but a few years older than she.

"You're not here because of me," she said sternly, while inside her heart was doing cartwheels.

"Actually, I had some business to attend to. But I couldn't leave town without seeing you. Your Aunt Constance said I'd probably find you someplace on Main Street, and she was right."

They know where I am practically every minute of the day.

Eager to leave the corner, she continued walking. Doug kept pace beside her. They hadn't gone more than ten paces when a woman stopped them.

"Hello, Erica. So nice to see you after all these years."

She stared at the well-dressed woman beaming at her. She looked familiar, but Erica simply couldn't remember her neighbor's name.

Then it came to her. "Oh, hello, Mrs. Taylor."

"I heard you were back home again." Mrs. Taylor smiled at Doug. "Is this your new husband?"

The blood rushed to Erica's face, probably turning it beet red. "No, this is a friend. My husband died. He was killed in an accident."

The older woman's face registered concern. "I'm so sorry, dear, I didn't know. Though, come to think of it, my daughter did say something about a car crash. Or was that Harriet Johnson's son-in-law?"

She continued down the block, muttering to herself.

"Mrs. Taylor lives around the corner from us," Erica explained to Doug. "She has trouble remembering what day it is. For years, she thought Jason was my brother."

"Who's Jason?" he asked.

She looked at him, surprised for a moment he didn't know. Sometimes, it seemed Doug Remsen knew everything about her life.

"He's an old friend." She frowned. "Who's turning into quite a nuisance."

"People change when there's a fortune around."

She sent him a sharp glance, wondering if he knew he'd scored a bull's eye. A thought occurred to her. "You called Aunt Constance?"

"No, I called you and you weren't in. Your aunt gave me the necessary information, though." Doug chuckled. "At first, she wouldn't tell me anything, but once I explained I was a friend of Terry's, she was more obliging."

She laughed, liking the idea of Doug and Aunt Constance talking about her for some reason.

"Doug Remsen, if I locked you up with a spy, you'd have him spitting out names and codes inside of ten minutes."

He grinned. "I'm not sure you mean that as a compliment, but I'll consider it one anyway."

He took her arm to cross the street.

She was delighted to have him close beside her. And glad she was wearing her new trousers, silk top, and colorful blazer.

They stopped in front of the blue BMW. He unlocked the passenger door, and she stepped inside.

"Where are we going?" she asked as he slid in beside her from the other side.

"Where would you like to go?" He turned the ignition. "I'm free this afternoon, if you are. I thought we'd drive someplace and relax."

His invitation sent her heart soaring. "I'd love to go to Montauk right now, but short of that, a park will do."

"Fine. I know just the spot."

They drove through the center of town. She thought she caught sight of Aunt Betty, but it wasn't her aunt at all. A minute later, she was certain she'd spied Jason in his car waiting to make a left-hand turn from the opposite side of Main Street.

Stop that, she scolded herself. *Forget about Betty, Constance, Sherman, and Jason.* She managed to push them out of her mind, but her mind wouldn't rest.

"Why wouldn't you talk to me on Wednesday?" she asked accusingly.

His eyes narrowed. The knowing, foxy expression had returned. "You saw that creep I was with."

She nodded.

"He's an addict. He'd sell his own mother for some crack. It's bad enough I have to talk to scum like that. I don't want him breathing the same air, let alone noticing someone I care about."

Care about?

For a moment, she was too exhilarated to speak. "I suppose I shouldn't have called out to you across a roomful of people."

"It wasn't the smartest thing to do, considering the line of work I'm in." His grin took away the biting edge of his comment.

Although she knew it hadn't been his intention, his words succeeded in frightening her. They confronted her with the undeniable reality that Doug lived in a world of crime and violence. As a law-abiding citizen, Erica had a natural abhorrence of crime. But it was the violence she feared. A shudder ran down her spine. She realized she wasn't frightened for herself, but for Doug. She didn't want anything bad to happen to him.

The sudden awareness of her feelings swept over her. She longed to tell him to be careful, but knew better than to express her concern for his safety. He would get annoyed, or worse, laugh at her sentimentality.

Instead, she concentrated on the moment at hand.

"Where are we going?" she asked as they left the town and turned onto the four-lane turnpike.

"To my favorite duck pond. I haven't been there in years."

"Don't tell me you come from around here."

"Long Island-born and bred. Summers at Jones Beach, winters at the Roosevelt Field Mall."

They laughed and talked about their childhoods. He had a brother and two sisters. His father had died two years ago.

"How are you adjusting to living with your aunts?" he asked as they turned onto a local road.

"Not too well," she admitted. "As soon as everything's settled, I'm going to move far away. To where, I haven't the slightest idea."

He gave an understanding smile. They chatted easily as they passed houses and shops. When they reached the old village above the duck pond, they drove along the narrow one-way road and parked.

They walked down the hill to the pond, stopping at the water's edge, where a quacking group of ducks swam about waiting to be fed.

The park was fairly crowded. There were a few elderly couples and young women with small children in tow, as well as groups of teenagers sprawled about on the grassy slopes, probably on their lunch hour from the nearby high school.

She smiled, pleased that Doug had thought to bring her here.

"I just love this place!" she cried, watching the ducks dive for pieces of bread that a small boy was tossing into the water. Without thinking, she added, "We should have brought some bread, too."

He laughed. "We'll have to remember that for next time."

Next time! She felt as though she were wandering through a lovely dream in the company of this handsome man—half-stranger, half-friend.

A sudden disturbance jolted her out of her peaceful reverie. She looked up. On the slope above them, three boys were playing frisbee and shouting insults at one another. She smiled and told herself she was reacting like an old fusspot to some good-natured fun, and pointedly ignored the trio.

"Want some ice cream?" Doug asked.

"Sure, why not?"

They stopped at the ice cream truck and bought chocolate-covered pops, which they ate as they slowly circled the pond.

She happened to glance up at the frisbee players again. Something odd about their manner held her attention. They had stopped playing and now stood huddled together beside a very large tree. Someone or something behind the tree held their undivided attention. One of the boys stretched out his hand and put something in his pocket. Then, all three turned to stare at her.

She looked away. She felt foolish, yet compelled to mention the incident, when Doug spoke first.

"Your aunt told me you had an appointment with Sherman Hartley this morning."

"I did. About my inheritance."

"A real stuffed shirt, don't you think?"

She stared at him, ignoring the boys and the ice cream that trickled down her hand.

"I agree, but how do you know Sherman?"

"I've met him once or twice. Mr. B has dealings with him."

"You're kidding!" She was shocked. "Sherman's so ramrod straight." She looked down at the melting ice cream and wiped her hand with her napkin.

He smiled. "That's probably why Mr. B chose him to handle some of his legit properties. I've met his son, too, but under different circumstances."

"Jason?"

He shook his head in disbelief. "Don't tell me he's the old friend you were talking about." When Erica nodded, he said, "I'd watch out for him, Erica. He tried to stick my boss for a couple of thousand dollars. Mr. B had to teach him a lesson."

Both Sherman and Jason were mixed up with Doug's boss. Was there no end to the surprises? The dirty secrets?

"This incident with Jason—was it recent?"

"A few months ago. Why?"

"I'm thinking that was why Jason holed up in Montauk."

Just then, the three boys dashed down the hill, yelling, and laughing. The tallest one slammed into her. Her ice cream went flying, and she would have fallen if Doug hadn't thrust out an arm to catch her.

The boy paused and was about to run off to join his friends, but Doug grabbed hold of him.

"I think you owe someone an apology," Doug said. His voice remained calm, but there was a steel edge to it.

She watched cold fear seep into the boy's freckled face. He stared down at the ground.

"I'm sorry, mister. Sorry, lady. I didn't mean to do anything."

Doug glared at the boy, forcing him to meet his eyes. "Make sure you don't crash into anyone again. Understand?" The menacing words hung in the air.

The boy nodded and fled when Doug released his grip. The three teenagers whispered and pointed at them from a distance.

She sighed with relief when they finally turned and left the park.

Doug put an arm around her shoulder and led her to a bench. "Are you okay?" He sat down beside her, his manner now gentle and caring.

"I'm fine. Really," she quickly assured him.

But his sudden ferocity had shaken her. Doug was used to physical violence. She shuddered as she wondered if he'd ever killed anyone. What was she doing, getting involved with another inappropriate guy?

They sat in silence.

She was about to ask Doug to drive her home when she noticed his forehead was furrowed, and he was deep in thought.

She turned back to the pond, and once again, fell under the spell of the place, its tranquility and picture-book loveliness. She was surprised at how calm she felt after the ugly incident with the boys.

It's because I'm with Doug, she realized. *Inappropriate or not, he makes me feel safe. Cherished.*

When he spoke, she thought she'd imagined his words. "I really did want to see you, Erica."

She smiled. "I'm glad."

"For Terry's sake as well as my own peace of mind."

So that was it, she thought ruefully. The underworld's code of honor. She should have remembered what he'd told her the other night. He was seeing her because Terry had asked him to keep an eye on her. Only, she'd twisted it around because of her romantic notions about the handsome gangster she was mysteriously drawn to, but didn't really know.

His expression turned grim. He squeezed her hand. "Tell me, has anyone tried to kill you since your drive out to Montauk?"

"Ow." Erica pulled her hand free. "There's no need to put it like that."

"Really? How should I put it?"

She hesitated. Sitting in the middle of a grassy, sunlit park, she couldn't be absolutely positive that someone had shoved her into the path of that oncoming car. And Doug seemed on the verge of getting furious again. She didn't want to deal with his anger after what had just happened.

But, he took her hesitation for what it was—reluctance to tell him about another attempt on her life. "Someone *did* try again. Where and when?"

She told him what had happened in town. "I didn't mention it to my aunts because I didn't want to upset them. Though, I had to concoct a story to explain how my face got bruised."

He scowled. "You're lucky it wasn't anything worse. Why didn't you call the police?"

He looked so earnest, Erica burst out laughing. "Since when are you so fond of the police?"

He gave a sigh of exasperation. "This isn't a joke, Erica. You should have called them. Their job is to protect you."

"From something that already happened? And what was I supposed to tell them? It could have been an accident. I didn't see anything. Nobody standing near me saw anything. And besides..." She faltered.

"Go on."

"I was afraid the police would think I was a bit demented or peculiar or something."

"No, they wouldn't," he said bluntly. "Not if you told them you were about to inherit twenty million bucks."

She had no answer.

He got a faraway look in his eyes. He seemed to be doing some deep thinking.

She knew Doug feared for her life, and she should be anxious and afraid. But somehow, his obvious concern had the opposite effect. Instead of wanting to hurry home to hide beneath her quilt, she felt safe. With Doug beside her, she had the urge to get up and dance around the duck pond.

Finally, he spoke. "Erica, much as I'd like to, I can't guard you twenty-four-seven." His expression was so intense, she could see the vein throbbing at his temple. "If anything, and I mean anything, happens again, call my cell. Do you still have the number?"

She nodded, chastened by his tone. He reached inside his shirt pocket for a small note pad. "If I'm not there, try this number." He scribbled it down and handed her the slip of paper. "Call me if you get a strange phone call. If someone looks at you the wrong way. Anything out of the ordinary. And for God's sake, be careful!"

He sprang to his feet. "Time to go."

She followed him to the car.

They'd been having such an enjoyable afternoon until he had to bring up the one subject that terrified her, left her confused and uncertain each time she tried to figure it out.

Doug, she was beginning to learn, faced issues with brutal reality. Unlike Terry, who had shied away from discussing anything unpleasant.

Thinking of Terry reminded her of his debt. "About the money Terry owed your boss," she began as they approached the BMW.

"Subject closed," he said firmly. "Consider it resolved, okay?" He opened the car door for her, then walked around to the driver's side.

She clicked her safety belt in place. She opened her mouth to ask who had taken care of the debt and why, then closed it. Doug wasn't going to say another word about the subject, no matter how many questions she asked.

"Thank you," she said belatedly. At least one problem was laid to rest.

They drove down the narrow road, passing a dusty old Buick, half-hidden by bushes. It looked like Jason's car. Amazing. She didn't think there could be two of them on all of Long Island.

Doug's mood lightened as they headed back to Manordale. "Your birthday must be coming up any day now."

"Tuesday," she told him. "I turn into an old woman of twenty-five."

"A rich young woman of twenty-five," he corrected her. "Beware of fortune hunters," he teased.

"They're already gathering around," she grumbled. Again, inspired by the comforting feeling that she could tell Doug anything, she found herself complaining about her aunts.

"So," she finished, "one's given me a list of home improvements, and the other's asked for a substantial dowry." She adjusted her glasses, which were sliding down her nose. "As though I were their aunt, and they my young nieces."

"Money does strange things to people," he commented. "But your aunts sound harmless enough." His voice turned sharp. "Of course, you have to be the best judge of that. And don't you forget it."

"It's gotten so I don't know who to trust." Only when she heard the words spoken aloud did she realize how long this thought had been preying on her mind, eating away at her. "Even Jason Hartley, my oldest, dearest friend, has been acting kind of weird. I don't know what to make of it all."

They stopped at an intersection and waited for the light to turn green. Doug's fingers brushed the side of her face. "Trust your instincts, Erica. I've found mine to be the best guide of all. And don't hesitate to call me if anything suspicious happens, no matter how unimportant it may seem. We don't want any more 'accidents', right?"

"Right."

She smiled. He cared about her, after all. Why else was he so concerned about her welfare?

Impulsively, she said, "The Hartleys are having a birthday dinner for me tomorrow night. They said I could invite anyone I wanted. Would you like to come?"

Her invitation issued, she stared straight ahead.

When the silence lengthened, she ventured to peer at him from the corner of her eye. His face looked closed, and she couldn't fathom what was going on inside his head. Finally, as she was about to insist on an answer, he spoke.

"It would be my greatest pleasure to share your birthday celebration, Erica, but I must decline." He took her hand in his. "It's out of the question. Please try and understand."

She feared tears would come streaming down her cheeks and betray her disappointment, but she managed to check them as she silently berated herself. *What a dumb move, inviting him to a family gathering.* Her cheeks burned with embarrassment. *Now he probably thinks I'm in love with him, which is absolutely ludicrous! Of course, he doesn't want to come, and who can blame him? Fool that I am, assuming he likes me just because he's been kind.*

And to ask him to the Hartleys, of all places, she persisted in tormenting herself. *He can't go there! Sherman knows him, knows he's a gangster. He'd throw Doug right out and tell my aunts, who would hound me to death for getting involved with criminals.*

Besides, she scolded herself with one last withering argument, *I really put him on the spot, giving him one day's notice. I'm sure he has better things to do on his Saturday nights than wait around for a last-minute invitation.*

They drove in silence. When they got to Manordale, she directed him to the parking lot where she'd left her car so many hours earlier.

"Goodbye, and thanks for a lovely afternoon," she said formally the moment the BMW glided to a halt.

She fumbled in her pocketbook for her car keys, and was totally taken aback when he tilted her face toward him and took her in his arms.

Their kiss lasted a moment, but left her delirious with happiness.

"Happy Birthday, sweet Erica. Remember to call me if anything upsets you. Promise?"

His unexpected action left her too dazed to do more than nod. She got out of his car and into hers, aware of his eyes watching her until she drove away.

CHAPTER ELEVEN

To Erica's surprise, both aunts seemed to temporarily forget their grievances just before they left for the Hartleys, and embarrassed her by fussing over her the way they used to. They stood side-by-side and beamed up at her as she descended the stairs in the flowered dress she'd worn with Doug the week before.

"Erica, darling, you look downright beautiful," boomed Aunt Constance. "That dress is the loveliest, isn't it, Betty?"

Erica tried for a smile. She hadn't wanted to wear this dress, but she had nothing else quite as festive. She wore it in honor of her birthday, she told herself fiercely. Not for the Hartleys or her aunts.

"Indeed, it is, Connie. And I have just the perfect lipstick for you to wear tonight."

"But I'm already wearing lipstick," she protested.

"You can wipe it off, can't you?" Aunt Betty said, hustling her back upstairs.

In the driveway, Erica pushed forward the front seat of her aunt's Camry and was about to step into the back, when she felt

Aunt Constance's heavy hand on her back. "Oh, no, girl. You sit in the front, next to your Aunt Betty. It's your special night."

"But, Aunt Constance," she began, embarrassed.

"Not another word," Constance said. "I insist."

Erica was forced to watch her aunt maneuver her massive frame into the backseat of the car, puffing with the exertion it cost her. Aunt Constance was still panting a minute later when Erica was fastening her seatbelt.

Did she always breathe that heavily? she wondered as Aunt Betty backed out of the driveway. Or was this further proof her heart condition had deteriorated?

She turned around to face Aunt Constance. "Did you remember to take your pill?"

"Of course, I did!" Constance snapped.

"Connie, she's only asking because she cares," Aunt Betty said smoothly.

Erica suddenly realized how often Aunt Betty had her own back, simply by stating the obvious.

"Hmm," was Aunt Constance's reply. "I'm fifty-eight years old. Old enough to remember to take a pill."

A headache, Erica thought. *I'll say I have a headache. Or a toothache.*

In the tense silence, her brain came up with one possibility after another, yet she discarded them all. There was no excuse powerful enough to relieve her of the unbearable evening stretching before her. Besides, she couldn't disappoint Monica at the last minute. The dinner was in Erica's honor, and there was nothing for her to do but attend.

"I wonder what delicacies Monica has prepared for this special occasion," Aunt Betty chirped as she steered her blue Camry down the turnpike.

Her two passengers remained silent, but Betty, once again in her Pollyanna mode, didn't seem to notice. "I hope it's one of those heavenly dishes she learned to prepare in her gourmet cooking class."

It was nearly eight, and the bright, sunlit sky had faded to a dull magenta. Erica tried not to think about the tiresome evening ahead. To distract herself, she concentrated on her aunts.

Aunt Betty was eagerly anticipating the evening's festivities. She looked especially attractive in a pink suit that camouflaged her paltry bosom and bony figure. Aunt Constance did not share Betty's good cheer. She dominated the backseat, holding herself as rigid as a general reviewing his troops. Like Erica, she was attending this dinner under duress.

"Since when do you go for rich, overcooked food and thick sauces, Elizabeth?" Constance asked querulously. "The last time we dined at the Hartleys, I was up all night with indigestion."

"That was because you took three helpings of the chocolate mousse, Connie, dear. Don't you remember?"

"Well, I couldn't swallow any of that seafood mess she called a main course. Don't you remember?" Constance asked, imitating Betty's high-pitched question. "And I was hungry by the time she served dessert, so I ate the damn mousse."

"I do hope this time Monica's a bit more aware that we all need to watch our cholesterol," Betty said diplomatically.

Erica held her breath and waited for Aunt Constance to take offense at this allusion to her heart condition, but she didn't. No one said another word.

Ill-at-ease in her silent prison, Erica rested her temple against the window and watched as the car turned onto a darkened country lane. The only glints of light came from the large houses they passed, well screened by trees and overgrown shrubbery, and set back from the road.

The truce that hovered over the three women was an uneasy one at best. Erica knew a full-fledged quarrel could break out between her aunts at any moment. All it would take was one barb too deep, one dig too many.

And while she was glad Aunt Betty was apparently over her bout of guilt and dejection, Erica hoped the restoration of her aunt's good humor wasn't based on the mistaken assumption that she could depend on Erica to ease her financial burdens. Especially since Aunt Betty had made a few more provoking comments about her desired wedding gift. Erica had managed to remain noncommittal on the subject. She bottled up her feelings of being exploited with the result that she'd gulped down Friday night's dinner as quickly as possible and had retreated to her room with a stomachache.

The Hartley house—a large white colonial with black shutters—stood on a rise of land well-forested with maples, white birches, beeches, and giant rhododendrons. Aunt Betty bypassed the deep, circular driveway and turned onto the blacktop leading to the three-car garage. Two cars were parked outside—a blue Cadillac that must have been Sherman's and a red Audi that Monica probably drove.

Erica sighed. Another blue car. She was stepping out of a blue car. Doug had a blue car. So did Jason, although it was nowhere in sight. She shook her head to rid herself of unpleasant thoughts. She couldn't worry about every blue car that crossed her path, could she?

"Erica, dear! Happy Birthday!"

Sherman strode toward them, short arms outstretched, his face aglow. Although his navy blazer was probably meant to give him a nautical look that conjured images of regattas and yacht clubs, his manner reminded her of a Greek restaurant owner greeting his favorite customers.

She allowed herself to be hugged and kissed as she mumbled the appropriate words of appreciation. When it was her turn, Aunt Betty giggled with girlish embarrassment. Hypocrite, Erica thought with distaste. Aunt Constance brought up the rear, carrying the walnut cake she'd baked for the occasion. She solemnly offered her cheek to Sherman, who then led his three guests past the oak door and into the house.

Although she'd been to visit several times before, Erica couldn't help but marvel at the beauty and spaciousness of the large center hall. It reminded her of an old-fashioned ballroom. The tiled floor of black marble reflected the six-tiered crystal chandelier shimmering above them. An oak staircase curved dramatically up to the second floor.

Monica was just as dazzling, with an array of diamonds and sapphires on her ears, neck, and wrist. Her low-cut hostess gown revealed her creamy white bosom, while cleverly concealing the full width and breadth of her hips and buttocks. Although bleached blonde hair cascaded down her back, giving her an aging Goldilocks appearance, her sweet smile was heartwarming.

"Welcome, Erica, darling, and a happy, happy birthday."

Erica was pressed to her perfumed breast and kissed on both cheeks. Was that something she'd learned in France? she wondered snidely, then suffered a pang of remorse. For all her airs and excesses, Monica seemed genuinely glad to see her.

Amid a flurry of greetings and compliments concerning lost weight, health, and new hair styles, Sherman took his guests' wraps and pocketbooks.

"I'll dispose of these, then mix us some drinks."

He left, and Erica found herself face-to-face with Jason. He was wearing the sports jacket and pants he'd worn the night they'd gone out to dinner, and a pale yellow shirt that did nothing for his sallow complexion. He seemed very pleased with himself.

"Happy Birthday, Erica. May this be the first of many joyous celebrations."

He bent down to kiss her. Too late, she realized he was aiming for her lips and not the cheek she had offered. She turned her head swiftly so that his lips landed on the corner of her mouth.

"Thank you, Jason," she replied in her frostiest tone, the one that, in the past, could be depended on to elicit an apology and a sheepish look for whatever transgression he'd enacted. But tonight, he remained impervious to her displeasure.

He flashed her an audacious grin. "You're more than welcome. I've a present for you, but you won't be getting it until later."

She flinched when he placed his hand on her shoulder, but he seemed not to notice.

"There's no need to stand about," he said buoyantly. "Let's go inside. We've several trays of Mrs. Wiggins's tartlets to devour, and I, for one, am starved!" He leaned closer to her in a conspiratorial gesture. "I don't know about you, but eight o'clock is way past my dinner hour."

He shepherded her past the three older women, who were all speaking at once. Erica was relieved to see Aunt Constance had given up the sulks and was booming away, holding up her end of the conversation. As they passed Sherman's study, Erica stopped, her attention drawn inside to the several paintings covering the walls. Jason paused beside her and followed her glance.

"Impressive, aren't they? There are plenty moreall over the house." He laughed. "Collecting art has become Dad's passion these last few years."

She waited for the usual sneering remark to follow. Instead, his tone, as he spoke about Sherman, remained respectful, bordering on awe. She was puzzled by this sudden shift in affection. Then, she chided herself. She should be delighted father and son were finally getting along. Still, it seemed unnatural, after all those years of sparring and hostilities.

Sherman stood waiting for them in the living room, next to the well-stocked liquor cabinet. "What will you have, Erica, on this special occasion?"

"Some white wine would be fine, thank you."

He beamed. "A woman after my own heart. I've chilled a wonderful chardonnay for tonight. I'll get a bottle. Be right back."

He returned with the wine, which he proceeded to uncork with a flourish. He poured some into a glass and handed it to Erica. "Here you are, my dear. Jason? What are you drinking tonight?"

While Sherman busied himself with his son's scotch and soda, she wandered aimlessly about the room. She stopped beside the grand piano, fingered the smooth, well-polished wood that covered the keys. *It's only a piece of furniture now*, she thought sadly. *I bet no one's played it since Regina died.*

Determined not to let morbid thoughts fill her head, she stood at an open window and contemplated the illuminated Japanese garden outside. How lovely and peaceful. She breathed deeply. If only she could remain here all evening, quiet and undisturbed, to restore her peace of mind.

"Hors d'oeuvres, miss?"

Erica gave a start. She smiled at the young woman, then studied the appetizers on the tray. She chose a tiny cheese quiche. It was heavenly. Mrs. Wiggins hadn't lost her touch! She was seventy if she was a day, and her culinary skill was as excellent as it had been when she'd catered Erica's parents' parties all those years ago.

She sipped her wine. It was perfect. Dry, not too fruity.

Her shoulder muscles relaxed and the knot in her stomach dissolved. It was only a dinner, she told herself. And so far, the food and drink were first rate, even though the company wasn't of her choosing.

She'd be enjoying herself thoroughly if Doug had accepted her invitation. She shook her head to rid it of this unbidden thought. Doug had made it perfectly clear that he couldn't—or wouldn't—come tonight. And she certainly wasn't going to waste time or energy thinking about Doug Remsen!

Alone for the moment, she strolled around the room. Except for the piano, the entire decor had been changed since her last visit. Now the room had a distinctive oriental ambience. It was evident in the quilted fabric on the sofa and chairs flanking the fireplace, as well as the flower-patterned drapes and in the exquisitely hand-painted screen in the corner. A porcelain Chinese lion stood on the glass and bronze table between the sofa and two arm chairs. The color scheme—muted shades of green, rust, maroon, and pink—was pleasing to the eye. It was a refreshing relief from Monica's earlier venture in overstuffed upholstery and ornate French period pieces.

Now, the only overdone aspect of the room were the paintings. They hung on every wall and covered nearly every inch of space. There were oils, acrylics, watercolors, lithographs, woodcuts, and silk screens. They varied from geometric patterns to abstracts, landscapes to nudes.

She was astonished by the obvious mastery and quality of each work of art, as well as by the haphazard way they were placed. A modern acrylic painting of bold, garish brush strokes hung next to a Renoir-type oil of two young women resting against a gnarled tree. Her eyes darted from painting to print, greedily feasting on the artistic beauty of them all.

Sherman came to stand beside her. "Wonderful, aren't they?" His voice rang with pride. "I know they aren't hung properly. Monica scolds me each time I bring home another painting. She says the house looks like a museum, and a poorly arranged one at that. But I can't help it. Whenever I see something that appeals to me, something I know is well worth the asking price, I have to buy it."

"They're extraordinary. Each and every one of them. You have a wonderful eye for art."

"Why, thank you, Erica." There was no mistaking the surprise and pleasure in his voice. "After dinner, I'll show you the other rooms, if you like."

"I'd like that," she said, meaning it.

She moved closer to study the large oil painting hanging over the fireplace. It was of a solemn, middle-aged woman done in earth tones, the simple, angular lines reminiscent of a famous artist. She gasped aloud when she read the signature in the right-hand corner.

Sherman chuckled at her incredulity, then returned to the liquor cabinet to prepare drinks for the others, who were now entering the room.

"Dad's making quite a name for himself in the art world," Jason commented, standing where his father had been a moment earlier. "A few museums have already approached him. They want to know if he'll lend them the Hartley Collection." He sipped his drink. "I'm amazed. His taste is impeccable, though I must say, I hate a good deal of it."

"But all these paintings!" She made no effort to hide her wonderment. "They must cost a fortune. Where does he get the money for them all?"

He patted her shoulder. "I'm sure I don't know, Erica. And it's none of our business, now, is it?"

Her ears began to burn. Stung as she was by Jason's reprimand, indignation grew in her heart. How dare he? Of course, it was none of her business how Sherman got the money for his art collection. By doing legal work for Doug's boss, for all she knew or cared. That wasn't the point.

Jason's attitude was the point. Since when did he see his father as some sacred cow, beyond speculation or reproach? Ever since she'd known Jason, he'd come whining to her with complaint after complaint about Sherman. And now this. It was very peculiar.

She felt a hand on her arm and turned to meet Monica's glowing smile. Erica smiled back. Her aunts were nearby, as well, but their eyes were glued to the large oil painting over the fireplace.

"And this is the picture you were telling us about, Sherman," Aunt Betty said slowly. She scrutinized the painting before speaking again. "Lovely. Marvelous flesh tones. And sure to be worth a million dollars in a few years. At least that's what a very close friend told me." She gave a little laugh. "And he should know."

So, Erica thought, Aunt Betty's boyfriend is another art connoisseur. Maybe he's short of cash because he keeps buying artwork he can't afford.

She shook her head, wishing she weren't so suspicious of everyone's motives. And what was she supposed to call him after he and Aunt Betty got married? Certainly not Mr. Jennings, which was how she'd addressed him on the few occasions they'd met. Ron, she supposed. She had no intention of calling him "uncle."

"Very nice picture, Sherman," Aunt Constance said brusquely. She turned to the young woman and her tray. "I think I'll try some of Mrs. Wiggins's appetizers."

Erica grinned. Trust Aunt Constance to remain true to form.

She spent the next fifteen minutes skillfully avoiding conversation by examining the artwork around the room. Sherman, obviously gratified by her interest, came over from time to time to comment about the picture she was viewing. At the same time, she managed to down a fair number of Mrs. Wiggins's tartlets. This might well be her last opportunity to eat these scrumptious tidbits. According to Monica, Mrs. Wiggins was planning to retire next month and move down to Florida.

The appetizers did more than placate her hunger and keep her occupied. They reminded her of her parents' parties, when Mrs. Wiggins would arrive early, laden with trays of her specialties, with plenty of extras for Missy and Erica to munch on.

She remembered those occasions well. How, all dressed up in her organdy party dress and black patent Mary Janes, she'd open the front door to greet her parents' guests and help Missy carry their coats upstairs. Then she would circle the living room—or the back yard, if it was warm enough—the silver platter in her hands, and offer hors d'oeuvres to the visitors.

"A penny for your thoughts." Jason startled her, and she nearly spilled her wine. "I didn't mean to scare you," he said. "Although, I must say, you're rather jumpy lately."

"Am I?" she asked coldly. "Have you nothing better to do than to watch me?"

"And not at all friendly, I might add."

She stared into his laughing eyes until he looked away. *Aha,* she thought triumphantly. *He's up to something. I'm sure of it now.* Jason had never been able to meet her gaze when he had a guilty conscience. The realization cheered her up considerably, even though she hadn't a clue as to what he had done or was currently plotting. It relieved her to know that at least some things remained constant in a world full of puzzling surprises.

The dinner was a disaster. Each course was drenched in a sauce or a dressing, often making it difficult to recognize what lay beneath. As far as Erica knew, no one at the table cared for this type of cuisine. Even Aunt Betty, who claimed she enjoyed gourmet food, preferred simple roasts and fresh vegetables, as did Erica and Aunt Constance. Jason was happiest eating junk food, and Sherman and Monica always claimed they were dieting.

Erica watched Monica with fascination. She absolutely gurgled with delight as the young woman she'd hired placed a seafood appetizer drowned in Newberg sauce before each person. Then, ignoring her own plate, she beseeched them to eat.

"I made this all by myself! Do you like it? Would you care for some more?" she asked each of themabout the drowned Caesar salad, the overcooked veal Francese, the heavily buttered green beans, and the soggy pilaf.

Erica, who detested sauces and was not really hungry after eating all those tartlets, picked at her food. *Poor Aunt Constance*, she thought, when she caught her aunt doing the same. Even if she weren't as sick as Aunt Betty claimed, she had no business eating anything set before her tonight. Aunt Betty, like Sherman and Jason, was making a noble attempt to eat everything she was served. But the strained expression on her face showed the effort it cost her.

"Would you care for more veal, Erica, dear?" Monica offered brightly. "We've plenty more in the kitchen, haven't we, Chloe?"

"Enough for five more people, Mrs. Hartley," Chloe answered. "Here's the wine you wanted, Mr. Hartley."

Sherman uncorked the bottle and held it up to Erica. "More vino?" He enunciated very clearly, the only telltale sign that he'd been drinking.

She nodded and passed her glass to him.

For perhaps the thousandth time, she wondered what had inspired Sherman to marry this mindless, overblown woman who was acting as though she'd just learned to cook and was celebrating her first dinner party. Monica seemed to mean well. Which was probably why she got on so well with her aunts who, for all their faults, had no patience with phonies and snobs. And

Monica was lively and good-natured, pretty in a gaudy, showy sort of way.

But she was so...common. Erica was prepared to take an oath that an original thought had never entered the woman's mind. Her conversation revolved around her furniture, her hair, her clothing, or her next vacation. She was the very antithesis of Jason's mother. Regina had been a sensitive, cultured, well-educated woman. And Erica had always thought Sherman valued culture. His latest passion bore that out. But the only cultured thing about Monica was the enormous pearl adorning her right hand, which at the moment, was fluttering inches from Erica's face.

Monica caught Erica's uneasy glance and mistook it for admiration. "Beautiful, isn't it?" She beamed as she flashed the ring before Erica's eyes. "Sherman bought it for me last year on our Caribbean cruise. It's one of my most favorite rings."

"It's lovely," she murmured, glad for once, she wore glasses.

"Oops, sorry dear." Monica became aware of Erica's discomfort and moved her hand. She smiled. "Now you'll be able to buy yourself jewelry. Anything and everything that catches your fancy."

"Erica's husband can darn well buy her jewelry!" Aunt Constance blared across the table. "That is, whenever she decides to marry again. No need for her to fritter away her inheritance."

Aunt Betty tittered. "Young women today are independent, Connie. They like to spend their money as they please, especially when there's plenty of it." She cast a sly glance at Constance to see how she was receiving this contradiction.

Erica sighed. If only they'd stop bickering, and stop concerning themselves with her life.

"Regardless of who buys it for you," Monica continued, oblivious to the rising tension in the room, "jewelry is a wonderful investment. Isn't it, Sherman?"

"I suppose jewelry slowly increases its value with time. However, I personally would advise Erica to invest in good artwork. That's certain to appreciate, especially after the artist dies."

Sherman must have realized Monica's smile had faded because he'd failed to support her. He patted her hand and added, "I must say, darling, this meal is absolutely scrumptious. Better than anything we ate on our trip."

Monica's face lit up immediately. "Do you really think so?" Reassured by his vehement nod, she gushed, "That makes me very happy, Sherman, dear."

"I mean it quite sincerely." He took another bite of his veal to prove his point.

Erica marveled at his patience with his wife's childish behavior. He seemed utterly enchanted. And Monica was too naive to be believed. It was difficult to remember that, at one time, she had actually managed Sherman's office.

"We could play cards after dinner," Monica was saying, "except I have this teensy-weensy problem of confusing poker with gin rummy."

Everyone laughed.

Erica swallowed a sigh of exasperation. Monica was irritating, but obviously some people found her amusing. Was she for real? Was she truly as flighty and as shallow as she appeared to be? Or was this how she thought Sherman wanted her to be, and the act got to be a habit? Perhaps she was a good deal more clever than she seemed. In which case, maybe she'd had something to do with Erica's accidents.

But that was ridiculous. Why would Monica want to hurt her? Erica nibbled at her lip. She was growing distrustful of everyone. If she kept this up, she would soon find some evil motivation behind Sherman's new hobby of collecting art. Almost in penance, she turned to smile at him.

"If you're still game, Erica, I'd be happy to show you the paintings upstairs," he told her. "Buying art, good art, is an excellent investment. It's a gamble, of course. But then, so is everything in life. However, the risk is minimal if you know your artists."

"As long as she steers clear of gamblers, she'll be fine," Jason quipped.

He had remained silent during most of the meal, busily eating all he'd been served, and he was the only one to ask for seconds. He'd also had plenty to drink, judging from the way his words slurred together.

Blood rushed to Erica's ears. "How dare you!" she spat across the table.

How dare he make allusions to Terry, a dead man! Or was he hinting at Doug?

A spark of insight struck her, and she put one more piece of the puzzle in place. Jason had been behind that tree at the duck pond! It was his car she'd seen as they drove away. He must have paid those boys to scare her.

But, why?

Sherman patted her hand. "I apologize for Jason, Erica," he said, then turned a grim face to his son. "You've been rude and insensitive. If anyone here ought to steer clear of gamblers, it's you. After all the thousands of dollars you've lost. Thrown away."

Nobody spoke. The silence was palpable as all eyes stared at the dirty plates before them.

Sherman's tone softened. "Enough said about this matter." He smiled as he looked around the room, encouraging them to resume conversation.

"I think we're all ready for coffee," Monica announced cheerfully.

Again, Erica wondered about her. Was Monica unaware of the tension in the room, or was she a hostess skilled at glossing over a difficult moment?

No matter. Erica grinned suddenly. Her world was turning topsy turvy. She'd never dreamed she'd enjoy hearing Sherman reprimand Jason.

In gratitude, she turned to her host. "I'd love to see the rest of the paintings, Sherman."

He beamed. "My pleasure, Erica. Right after coffee and dessert."

CHAPTER TWELVE

The candles in the ornate silver candelabra were flickering. Two, Erica noticed, had already gone out.

"Have some more chocolate mousse, Constance," Monica urged. "I made it especially for you. I remember how much you loved it the last time."

Aunt Constance hesitated. "I really shouldn't," she said softly.

Don't listen to that moron, Erica silently instructed her aunt. She longed to shout out her advice, but didn't dare. Not that her words would protect her aunt from Monica's irresponsible prompting. Constance would eat more than was good for her because she had a passion for rich desserts.

"Just a little bit, dear," Monica coaxed as though she were encouraging a recalcitrant baby to eat its cereal. She stretched out a bejeweled hand. "Let's have your plate, Constance."

"Monica," Erica began in spite of herself, but it was too late. Monica had filled the small dish with mousse and was topping it with a dollop of whipped cream.

In a flare of anger, Erica pushed back her own dessert dish and rose from her seat. Her aunt was a grown woman, yet she had not one shred of common sense when it came to her health.

"Shall we go, Erica?" Sherman stood also. His gentle question made it appear as though they had agreed to leave the table together.

"Of course. Excuse us," she mumbled, and followed her host into the hall.

The upstairs rooms were plushily carpeted and decorated in muted tones. Here, too, art hung on every wall. Sherman led Erica to one of the guest bedrooms.

"Actually, it was Regina who introduced me to collecting art," he said. "We were married as soon as I graduated from law school, and we took an apartment in Queens. There we were, living on the pittance I earned at one of those large firms, plus what Regina made giving piano lessons." He laughed. "Between the two of us, we barely had enough money to take in a movie after paying the rent. Instead, we'd travel by subway to Manhattan, where we wandered from gallery to gallery.

"Regina would stand as though hypnotized before whatever painting caught her eye. I'd ask her what was so special about that particular piece of art, and she'd explain—in great detail and with much enthusiasm—why she was drawn to the work. She'd go on about the composition, the brush strokes, the colors, and God knows what else." He shook his head admiringly. "She knew more about art than any dealer I've ever met."

She nodded, pleased to hear him speak in such complimentary terms about his first wife. He pointed to a small lithograph of a mother holding her young son in her arms. They were smiling at each other, their mutual love and joy apparent.

"That's the first piece of art we ever bought." He chuckled. "It cost us a month's salary—hers and mine combined—but Regina insisted we get it to celebrate our first anniversary. And damn it, if she wasn't right! It's worth five times what we paid for it. Of course, that was years before she got her grandmother's inheritance." His voice grew cold. "And long before I started collecting myself."

He strode from the room. "Come along, Erica," he called over his shoulder. "No need to rehash ancient history."

She followed him out. She had sensed he and Regina had been estranged at the time of her death, and now she was certain what she'd suspected was true. Erica shrugged. It was sad, but that often happened with married couples. In another sense, she was gratified. By speaking of his life as a newlywed and alluding to past unhappiness, he was regarding her as an adult, and no longer the young girl he had watched grow up.

They walked past the master bedroom and Monica's sitting room to the smallest guest room at the end of the hall. The only furniture here was a scarred bureau, a simple table, and a high riser covered with a faded bedspread, all bits and pieces of a less affluent era. But the walls were another matter. They were covered with miniatures—small paintings, prints, and enamels.

She drew closer, fascinated by the care and effort that went into each work of art.

"Isn't this exquisite!" she exclaimed over one in particular. It was an oil painting of a girl of about sixteen, sailing high on a swing, smiling as if she hadn't a care in the world. The details were incredible. She could make out strands of her long brown hair flying behind, the lace of her white dress, the bark of the branch from which the swing hung. But best of all was the sense of suspended action. A moment captured forever.

"Lucky girl," she mused. "She has no idea what life has in store for her."

He ignored her cynical tone. "You have impeccable taste, my dear. I bought this lovely painting in London two years ago. Cost me a pretty penny, but it's worth every pound I spent."

He removed it from the wall and handed it to her. "It's yours, Erica. For your twenty-fifth birthday."

His generosity left her speechless. She held the unexpected gift, then offered it back to him.

"Don't you want it?" he asked, clearly amused to see how affected she was by his gesture. "I had the impression you really liked it."

He sat down on the high riser.

She did, too. "I love it. I really do!" she said fervently. She felt compelled to explain herself so that he wouldn't think her foolish. "It's one of the most beautiful pictures I've ever seen, only...it's yours," she finished lamely.

"Yes, mine to give to you, if I so choose," he said, a touch of his pomposity returning. "Monica and I wanted to give you something you really liked, and since you'll soon be able to buy anything your heart desires, we decided to let you choose."

She gulped. Each of these paintings was worth hundreds of thousands of dollars. "You mean, you were planning to give me whichever painting I liked best?"

He laughed. "Not quite any painting, I must admit. But I had an inkling of the few you might like, so let's leave it at that." He patted her hand.

But she couldn't let it go that easily. She wasn't used to receiving gifts, and she continued to demur at his unexpected show of munificence.

"I don't know, Sherman. This is a very expensive gift."

He stood suddenly, as though recoiling from her remark, and walked to the other end of the small room. She knew she had offended him.

"Don't behave like a ninny, Erica," he said impatiently. "Your father was one of my dearest friends. I owe it to his memory to do the little I can for his daughter."

"It is I who owe you so much," she now insisted, deeply moved by Sherman's loyalty to her father, all these years after his death.

"Good, good." He took a roll of brown paper from the closet and deftly wrapped the small painting as he spoke. "Not another word on the subject. Except one. I'd appreciate you not mentioning your little gift to anyone downstairs. And it would please me if you opened this package on your birthday. Tuesday morning, and not before."

Before she could respond, he handed over her new possession. "Here you are, and a very happy birthday to you." He bent down to kiss her cheek.

She nodded, although his words made her uneasy. Why was she to keep his gift a secret? And from whom? Monica? But he'd just told her they had both decided to give her a painting.

He interrupted her speculations. "Come. I still have many more paintings to show you. They'll begin to wonder what's keeping us."

She gazed politely at the large abstract paintings hanging in the master bedroom—harsh and incomprehensible in her opinion, which she kept to herself. But she found the primitives in Monica's sitting room colorful and uplifting.

The last room they came to was Jason's. The same Mexican blanket covered the narrow bed as it had years before, a pair of jeans lay sprawled across the chair beside the window.

Sherman pointed to a lithograph of children playing in a circle. "You probably remember this, since we bought it when Jason was two. Not very important, but I've kept it for sentimental reasons."

Erica nodded.

"Actually, I began collecting art in earnest only a few years ago. When I could afford to." He sounded apologetic, although she didn't know why.

Dutifully, she glanced around the room. The only other pictures were two boating scenes and a watercolor of a sand dune, none of which was unique or appealing. Even Sherman's exuberance seemed to have petered out. She waited for him to finish talking about the pictures so they could go downstairs.

Instead, he sank onto the bed and pointed to the chair. Perplexed, she pushed aside Jason's pants and sat facing him.

"Before we join the others, I'd like to express a sentiment that's been growing in my heart these past few days."

She said nothing, but continued to watch him, as fascinated as a rabbit captivated by the headlights of an oncoming car.

He paused, then continued with some embarrassment. "I know it's much too soon, what with your husband's untimely death and so on..."

Her mouth fell open, knowing yet dreading what she was about to hear.

"You and Jason have been dear friends since childhood. I've no doubt the two of you are deeply attached to each other in important and fundamental ways."

He gazed searchingly into her eyes, as if willing her to speak. But now, her silence was deliberate. She refused to help him express what was obviously difficult for him to put into words.

He looked down at the floor as he stumbled onward. "I haven't been the best of fathers." He coughed, hoping she'd contradict him.

She didn't.

"At any rate, I love Jason very much. He's my only child, and I'm delighted to say we've gotten along better these last few weeks than ever before."

He looked at her beseechingly. She stared stonily ahead, refusing to meet his eyes.

"He's a dear boy, a bright boy, but he needs a firm hand to guide him. You're level-headed, Erica, and I know how fond Jason is of you." He laughed. "And I appreciate the spunk you've shown since you've returned to Manordale."

Spunk. What spunk? If I had any spunk, I'd get the hell out of here.

"Frankly," he went on, his manner growing more confident as he took her silence to signify agreement, "I think you'd be the ideal wife for Jason. He shows every indication of becoming a productive citizen. He could, too, with you to keep him on the right track."

And what about me? she thought bitterly. *Does anyone care what I want or need?*

Still, she forced herself to speak calmly. "What you're proposing, Sherman, is out of the question. I'm very fond of Jason, but only as a friend."

"Of course, you're fond of him. I wouldn't be having this conversation with you if that weren't the case," he said a bit impatiently. "But very often, Erica, friendship can turn into something more...romantic. I know Jason cares for you. He's told me several times how glad he is that you've come back home. He claims he's never really appreciated you before."

His small eyes bore into her, made her squirm with discomfort. Why was he going on like this, putting her in a false position? It was time she set him straight.

"I think you've misunderstood what Jason told you," she said coldly. "We're friends, nothing more. I could never care for Jason in a romantic way. I used to feel sympathy for him. I tried to help him in the past, and he was a good friend to me. We listened to each other's problems, that was all."

She stared back at Sherman, as though defying him to contradict her. She suddenly realized she'd put everything in the past tense. Was that how she felt about Jason? A childhood friend she'd outgrown?

But Sherman, to her growing annoyance, remained un-daunted. "The essential element you're choosing to ignore," he said pedantically, "is that you and Jason understand each other. You can relate to one another on a deeper level than most people can, because you've known each other since childhood." His voice rose with excitement. "Frankly, seeing the two of you married is something I would welcome with all my heart."

She shook her head vehemently. "Sherman, Jason is a weak and unhappy person, and I'm afraid he'll never change. I've cared for him like a brother, but please believe me, I would never, *never* marry him, and that's final!"

He sighed and rose heavily from the bed with obvious disap-pointment.

"My dear, don't take my musings to heart. I'm sorry if I've upset you. It was only a thought. A wish. I suppose celebrating your twenty-fifth birthday has made me ponder on the brevity of life, and how I'd like to enjoy my grandchildren before I'm too old."

Grandchildren! What nerve! As though I'm supposed to turn into a brood mare in order to please him.

"We'd better go downstairs and join the others," he said. "They'll be wondering what we've been up to."

She swept past him, eager to leave the room, but he grasped her shoulder. His grip was surprisingly strong.

"Just one more thing, Erica, before I forget." His voice had lost its warmth and there was a sardonic ring to it. "Jason tells me you've become friendly with Doug Remsen. I'd be careful, if I were you. I understand the last woman he was involved with ended up in the hospital with broken ribs. A bad temper, I hear. I wouldn't want anything like that to happen to you."

"Now look here," she sputtered. "I'd appreciate your staying out of my affairs—er—business." She felt her face growing hot, and was furious with herself for not keeping her cool.

"Certainly, Erica," he said smoothly. "I was speaking from concern."

"And tell your son to stop spying on me."

Was that a flicker of fear in his small blue eyes? She wasn't sure, although she fervently hoped it was.

"Please don't be hard on Jason. He only followed you yesterday because he cares for you."

"Is that why he paid those boys to knock me down?" she asked angrily. "Or did he leave that part out of his report?"

She rushed down the steps, unaware that she was clutching her small painting to her chest until she was near the bottom. She was furious with Sherman for trying to tell her how to lead her life. And he had no right to accuse Doug of physically abusing a woman. Sure, he had a temper, but...

She shuddered. As far as she knew, Sherman never lied. Although, he'd certainly had made good use of his wily lawyer tricks to lure her upstairs so he could urge her to marry his son.

Aunt Betty met her at the foot of the staircase, her face drawn and pale.

"I was just coming up to get you. Connie is feeling ill. She says it's just indigestion, but I'm taking her straight home. She's lying down in the living room."

"Oh, my God!"

Erica ran to Aunt Constance.

Monica was hovering over her, fussing with the cushion beneath her head. "I'll get your water now, Constance," she said, and hurried off.

Constance nodded, seemingly unable to speak. Her hand gripped her side in pain.

"Oh, Aunt Constance," Erica moaned. She knelt beside the large, inert figure and took her free hand.

"It's my own fault. I shouldn't have eaten all that damn mousse."

"Are you all right? Should I call a doctor?"

"Don't worry, girl," she whispered so that only Erica could hear. "It's not my heart."

She nodded, relieved by her aunt's forthrightness.

"Betty's taking me home now, but I don't want your evening ruined. Stay a while. Jason's offered to drive you home later."

"But I'd rather go with you now," she said frantically.

"Nonsense. It's only ten o'clock. Monica would be hurt if we all ran out on her. Besides, you're the guest of honor."

Erica felt Monica's hand on her back and moved aside. She cringed as Monica, in a singsong, childish voice, said, "Here you are, Constance, dear. Bottoms up!"

Aunt Constance struggled into a half-sitting position against the sofa's arm and drank the water. "That's better," she proclaimed.

"I'm so pleased," Monica replied. She turned to Erica. "I was hoping you'd stay with us for a while. After all the anticipation, I hate to see the evening end so soon."

Erica looked around. Jason and Sherman had come into the room. The three Hartleys fixed their eyes on her, imploring her to stay. She needed an excuse, any excuse, to release her from this disastrous evening, but her mind remained blank.

"Of course, she'll stay," Constance declared, settling the matter. "I'm ready to leave, Betty, any time you are."

She helped her aunt to her feet. "I'll walk you out to the car," she murmured.

"Now, don't run off and abandon us," Jason said lightly.

"Don't worry, I'll be back," she answered gracelessly, giving vent to her displeasure.

She yearned to jump in the car and drive off with her aunts. She'd had enough of the Hartleys to last her a lifetime. In the hall, she caught Monica and Sherman exchanging anxious glances. Were they concerned about Aunt Constance or upset about something else?

Aunt Constance allowed Erica to help her into the car. "You go back inside and have a good time," she mildly admonished.

Erica made a sour face. "I'll try."

CHAPTER THIRTEEN

To Erica's surprise, the next hour and a half flew by. A mood of ease and light-heartedness seemed to have settled around them as Sherman recounted one humorous anecdote after another, sending his audience into fits of laughter. And Monica, Erica discovered, when released from the self-imposed pressure of being the perfect hostess, had a wit of her own.

At eleven-thirty, Monica caught herself yawning and apologized profusely. "I'm sorry, Erica. I don't know what's come over me. And we've been having such a lovely time."

Jason put an arm around his stepmother's shoulders. "Of course, you're tired. You've been on your feet all day preparing this divine dinner, and now you're completely bushed."

Was he overdoing the considerate act, or was she being less than kind? Jason had behaved himself for the second part of the evening. He'd said little, but remained attentive to Erica's comfort. Did she want more brandy? Was she comfortable with the window open?

Monica yawned again, but this time she laughed. "I suppose you're right, Jason. It's been a busy day."

"I don't want to keep you up," Erica said quickly. "Could you please drive me home, Jason?" She turned to her old friend who, by virtue of his recent kind behavior, was back in her good graces.

"Sure enough, Ricky," he said obligingly. "I'll get your sweater."

She hugged Sherman and Monica, and thanked them for their hospitality, her small painting tucked discreetly under her arm. Though she was pleased that the evening had ended on a relaxed and friendly note, she was eager to get home.

"It was our pleasure to have you," Sherman repeated.

He and Monica walked her to the front door where Jason was waiting. He helped her with her cardigan, leaving a friendly arm around her shoulders as they stepped outside.

The night was cool, the sky full of stars.

He drew a deep breath. "Beautiful out, isn't it? We even have Dad's Cadillac at our disposal since mine's in the shop."

His words sent a chill down her back.

She pulled the sweater tightly around her shoulders. "What's wrong with your car?"

Silly, she told herself. She'd seen his car after Terry's accident. Had been inside it twice, in fact, when Jason had driven her to the morgue, and that awful evening they'd gone out.

Or had they used Monica's red car, now parked two feet away? She couldn't remember. But Jason's car had been at the duck pond yesterday. Sherman had as much as admitted Jason had followed her there.

Before she could sort any of it out, he said, "I brought it in for a lube and an oil change, and a new muffler. It won't be ready until Monday afternoon."

His response sounded offhand. No false note that she could detect.

He opened the passenger door, and she stepped inside. "Dad thinks I'm crazy to put any money into it." He walked around to the driver's side and got in. "He says I should get a new car for my new image, but I'm too attached to the old Buick." He gave a little laugh. "Besides, Tough Tony tells me she has two good years left, and he sure as hell knows what he's talking about."

"Who's Tough Tony?"

He switched on the motor before he answered. "Dad discovered him years ago, at the gas station near his office. The man's seventy-five if he's a day. Dad says what goes on under the hood of a car is as plain to him as the back of his hand. And he can fix anything. The old buzzard's sparse with words. Acts like they're pieces of gold."

"Where did he get a name like that?"

He shrugged. "Probably from his younger days, when he was in a different line of work. I think he spent a few years in prison."

I bet he did, she thought grimly. *And I wouldn't be surprised if he once worked for Doug's boss.*

To divert her thoughts from ex-convicts and cars needing repairs, she asked the first question that popped into her head. "How can you buy a new car? I thought you were low on funds."

He laughed easily as he swung onto the turnpike. "Technically, I am. But that's about to change. Dad's lined up three interviews for me. By this time next week, I should be gainfully employed."

Impulsively, she squeezed his hand. "Oh, Jase, I'm really glad for you."

They stopped at a red light, and he turned to face her. "It just shows how your life can change for the better when you least expect it. I came back here because of your husband's accident."

She winced at the reference to Terry's death, but he didn't seem to notice.

"Though I was getting pretty lonesome out at Montauk, wasting my time on that dumb play. Coming home to Manordale turned out to be the right move."

The light turned green, and the Cadillac rode smoothly on its way. "And I began to see Dad in a new light. Not as the stuffed shirt I'd been fighting all my life. More like a mentor. A counselor. Someone who really cares about me."

Good God, she thought in amazement. *I can't believe this is Jason Hartley, extolling the virtues of his father. The same father who ridiculed him and chipped away at his self-confidence all those years.* For a moment, she wondered if Jason was pulling her leg. If he was simply making use of his father and his connections.

A glance at his face told her he'd meant every word he was saying.

She reflected back on the evening. Jason and Sherman had shown nothing but a cordial respect for each other. Still, something was fishy. The change in their relationship had come about too suddenly. Too quickly. What really was the basis of it all?

"And," Jason said, interrupting her thoughts, "Dad's right. It's about time I stopped bumming around like an adolescent kid. I never told you, Erica, but I got involved in some bad deals a while back. Had a few close calls with some nasty people."

She tried to remember exactly what Doug had said about Jason, when he turned to give her a warm smile.

"But I'm through with all that now. I promise."

When he reached for her hand, she pulled free of his clasp. Something was very wrong. Why was he treating her like a date? Again.

After a minute of silence, he said, "Did you know that for years I was jealous of you?"

"Me? What could you possibly have been jealous of?"

"You always had drive. Knew exactly what you were going to do. I'll never forget the day you told me—no, announced—you were going to become an accountant. A CPA, no less. So you'd be able to earn money and be independent." His smile turned crafty. "But you never became an accountant, did you? Just an office girl for some little magazine."

"Office girl?" she bristled. "I was a senior editor, and wrote plenty of articles. And it was no little magazine, I'll have you know."

"What I know is you never could become an accountant. It's too boring and monotonous. And doesn't suit your fiery temper."

"Fiery?" she sputtered. "I don't have a fiery temper!"

"'I don't have a fiery temper!'" he imitated, then burst out laughing.

His laughter was infectious. Before she knew it, she was laughing along with him.

He slapped her knee. "That's more like the old Erica I used to know."

"And that's the old Jason coming through," she quipped back.

They drove along in relaxed silence until he spoke again. "Don't take this the wrong way, but your mad dash out to Montauk was like something out of a movie. It was so dramatic—the way you told me, in no uncertain terms, I'd better lend you twenty thousand dollars to pay off your husband's debt or else."

And you're letting me know you resent me for it, and always will, she thought, then marveled how this bit of insight hadn't occurred to her on her own. He had every right to be angry. She bit her lip in embarrassment, remembering how she'd threatened to tell Sherman about Jason's driving accident all those years ago if he refused to lend her the money. Heat spread across her face. She was glad he couldn't see her face.

He seemed to take her silence as a reproach for having brought up the subject of her dead husband. A wistful note crept into his voice. "I hope someday I'll have someone as loyal in my corner. You were as fierce as a tigress—eyes flashing behind those oversized glasses, your hair blowing every which way as you paced and turned. You were totally devastating."

"Devastating?" she chortled, regaining her composure. "I was frantic and worried and upset. I only did what I thought I had to." When she spoke again, her tone was contrite. "I'm terribly sorry for behaving in such a high-handed manner. It just occurred to me how downright nasty it was for you on the receiving end."

"Forget it, Ricky. I've done a few obnoxious things myself. Let's be friends again." He patted her hand.

This time she didn't pull away.

"Agreed." She sighed and relaxed deeper into the cushioned seat. It was nice having Jason back on her side.

The Cadillac hummed along with the light flow of traffic. When she glanced out her window, she was surprised to see they had long since passed the turn to her house.

"Hey, Jase, forget where I live? We're at least a mile past Redwood Lane."

He grinned sheepishly. "I thought you were having a good time."

"What do you mean?"

"Since it's so early, I thought we'd stop someplace for a drink. To celebrate your birthday properly."

"I'm tired and I'd like to go home. I thought the games were over and we were friends again."

"I'm sorry, Erica," his voice came out muffled. "It was damn selfish of me to think that you would... Forget it! I'll turn around and take you home."

He sounded so sad and forlorn, she was moved in spite of herself. "Is something wrong?"

He acted as if he hadn't heard her. When she repeated the question, he nodded.

"I thought, since we were friends again, we could talk like we used to."

"About what?"

He drove slower. "Lately, I'm feeling kind of jittery, and I haven't been sleeping well. I suppose it's all these changes. Those interviews Dad's arranged. They're with firms he represents. It was great of him to set it all up. I appreciate it and all. But..."

"But?" she prodded.

Silence.

When he spoke, his voice was barely audible. "I don't know if I can handle it." He swung into the left-hand lane, intent on turning back.

She touched his arm. "Let's go for that drink, Jason, talk about your interviews and things."

"Do you mean it?"

His relief and gratitude were apparent. She felt a pang of sadness. Same old Jason. He still needed a sympathetic ear, someone to bolster his faltering ego.

"Of course, Jason. That's what friends are for."

He continued heading down the turnpike. Seemingly encouraged by her change of heart, he told her of the three positions for which he'd interview, thanks to Sherman's arrangements.

"Which do you think would suit me best?"

She bit her lip as she thought. "It's difficult to say. The marketing research job sounds interesting. It's something I would like. But maybe you'd prefer writing copy in an ad office. Or go for the excitement of Wall Street. You'll get a better sense of each company at the interview."

She warmed to her subject, glad to be able to offer him practical advice. "Meanwhile, channel your nervousness and put it to good use. Google each company, then ask them questions based on what you've learned. They'll be impressed that you bothered to do your homework."

When he made no comment, she stared at his profile, trying to fathom what was going through his mind. In the dim light, she noted his face was drawn, his brow wrinkled.

Finally, he spoke, in a voice drained of all emotion. "Yeah, I know all that."

"Sorry, Jason. I didn't mean to suggest that you didn't."

Damn, she hadn't meant to get carried away. But it was more than that. Her intuition told her something was wrong.

"Don't be silly," he said. "It's nothing to do with you. It's just…"

Again, he stopped, and she had to encourage him. "It's just what, Jason?"

"Just that I don't know what the hell I'm getting myself into. It all sounded so great the way Dad put it—having a job with a prestige firm, buying a condo. Vacations, a new car."

He took a deep breath. "I don't think I can hack working in an office all day, five days a week. Two, three weeks off for vacation. Wearing a jacket and slacks all the time. It's too much to ask of me."

She let out a sigh of exasperation. Here he was, twenty-seven years old, with no more ambition than a house cat. "You have to settle down some day. It may as well be now."

He opened his mouth—to make a sarcastic comment, she would bet—but he closed it again without speaking. They drove on in silence, him clearly bristling under her disapproval.

She stared at the road ahead of her, regretting she'd agreed to extend the evening. And where was he taking her? She wished he would finally stop so they could have this drink and get it over with.

Finally, to break the heavy silence, she asked where they were going.

"I thought Fiorello's, unless you have an objection."

"Fiorello's!" she shrieked. Why did he have to pick the place where she'd gone with Doug?

"What's wrong with Fiorello's?" he asked defensively. "You haven't been there in years. The new owners did a nice job of redecorating. In fact, the bar's the most popular singles place around, especially on weekends."

"I thought it was a restaurant. And I couldn't see going there after that enormous dinner we've eaten."

"For your information, they make the best drinks east of Manhattan." His voice was sullen. "But if you don't want to go there for some strange, weird, mysterious reason—"

"No, no!" she protested, not wanting a hassle. "Fiorello's is just fine."

About fifteen cars were parked in the lot behind the restaurant. None of them a blue BMW, she was quick to notice. He kept his hand under her elbow as they walked toward the rear entrance. Though she didn't care for his proprietary gesture, she decided not to make a fuss and went along compliantly.

The atmosphere was exactly as she remembered—the lighting turned low, romantic music playing softly in the background. The same maître d' approached.

Jason told him they wanted to sit at the bar.

Here I go again, she thought. *Same restaurant, same dress, different man.*

The long room was even darker than the restaurant. A dozen or so young people sat on stools along the bar, chatting or watching a comedy show on the huge TV. The small round tables nearby stood empty, though most of the booths along the back wall were occupied. In one, a man and a woman were locked in a passionate embrace.

Erica stifled a groan. She hoped Jason wasn't thinking this was another "date" he'd arranged.

Two brassy-looking twenty-something women stopped their conversation to eye Jason as they walked by. He appraised the women in turn.

"The unlucky ones," he said dismissively, not bothering to keep his voice down. "Nobody wanted them tonight."

"Maybe they wouldn't settle for what was available," she cracked back.

They sat down in a booth.

"Is that what you plan to do?" Jason asked maliciously. "Go to bars to meet men? Oh, I almost forgot," he said in mock surprise. "In three days, you'll be a rich woman. You won't have to come to places like this. You'll be flying off to Monte Carlo or Paris or Dubai." He laughed unpleasantly. "But I bet one place is the same as the next when you're man-hunting."

She stiffened. She opened her mouth, but no words came forth.

He had turned on her again, becoming nasty and sardonic without provocation. She hadn't seen this side of him until very recently. Well, she sure as hell didn't have to hang around for insults and abuse. Her heart pounded against her ribs as she rose to her feet. But before she could speak, he grabbed her hand and started babbling an apology.

"Don't go, Erica. Please stay. I'm sorry. Damned sorry I've been saying such stupid things. I don't know what's gotten into me. I'm nervous and jittery and taking it out on you."

The waiter appeared, a smile plastered on his tired face. "Good evening, folks. What can I get you?"

"A vodka martini for me," Jason said, "and a glass of chardonnay for the lady." He turned to her. "Right?"

She sighed audibly and sat down. Jason! He was impossible. But he had apologized, and there was no reason to make an issue of it.

The waiter turned to go.

Jason called after him. "Please see that the wine glass is well chilled for the love of my life." He looked at her, a gloating smile on his lips.

His arrogance had her fuming with fury. "I'm not your love!" she snapped. "You're not even my friend! I know you set those boys on me in the park. You're damn lucky I didn't tell Doug. He has quite a temper."

He gave a rueful laugh. "So I noticed. It was a dumb thing to do. I just don't want to see you getting mixed up with another gambler. I do care about you, you know."

When she gave no answer, he reached inside his shirt pocket and took out a pill.

"Oh, no," she groaned. "Not that again."

He swallowed the pill without water, then smiled. "Don't be silly. I don't take anything stronger than aspirin these days. I'm just a little edgy since I got back from Montauk, and having trouble sleeping. I told you, remember?"

Her eyes narrowed as she studied him. "You're acting weird. What's really bothering you?"

Their drinks arrived, and Jason took a hearty gulp of his martini. "Everything I told you before—my new future, stuff like that." He spoke mockingly as he reached out to cover her hand with his. "And I'm afraid of letting Dad down."

"What do you mean, letting him down?" She struggled to extricate her hand, but his grip held it firmly beneath his own. "Let go of me, Jason," she said between clenched teeth.

"What? Oh, sorry, Erica. I didn't mean to hold you prisoner."

"Well, you sure as hell tried."

"I mean," he went on as though nothing had happened, "Dad seems so happy that I'm showing an interest in getting a job. He sees me as some sort of business manager or executive in five years. All I can see is having to prove myself to some insensitive clod who will probably swagger around the office, making sure I know just how important and powerful he is."

He swallowed the rest of his drink, then raised his hand to catch the waiter's attention.

"The clod might be a 'she'," Erica murmured.

When the waiter hurried over, Jason ordered another martini. He turned back to her. "What did you say?"

"Never mind. And I wish you'd calm down. Going on a few interviews doesn't require all this boozing and pill popping."

He ignored her comment. He drummed his fingers on the table, apparently lost in his own thoughts.

Then, he turned to her abruptly. "Do you have any cigarettes?"

She laughed. "Why should I? You know I don't smoke, and you don't, either. Besides, you can't smoke in here."

"I'll go get some. Be right back."

He sprang from his seat. When he returned, he was inhaling and coughing simultaneously. He almost collided with the waiter, who was placing Jason's drink on the table.

The older man moved quickly out of his way, and asked Jason to put out the cigarette.

She was growing alarmed. "Jason, calm down. You're acting like a nut."

He slid into the booth. He snuffed out his cigarette, then guzzled half his drink.

"What's wrong?" she asked, beginning to really worry. "It's not just the interviews. Something's wrong, isn't it?"

He reached inside his jacket and placed a tiny square box on the table. He swallowed a chestful of air, then gazed into her eyes. When he spoke, his voice was low and mournful.

"Erica," he implored. "Will you marry me?"

CHAPTER FOURTEEN

Sunday morning, Erica awoke with a groan. She willed herself to fall back into a dreamless sleep, but to no avail. Last night's farcical scene flashed through her mind, making her groan again. If this were someone else's life, if she weren't so angry with Jason, she could laugh. Perhaps she should laugh.

No! This was a serious matter. She had suffered an irretrievable loss. Jason was no longer her friend. She would never speak to him again.

She had always known he was weak. His insecurities and problems were partly what had endeared him to her. He had often depended on her support and common sense, and knew he was welcome to them. But what he had proposed last night—*proposed, hah!*—had been totally ridiculous.

And bordered on the incestuous.

Even though he'd made no pretense of suddenly falling in love with her. Merely of needing her. And finally admitting, when pressed, that it was her inheritance he "needed" most of all.

She'd stomped out of the bar, not giving him a chance to open the little box set before her. She had no desire to see the bauble he'd bought with his father's money in hopes of winning her fortune.

He'd chased after her, trapping her in the small vestibule where she waited for a taxi. "Erica, please," he'd begged. "All I'm asking is that you think it over. Not right now, of course. But soon."

When it became clear that she wouldn't respond, much less look at him, he'd turned angry and abusive. He'd called her a "selfish bitch," and worse, until the maître d' escorted him out of the restaurant.

In the taxi, tears of anger and humiliation had burned her eyes. How dare he? How dare Sherman? How dare they scheme to have that pathetic creep ask her to marry him? Just so he wouldn't have to work another day of his life!

She sat up in bed and decided Sherman must have planned it all. Jason was incapable of such machinations, while his father undoubtedly maneuvered and rearranged facts every day on behalf of his clients. But where was his good sense when it came to his son? Why assume Jason would succeed at making Erica his wife when he'd failed at everything else?

Her eyes narrowed with fury. To think that Sherman had so little regard for her. He considered her nothing but a pawn. A mere puppet to be manipulated. To dance to their tune! She wanted no part of him, as well. She picked up the little painting, considered returning it, then placed it back on her bureau and leaned it against the wall. The painting was hers. She had more than earned it.

In a sudden burst of energy, she sprang out of bed and pulled up the shades. Sunlight poured into her room. A perfect May day, she was forced to admit in spite of her foul mood.

A shower and wearing one of her new outfits did much to improve her spirits.

She stopped at Aunt Constance's room to see how she was feeling, and found the double bed was made, the corner of the flowered comforter neatly folded back. *She must be better*, she thought with relief. Thank God last night's pain had probably been nothing more serious than a bout of indigestion.

Although her physical well-being had been restored, a glowering, angry Constance greeted Erica in the kitchen.

"'Morning, Erica. I was wondering when you'd finally come downstairs."

Although puzzled and a bit hurt by the brusque remark, she chose to ignore it. "I'm glad you're feeling better," she said, and poured herself a glass of orange juice.

"My stomach has settled down. But if I don't have a heart attack one of these days," her aunt said darkly, "it'll be no thanks to your Aunt Betty."

"What do you mean?" She stared at her aunt. "Did you and Aunt Betty have an argument? Where is she?"

"Gone."

"Gone? Gone for the day? With a friend?" she added hopefully.

"No, Erica. I mean gone for good." There was no missing the smugness in her tone. "She packed her suitcase and said we'd be hearing from her eventually. Took her briefcase and computer, as well."

"Did you and Aunt Betty have a fight? When did she leave?"

Erica felt forsaken. Abandoned. Anxiety rose in her throat, forcing her to take deep, heaving breaths. Certainly, Aunt Betty was free to leave the house whenever she wanted, and Erica certainly didn't need Aunt Betty to look after her. But it was odd for her to go off like this. Odd and disconcerting.

"Betty and I had a heart-to-heart talk this morning. I finally got it out of her." Aunt Constance was gloating now. "All about her and Ron." She gave a snort of indignation. "He's a principal, mind you, and old enough to retire, carrying on like a backstreet Romeo. They're two fools, just as they were seventeen years ago.

"Betty wanted to know if I was angry with her. 'Angry?' I asked her. 'Why should I be angry if you choose to be an adulteress? The only reason I'm angry,' I said, 'is because you do it in such a sneaky, pussyfooting, childish kind of way.'"

"She didn't want to hurt you, Aunt Constance. That's why she kept it a secret."

"Don't tell me you knew about her and Ron!" Further incensed by this new revelation, her aunt turned her anger on Erica. "Why didn't you say so instead of keeping me ignorant like a fool, not knowing what was happening in my own house? Excuse me. *Your* house."

Erica groaned. "Let's not start that again. I'm really not up to it."

Constance's jaw snapped shut.

Although she was no longer hungry, Erica toasted an English muffin and made herself a cup of coffee. Her aunt went to the sink and noisily loaded the dishwasher.

The heavy atmosphere bore down on them. Erica wracked her brain to think of something innocuous to say, and was relieved when her aunt spoke again.

"How was your evening last night? I didn't hear you come in. It must have been pretty late."

"I came home around twelve-thirty." She resented this old habit of being expected to "check in," but was unable to stop herself. "By taxi, I might add."

"Oh?" Constance eyed her inquisitively. "I thought Jason was driving you home."

"He started to," she said, then proceeded to tell her aunt what had happened.

Aunt Constance showed no sign of surprise. "I've always said Jason has a screw loose, but your Aunt Betty, with her usual lack of judgment, was so positive he'd changed. Of course, it was Monica who convinced Betty to consider Jason in a different light." She rolled her eyes at Erica. "Just the other day, the two of them were practically planning your wedding. Can you imagine Betty being part of that? As if you'd ever consider marrying that boy."

The Hartleys had gone so far as to draw her aunts into their scheme. She felt a flair of anger against them all, especially against her Aunt Betty, who should have known better.

Aunt Constance's voice turned gentle. "I know you think I interfered too much in your life, Erica. Betty told me so often enough while you were gone, and I suppose she was right. But this time, I kept out of it while she went along with the dinner, trying to bring you and Jason together." She looked sheepishly at her niece. "That was another thing we fought about this morning."

Erica's cell phone rang, interrupting her impulse to fling her arms around her aunt in gratitude.

"Good morning," she practically sang when she saw it was Doug.

Her aunt must have figured out who had called, because her scowl was back.

Erica went into the dining room, and shut the swinging doors for privacy.

"Good morning, Erica. I hope I didn't wake you."

"No, we were just finishing our breakfast. How are you?"

"Just fine." He sounded fine and pleasantly relaxed. "Enjoy your dinner last night?"

"Not exactly. It's a long story. I'll tell you about it some other time." She blushed, suddenly feeling she'd been too forward by implying there might be a future time they'd be together.

"I'd like to hear all about it. And I've something to discuss with you—an idea that just occurred to me. I'm curious to find out what you think."

A chill went through her heart. There he went again, scaring her. "What is it?" she asked breathlessly. "Do you know who—?"

"Nothing for you to worry about," he cut in smoothly. "It was only a thought." His voice quickened. "Are you free tomorrow? I don't have to work until the evening. I was hoping I could see you."

"Tomorrow's great," she answered. "I've nothing planned." She pushed open the door and found Aunt Constance standing there, eavesdropping unashamedly to Erica's end of the conversation.

"Great! Then we have the entire day to ourselves. How about I pick you up at nine, and we drive into Manhattan?"

"I'd like that very much," she said, ignoring Aunt Constance's snort of disapproval. An entire day with Doug. "I'll set my alarm clock."

"Do that," he quipped. "I'm always on time."

She heard voices in the background.

"Hold it a second." When he spoke again, his manner was brusque. "I have to go now. See you tomorrow."

The phone clicked, and he was gone.

Too bad their conversation had been cut short by what was obviously an unexpected interruption. Still, Doug had called, and they were going to spend all of tomorrow together. She was grinning as she returned to the kitchen.

"I gather you're going out with Doug Remsen."

She was taken aback by the hostility in her aunt's voice. "Yes, I am," she forced herself to answer civilly. "Why are you so angry?"

"If I'd known what I know now, I wouldn't have given him the right time of day when he called asking for you on Friday."

"What do you mean?" Her face was burning and must be blazing red. Aunt Constance knew!

"I happened to mention his name to Sherman, and the poor man nearly had a fit." Aunt Constance glared at her niece. "Sherman knew who he was, all right. He told me your Mr. Doug Remsen's a strong arm for some gangster—a most unsavory character—and if you were his daughter, he'd forbid you to have anything to do with the man."

"Forbid me?" This time she made no attempt to contain her outrage. "And did your precious Sherman tell you what kind of dealings he has with Doug's boss? No, of course not. I tell you, I'm sick and tired of Sherman Hartley meddling in my affairs. The day I sign all those legal papers is the last time I ever set eyes on that pompous fool!"

"Sherman's only looking out for your own good," Constance said sternly, "and that's not the issue at hand. How do you know this man?"

Flustered, Erica said, "I told you. He knew Terry. Through business."

"Business? Hah!"

Arms crossed, Aunt Constance resembled an unforgiving Buddha. In the pulsating silence, Erica gave a start as the motor of the old refrigerator clicked on. She felt twelve years old again. Guilty and unsure of herself before the implacable stare of her aunt.

"Look, Aunt Constance," she began nervously, "you don't know anything about Terry or Doug."

"Tell me. I'm listening." Her aunt's voice was icy.

Erica searched for the right words, and couldn't find them. "I can't. It's too complicated and you wouldn't understand," she finished lamely.

It was the worst thing she could have said.

"I wouldn't understand?" Her aunt's eyes fairly bulged out of their sockets. "I'm tired of people telling me I won't understand. First Betty, now you. I'm not stupid. I'm not incompetent." She pounded the table to emphasize her point, and made the dishes rattle. "Do you think that just because I have a touch of heart trouble I'm to be treated like a child? Well, do you?" Her fierce expression demanded an answer.

"No," Erica mumbled. She wanted to throw her arms around Aunt Constance's massive shoulders and stop her from upsetting herself. Erica's anxiety for her aunt's health mounted. Her palms grew moist, her heartbeat accelerated. Aunt Constance shouldn't be carrying on this way. What if she had a heart attack right now? What could she do to save her? Erica wished she weren't the reason for her aunt's wrath. "Please calm yourself," she said. "It isn't worth all this fuss."

"Calm myself?" Her words inflamed her aunt even more. "I resent your treating me like I'm an imbecile. And I'd like to know why your face lights up like Christmas whenever this Doug Remsen—this gangster—calls."

Erica decided to try a new tack. "Doug wants to help me. He's looking out for my welfare. He's the only one who's trying—"

"Well, I like that," Constance broke in, bellowing her outrage. "If I don't care about you, I'd like to know who does."

"That's not what I mean," Erica said doggedly. She hesitated, afraid to say too much, then decided to take the plunge. After all, she couldn't possibly upset her aunt any more than she was right now.

"I've had a few accidents. Doug thinks someone close to me is trying to harm me."

"Accidents?" Aunt Constance repeated, sounding puzzled. "This is the first time I've heard of any accidents."

Reluctantly, Erica told her of the two attempts on her life. Aunt Constance remained silent for what seemed like minutes, her brow wrinkled in concentration. When she finally spoke, her voice was calm.

"This is serious, Erica. Why didn't you tell Betty or me? Or the police?"

"I didn't want to upset either of you. I told the police about the first incident, but I never bothered about the second since nobody saw anything and I was beginning to wonder if I'd imagined it all. And nothing's happened since." She bit her lip. "Doug thought I should have called them. He thinks someone here in Manordale is after mefor my inheritance."

"That's preposterous!" Constance boomed. "The only people who stand to gain are Betty and me. I certainly wouldn't kill you for any amount of money, and I'm willing to swear that Elizabeth, for all her faults, wouldn't, either."

She shuffled out of the kitchen, her cloth slippers flapping against the tiles. In the hall she turned very deliberately and declared, "I'd consider the motives of your friend, Mr. Doug Remsen, if I were you. Perhaps he's staging the 'attempts' on your life in order to play Hero to the Rescue. Get you to marry him out of gratitude. You'll end up living unhappily ever after—or until he squanders your money and leaves."

"Stop it! How could you say such a thing?"

Erica rushed after Aunt Constance, explaining that Doug wasn't like that. She'd gotten halfway up the stairs when her aunt interrupted.

"Erica, think something through, for once in your life. This Doug Remsen's trying to make you suspicious of people who love you, people you've known all your life. He's the one who's up to no good. Use your head, girl! It's the only thing that makes any sense."

Erica froze, her mouth open with unspoken rebuttals. Constance entered her bedroom and slammed the door, leaving Erica nothing to do but finish her breakfast.

But she couldn't eat. She tossed her muffin into the garbage and stacked the dishwasher with more vigor than the task required as she seethed with indignation. Aunt Constance was worse than ever! She'd never given Erica a chance to say one word in Doug's defense. She was prejudiced against him though she'd never met him. *Thank you, Sherman Hartley.*

Aunt Constance was too quick to cast Doug in the role of villain, while Erica was certain of one thing and one thing only: Doug, whatever his reasons, had her best interests at heart.

She went upstairs and knocked on her aunt's door. "I'm going out," she said loudly. "I'll be back around three or four."

She waited with one ear cocked against the closed door. Nothing.

She sighed. There wasn't anything anyone could do when Aunt Constance was in one of her sulks.

A balmy breeze ruffled her hair as she stepped outside. The lawn, she noted, was checkered with bare patches. The shrubbery needed a good pruning. She made a mental note to find an experienced gardener to revitalize the property that had once been the envy of every homeowner on the block.

And then what? Do I repair the roof, order new carpeting, replace the old refrigerator? Must I stay here?

At that, she shook her head a vigorous no. It was impossible for her to live with Aunt Constance any longer. The way that woman took offense and flew off the handle! And still insisted on telling Erica how to lead her life. There was zero privacy.

She climbed into her car and headed for town, her destination, the travel agency in the new mini mall. For the last few days, an idea had been percolating, and today she decided to give it her full attention. She would spend a month or two traveling leisurely through Europe. She'd leave in June, or even the end of May—as soon as she had access to her inheritance. A trip would be perfect. She needed to get away from Manordale, away from the schemes and manipulations of people who, for their own selfish reasons, wanted to run her life.

Her pulse quickened as she remembered visiting Paris, her only trip abroad, when she was ten years old. It had been spring, just as it was now. A scene came rushing back, as clear as a movie, of strolling down the Champs Elysées with her parents. People laughed and spoke in a language she loved hearing, though she couldn't understand a single word.

She hummed along with the radio as she drove into town, her head swarming with plans. She'd go back to Paris and see the rest of France, too. Along with England, Scotland, and Wales this time. As well as Belgium and The Netherlands. She'd take a boat trip up the Rhine. And go anywhere else she damned well pleased.

She glanced at her watch, saw it was almost eleven o'clock. Now, if only the travel agency were open.

To her delight, it was. An attractive young woman, whose long fuchsia talons matched the flowers on her tunic, became most enthusiastic when Erica explained what she wanted.

"Sounds wonderful! Do you want to take a tour or travel on your own?" the agent, who introduced herself as Nancy, asked.

Erica thought. "A bit of both."

"Good idea. I have some tours that haven't filled up yet. Let me get you the brochures, then you can decide what you like."

Erica readily agreed, and spent the next two hours discussing cities, sights, connections, and hotels with Nancy. By the time she left, she was overwhelmed by the many possibilities that travel and money had opened to her. With her arms full of colorful brochures and the tentative itinerary they'd drawn up, she promised to return later in the week, after she'd sorted them all out.

"Don't wait too long," Nancy advised, "or we'll lose some of the tours."

"I don't intend to wait," Erica told her. "I need to get away from here."

She felt decisive. In command of her own life once again. As soon as she left Manordale, she'd be able to put everything that had happened to her in perspective. And with no one to badger her, she'd make some serious decisions regarding the house and her future.

She tossed the brochures into her car and was about to drive off when her eye caught a red car speeding toward the far exit. It made a quick right onto the street. Where was the driver going in such a rush?

She was famished. Instead of driving off, she stayed in town for something to eat. She walked along Main Street, toward the diner where she and Aunt Betty had eaten on Friday.

There was the red car again! It slowed down as it passed her, but in the sun's glare, she was unable to see the driver's face. She remembered the blue car and shivered. But this one was red, not blue.

The diner was pleasantly cool. She finished off a tuna fish sandwich and treated herself to a chocolate malt. Then, she found herself back in the boutique where she'd been so success-ful a week ago.

Martha, the saleswoman who had previously helped her, greeted her like an old customer. She showed Erica a cotton sweater and skirt outfit that had just come in. She liked it and went to try it on.

Martha carried more new arrivals into the dressing room.

An hour later, Erica returned to her car with the sweater and skirt outfit, and three sleeveless tops. She was thoroughly pleased with herself.

She drove to the town park and walked along the nature path, then watched elementary school children play soccer. It felt good to be alone. To enjoy the pleasures that life had to offer. It was close to four o'clock when she returned home.

"Aunt Constance, I'm home," she called out as she stepped into the house.

No one answered. The house seemed strangely silent.

She wandered through the downstairs rooms, then climbed the stairs. She dropped her brochures and packages on her bed, then peered in the bathroom and in Aunt Constance's room. Her aunt was nowhere to be found.

Erica's heart filled with fear. "Aunt Constance? Aunt Constance!"

She had to be here. Where could she have gone, all by herself? The basement!

Erica flew down the two flights of steps in record time. Could her aunt have fallen and hurt herself? Sprained her ankle, with no one to hear her cry for help?

She discovered a note propped up against the sugar bowl on her second tour of the house. It was brief and to the point.

Erica,

I was greatly disturbed by what you told me this morning. It pains me that you should believe either Elizabeth or I would wish to harm you. I am completely opposed to your seeing this Doug Remsen. However, you are a grown woman, and this is your house.

Given these realities, I've no alternative but to leave. I have made arrangements to stay with a dear friend until I can get my bearings. No need to tell you this person's name, as I do not want

*you to call me. Right now, I require tranquility and the company
of someone who will offer me kindness and support. Your aunt,*
    Constance Harding.

She tossed the note aside, torn between the urge to shake her
aunt in exasperation and burst out laughing. Aunt Constance
felt she had to get away! Erica appreciated the grim irony. She'd
left her aunts three years ago, and today, they both took leave of
her.

But she had no intention of leaving Aunt Constance's
whereabouts a secret. Who could this "dear friend" be? she
wondered, as she thumbed through the telephone book for the
numbers of her aunt's organization cronies.

Mrs. Edelstein's name was crossed out and "deceased" was
written beside it. Mrs. Truscott's phone number had been
changed to a number in Florida, but there was still Mrs.
Harris. Erica remembered meeting her years ago—a small,
skin-and-bones woman with sharp, hooded eyes. Remembered,
belatedly, that she was prone to hysterics.

"You say you don't know where Constance is?" Mrs. Harris
shouted into the phone. "Why, that's terrible, simply terrible!
Doesn't Betty know where she is?"

Erica had to admit she didn't.

"You have no idea where she's gone to?"

She repeated that she didn't, which was why she was calling.

"But Constance doesn't drive any longer," Mrs. Harris persisted.

She could only sigh and agree. When Mrs. Harris suggested
that she call the police, Erica got off the phone as quickly as she
could.

It occurred to her Monica might be the kind and supportive
friend.

No, Erica decided, but made the call anyway. The phone
rang twice, then Monica answered. There was no mistaking that

coy, little-girl voice. When Erica identified herself, Monica grew excited.

"Oh, Erica, dear. I was just telling my sister how lovely you looked last night."

Just in time, she remembered her manners. "Thank you for a lovely evening, Monica. Dinner was delicious. I shall never forget last night as long as I live." At least the last sentence was sincere and perfectly true.

"I'm so glad, dear," Monica cooed. "How is Constance feeling? I did try calling her earlier and got no answer, so I assumed she was feeling well enough to go out."

"She's fine," she said quickly, intent on avoiding another frantic conversation. "I'll tell her you asked after her."

Constance wasn't there. Erica bit back her disappointment. The Hartleys had been her last hope.

"I'd love to chat with you," Monica was saying, "but my sister and brother-in-law are here, and we're just about to go out to dinner. Give Betty and Constance my love."

Erica said goodbye, grateful that there had been no need to explain that both her aunts had left home. Run away. She giggled. As if she were a horrible ogress from whom they needed to escape. Most likely, they needed a vacation from each other.

Although she was no longer as worried about Aunt Constance, Erica discovered she couldn't relax. She paced about the house, munching cookies, switching the TV on and off. She wished there were someone she could call. The trouble was, aside from Jason, she'd made no close friends in Manordale. Doug was the only person who understood what she'd been going through these last few weeks. The only person who knew Terry and what her life with him had been like. But she didn't want to bother Doug. She'd be seeing him tomorrow.

She felt a flush of anger as she recalled Aunt Constance's parting shot. It wasn't true. Doug had no designs on her. He wasn't after her money.

Are you positive? a little voice inside her head asked. *Are you absolutely certain that his motives are pure? After all, he's not exactly an honorable, law-abiding citizen. And he's used to taking what he wants, with little regard for the consequences.*

She threw herself on the family room couch and wondered about this. Here she was, elated because she had plans with Doug, when the fact was, she knew nothing about him except that he treated her kindly and seemed genuinely concerned about her safety.

You know more than that, the little voice rasped malevolently. *You know he's a criminal, that he's capable of violence, and that he has a terrible temper.*

She shuddered. What was wrong with her that she kept falling for gamblers and gangsters? Was it some defect in her personality? Some perverse, self-destructive need to flirt with excitement because her own life was barren and drab?

A terrible thought came back. Maybe Doug had killed Terry, and he was cozying up to her out of guilt. Or to erase any suspicions she might unconsciously harbor.

"No, no, no!" she shouted aloud. "Aunt Constance is dead wrong about Doug!"

She raced to the front door and flung it open, as if fresh air was an antidote for her poisonous thoughts. The sun was still shining, but there was a decided chill in the air. She grabbed her cardigan from the hall closet and hopped into her car. It was foolish to remain in that empty house, brooding and speculating on what could be when she hadn't a shred of evidence to back it up.

She took in an early movie, then treated herself to dinner at the new Japanese restaurant in the next town. The meal was delicious. She dawdled over her last cup of tea, much to the annoyance of the waiter, so it was dusk when she arrived home. Reluctantly, she pulled into the driveway and stood at the front door, fumbling for her ever elusive keys.

Noises came at her, loud and staccato. They sounded like firecrackers. Or bullets.

When the third shot rang out, she threw herself down on the top step. Concrete grazed her chin. She heard two more shots, then the rev of an engine, and a car speeding away.

She remained in a fetal position, panting, her legs too weak to support her.

A door slammed, and voices approached. She managed to open her eyes.

"Erica, are you all right? Are you hurt? Should I call a doctor?" Frail but determined arms helped her to her feet.

"Thanks, Mr. Garrett. I'm okay," she whispered to her neighbor of twenty years, an elderly man with whom she exchanged greetings, but whose house she'd never entered.

"Lands' sake, what's going on?" Mr. Garrett's straight-talking wife didn't hesitate to get to the point. "We heard shots, then came rushing out to see what happened."

"They *were* shots, weren't they?" Erica asked.

Mrs. Garrett's lips narrowed to a grimace. "They sure as hell were. I'm calling the cops, Herbert. Lousy hoodlums. We're not even safe here in Manordale. Not even safe in our own home."

Erica's eyelids grew heavy. A downy cloak covered her, and she knew no more.

CHAPTER FIFTEEN

Erica opened her eyes and glanced around the unfamiliar room, which reeked of camphor. Doilies were scattered about the sofa where she lay. She gasped at the sight of two policemen standing at watchful attention on either side of the living room doorway.

"She's coming to, Herbert." Mrs. Garrett's excited voice echoed in Erica's ears as though she were speaking in a tunnel. "That's it, Erica! Wake up, girl!"

Erica brushed her neighbor's hand from her cheek and sat up slowly. "I'm all right, Mrs. Garrett. Thank you." She reached for her glasses, resting on the ornate wooden table.

The two policemen stepped forward. The older, shorter man addressed Erica.

"I'm Officer Frost, ma'am. If you're up to it, we'd like to ask you a few questions."

Mrs. Garrett was at him like a tiger protecting her young. "Leave her be! Can't you see she's not herself?"

"It's all right," Erica said quickly. "Just give me a minute."

She shivered, remembering what had just happened. She was grateful that the Garretts had heard the shots and called the police. With her neighbors as witnesses, the police would have to take her seriously when she told them about the other attempts on her life.

"Have some water, Erica." Mr. Garrett wove his way past the two policemen and his wife, and handed her a glass.

She sipped slowly, glad to have a moment to think. She would have to answer the officers' questions. She wanted to answer them and help them find whoever was trying to kill her, but she would do so in the privacy of her own home.

"How did I get here?" she asked, avoiding the issue temporarily. She turned to the Garretts hovering before her. "You didn't carry me, did you?"

Mr. Garrett shook his head. "My wife called the police and they came, quick as lightning. Since no one was home at your house, these officers brought you here."

Erica rubbed her bruised chin. "How long have I been unconscious?"

Mrs. Garrett clucked. "Only a few minutes. Are you really all right, Erica? Feel free to rest here a while, 'til you get your bearings."

Officer Frost gazed down at Erica. "We'd like to talk to you as soon as possible."

"Fine," she agreed, "but I'd like to go home now, if you don't mind." When she tried to stand, her knees buckled, and she sank back onto the sofa. "I'll need a few minutes," she murmured.

The policemen nodded and stepped back. Mrs. Garrett took their place.

"You relax and take your time," she told Erica, then turned to glare at the two officers. "You leave her be, or I'll call the precinct right now and file a complaint with your superior. Harassing a poor, innocent girl who almost got shot to death. Go chase after the criminals, why don't you?"

"Now, now, Essie. Don't take on so." Mr. Garrett led his wife to an overstuffed chair a few feet away.

"I'm all right, Mrs. Garrett. Really, I am." She wondered why it was her fate to have to contend with so many bossy, belligerent older women.

Ten minutes later, she felt strong enough to walk home. She thanked her neighbors and let out a yelp of surprise at the sight of several curious onlookers milling around her house. To her relief, Officer Frost's partner sent them on their way.

She was more upset than she'd realized. Standing at her front door, she started to shake. Her hand trembled so badly, Officer Frost had to take her key and unlock the door.

But the door was unscarred. There was no damage from bullet holes, only the cracked and peeling white paint she'd faced each day of the last few weeks.

Even with two armed men at her side, she shuddered as she switched on all the downstairs lights.

Outside, two cars squealed to a halt. The doorbell rang.

Had someone managed to find her aunts? She fervently hoped so. She'd never missed them more than she did this very minute. She had never felt so vulnerable and alone.

Instead of Aunt Constance and Aunt Betty, four more uniformed officers and a plain-clothed detective entered the house. Briefly, they conferred with Officer Frost and his partner in the hall. Then, while Officer Frost remained with her, the others dispersed to examine the house and the grounds, and to question neighbors.

The detective, a bald, paunchy, middle-aged man, approached Erica.

"Hello, Mrs. Parker. I'm Detective Sawyer. Can we sit down someplace quiet where we won't be disturbed?" He nodded to Office Frost. "Jim, join us and take notes."

She led them to the family room, glad to leave the sight of men roaming about the house. *They won't find anything*, she thought. *There's nothing to find.*

"Do you know why anyone would want to shoot you?" the detective asked when the three of them were seated. His manner was mild, as though he asked this sort of question every day.

He probably did, she realized.

"I've no idea why someone would want to shoot me.".

The detective stared at her with kind, soulful eyes. Basset hound eyes, she thought.

"My men are looking for bullets and bullet holes, but so far we haven't found any." He cocked his head, welcoming her to comment on this.

"I didn't see any marks on the door when we came in. I could have sworn the shots were fired right behind me, so..." She stared at him fearfully, the tears building up in her voice, in her eyes. "You do believe me, don't you? I mean, there were shots. I couldn't have imagined it all."

He patted her hand reassuringly. "Or course, you didn't. Two of your neighbors heard them, as well, and called us, independent of each other." He scrutinized her more carefully. "Why shouldn't we believe you?"

She let out a deep sigh. She yearned to pour out her entire tale to this sympathetic man, but she was thoroughly exhausted. "It's a long story," she mumbled, huddling into the sofa.

"That's okay. We've plenty of time." He must have realized how distressed she was because he asked, "Would you like to drink something before we start? Is there any brandy in the house?"

She shook her head. "But I could go for some hot cocoa. Aunt Constance always makes me some when I get upset." She remembered, suddenly, she hadn't had any since the day after Terry's funeral.

She closed her eyes. A policeman had come to see her then, too.

"Would you mind making me a cup of coffee?" Detective Sawyer asked, breaking into her thoughts. "I don't mean to impose, but as long as you're going to boil water..."

His voice startled her. Cautiously, she got to her feet. "Of course," she said, flustered. "I should have offered."

She felt more like herself as she performed the simple tasks of boiling water and spooning out instant coffee for two and cocoa for herself. She smiled when she realized Detective Sawyer had sent her into the kitchen to give her something to do—something easy and ordinary to calm her nerves.

He came in minutes later and sat at the kitchen table.

"I'm sorry, but it seems we've finished off the cake," she apologized.

He patted his paunch. "Just as well, wouldn't you agree?"

They both laughed. The detective sipped his coffee.

She looked at him expectantly. "Aren't you going to ask me questions?"

"Sure. If you think you're up to it."

"I am."

He called Officer Frost to join them, and began. "Did you happen to see who shot at you?"

"No," she said promptly. "I was facing the door." She paused. "I do remember hearing a car stop as I was about to unlock the front door, but I thought nothing of it."

"Did you see the car?"

"No."

Detective Sawyer sighed loudly. "Let's try it from the other end. Can you think of anyone who would want to hurt or frighten you?"

She looked down, hoping he *wouldn't* notice the blush heating her ears. "Well," she began, wondering why she was embarrassed—no, ashamed—instead of angry. "Funny things have been happening. A friend thinks it's because, on my birthday, which is Tuesday, I come into a large inheritance."

She laughed nervously. "It doesn't seem worth it all, especially since everyone's been trying to direct my life and...and poor Terry..." She looked at the detective. "Someone murdered my husband."

"I'm so sorry."

He knew. Of course, he knew.

She blinked back unshed tears. Now was not the time for waterworks, she scolded herself. Now was the time to get the entire story out, so the police could find who was after her, and she could get on with her life.

But she found she couldn't talk because she was hyperventilating, heaving huge gulps of air that shook her entire body. Her chest was tight.

Detective Sawyer patted her back and murmured soothing words until her breathing returned to normal. When he spoke, his voice was filled with concern.

"Mrs. Parker—Erica—there must be someone you can call. A friend or relative who could come and stay with you tonight."

She gazed into his sorrowful eyes and sensed his sympathy. She considered calling Doug, but Aunt Constance's retort had retained some of its sting, and she thought better of it. Much as she disliked the idea, Doug was a suspect like the others.

"There's no one I can call. Or trust." The last two words fell from her mouth of their own accord. "Both my aunts who live here seem to have gone away—I don't know where—and I'm terribly afraid. I don't want to stay alone tonight. I really don't."

To her disgust, tears streamed down her face. *He must think I'm a high-strung, fragile neurotic*, she berated herself.

"Interesting, this happening when both of them are away," Detective Sawyer mused. "Don't worry yourself. I'll arrange to have two officers stay with you tonight."

She sipped her cocoa while he made the call. Her body was heavy. She could barely hold up her head. She longed to crawl into bed and sleep.

"They'll be here in a few minutes." The detective gave her a crooked grin. "I called in a favor and asked for two of our best officers. I guarantee, you'll be safe with them."

While she was thanking him for his thoughtfulness, a policeman entered the kitchen.

"Excuse me," Detective Sawyer said, and followed him out to the hall.

She made no attempt to catch the few audible words as they conferred in low voices. She was drained of all curiosity, of all feeling, as though the evening's events had happened to someone else, and she was observing it all from a distance.

Detective Sawyer returned. Instead of sitting down, he reached for his coffee cup and put it in the sink.

"Are you going to ask me more questions?"

"Tomorrow morning will do, after you've had some rest. Unless you've an urgent appointment. In which case, we'll talk later in the day."

"No urgent appointment." She had no intention of going out with Doug or with anyone else until this matter was settled.

"In that case, I'll stop by around eight-thirty. My men will continue to canvas the neighborhood then. They're out now, trying to find out if anyone saw anything. So far, nobody did, although plenty of people heard the shots."

It was close to ten o'clock when Detective Sawyer and the six uniformed policemen drove off, leaving Erica in the charge of her "bodyguards," as she secretly called Officers Gonzalez and Johnson. Mary Gonzalez was young, Salvadoran, and barely grazed the height requirement of the police department. But her obvious competence and firecracker personality inspired Erica with confidence, as did her tall, black, and equally young partner, Rich Johnson.

They gave the house a thorough inspection, then told her to feel free to follow her usual night-time routine. Erica was glad to escape upstairs. Although she was completely exhausted, she took one of the sedatives Aunt Constance had gotten for her when Terry had died. Then she drew her shades and prepared for bed.

The pill dulled her jangled nerves. She felt curiously at peace. There was nothing more for her to do. The police would handle everything.

Doug, she thought as she drifted off to sleep. *I should have called Doug and told him not to come.*

She awakened the next morning to find him gazing down at her and saying her name.

"You forgot to set your alarm," he teased. "It's after nine."

She rubbed her eyes, afraid to open them again to discover she was dreaming. But she wasn't.

Doug's handsome face, beaming with undisguised pleasure, made her heart soar with joy. She remembered her suspicions of the night before, and her face heated. In the sunlight that blazed through the open shades, she recognized the truth. Doug might work for a gangster and carry a gun, but he would never harm her.

To mask her sudden insight, she said with mock concern, "How did you get in? I thought I was under police protection."

She sat up suddenly, the comforter tucked about her. "Oh, my God! I've overslept. I'm keeping Detective Sawyer waiting."

Mary Gonzalez sailed into the bedroom. "Morning, sleeping beauty." She flashed Erica a grin. "We thought we'd let you sleep in, given the scare you had last night. But enough is enough. Time to get up."

Erica nodded. "I'll hurry and get dressed."

"There's fresh coffee waiting."

When Mary left the room, Doug said, "It's a beautiful day, Erica. A great day to stroll around Manhattan."

"But we can't," she said anxiously. "Not after last night. Didn't they tell you what happened? Someone tried to kill me. Only there aren't any bullet holes. I'm sure the police won't like my wandering about the city."

"I've had a talk with your Detective Sawyer, and he sees no reason why we should change our plans." He narrowed his eyes, giving him that foxy look, and observed her carefully. "That is, if you still want to."

Her almost imperceptible nod seemed to boost his spirits even more. "Then get dressed quickly and hurry down. I'll be waiting."

But it was Detective Sawyer who stood waiting for Erica at the foot of the stairs. He brushed aside her apologies, and handed her a cup of coffee as he led her into the family room.

Neither Doug nor her "bodyguards" were anywhere in sight.

"We have some news for you this morning. My men went out about an hour ago. A Mr. Barclay, who lives halfway down the block, is positive he saw a blue Cadillac speeding by just after he heard the shots. Thought nothing of them, just a car backfiring. And a lady from around the corner, a Mrs. Nelson, was out walking her dog near your house. She spotted a young man in a car. Can't swear what it was, but she noticed he held something shiny outside the driver's window as he drove past."

She stiffened. Jason! It had to be Jason playing some stupid game.

Detective Sawyer sighed. He needed a shave, and his shirt was crumpled. He looked as though he hadn't slept all night. "Have any idea who it could be?"

He yawned, probably missing the frown that momentarily crossed her face.

"I really couldn't say," she said primly. *Why was she still defending Jason? Because she wasn't absolutely sure he'd done it? She didn't want to ruin his chance to start a new life?*

"Still no bullets or bullet holes. The men searched high and low." He mused. "I wonder if it could have been a starter pistol."

She gave a snort of disgust. That clinched it! Jason had bought the damn thing in his senior year of high school, and took delight in shooting it off school grounds, and scaring everyone, until Sherman had threatened to toss it in the garbage if he didn't stop his nonsense.

She returned from her reverie to find the detective's eyes boring into hers. "Sound like anyone you know?" he asked.

She shook her head, claiming ignorance. Something kept her from telling this kind detective exactly what was running through her mind. Probably because she was afraid Detective Sawyer would consider it a sick joke and be disappointed with her for even knowing someone as despicable as Jason.

"Well," he said between a sigh and a yawn, "my men have checked, and there's no evidence of bullets. It sounds like a prank to me. And you were chosen at random." He rose from his chair with effort. "At least we can rest assured about one thing, Erica. Nobody's out there trying to kill you."

She grimaced. She should have told him of the two attempts on her life, but one involved an assailant wearing a Darth Vader mask, and the shove into traffic couldn't be proved. She'd feared this had been a third attempt, but it seemed it was only a prank.

"Do you think it's all right for me to go into Manhattan?" she asked.

"Sure, I don't see why not. Your boyfriend seems hot on the idea, and there's no reason to stop you now."

Her boyfriend. The words rang like chimes inside her head. They filled her with a strange delight and a determination to get on with her life.

She stood. Detective Sawyer did, too.

She led him to the front hall where Doug was waiting.

"Interrogation over?" he asked.

She nodded. "Detective Sawyer thinks I was the victim of a prank and there's nothing to worry about. From what he's told me, I agree." Relieved that last night's event hadn't been an attempt on her life, she exclaimed, "So, let's go to Manhattan and celebrate!"

But Doug wasn't amused. He shifted his attention to Detective Sawyer. "I hope that doesn't mean you're planning to take your men off the case," he said roughly.

"Looks that way," Detective Sawyer answered calmly. "Any reason why I shouldn't?"

"Erica, didn't you tell him?"

"There's nothing to tell," she interrupted swiftly.

"Then I will, at least, about the incident I witnessed." Doug proceeded to report what had happened with the boys at the duck pond to the detective. He finished by saying, "Jason Hartley paid them to scare Erica."

She stared at him as he spoke, wondering how he knew Jason had been responsible for the incident at the duck pond. She hadn't told him. Maybe Doug caught sight of Jason there, only he hadn't mentioned it to her for fear of upsetting her more?

Detective Sawyer listened intently to what Doug had to say. "I'll have a word with Jason Hartley," he said.

His words encouraged her to tell him about being shot at on the way to Montauk, and the shove into traffic that no one seemed to notice.

The detective's face grew grimmer as she reported each incident.

"Let's not forget Erica's about to become a very rich woman in a few days," Doug added.

"I'll follow up on everything you've told me," Detective Sawyer said. He turned to Erica. "And you didn't think to fill us in on all this?"

"Since I have no proof, I was afraid you would tell me I was imagining things."

Detective Sawyer offered her a sad smile. "I'm sorry you felt you couldn't trust us with the truth."

As soon as the police left, Doug took her in his arms and held her tight. "Why didn't you call me last night?" he scolded. "I told you to let me know if anything happened."

"I was terribly frightened. Neighbors took me into their home, and I fainted. Then the police came and stayed with me all night."

"So they told me. Where were your aunts?" he demanded. "Where are they now? It sure is a strange time for them to disappear."

She nodded. "That's what Detective Sawyer said. You're beginning to sound like him."

Doug shot her a penetrating glance. "Erica, starter gun or not, you were targeted and meant to be frightened."

"I was, wasn't I?" Her nostrils flared with fury. "And I know who was behind it."

He stared, her anger obviously taking him by surprise.

She flung open the front door. "Let's go! I'll tell you all about it in the car."

They were exiting the neighborhood by the time she'd finished explaining about Jason's starter pistol. "That bastard! It was his way of getting back at me because I won't marry him. Just like he paid those boys in the park to run into me."

"A real upstanding guy," Doug said sarcastically. "What's this about his wanting to marry you? I thought he was your lifelong friend."

"He used to be my best friend, but after last night..." She changed course to ask, "Could we please stop for some breakfast? I'm famished."

That evoked such uproarious laughter, she feared they would crash into oncoming traffic.

"You're an amazing woman, Erica Parker. Your stomach never stops working, no matter what."

She directed him to the diner that had been her favorite eating place through four years of college, and was pleased when the Greek owner gave her an effusive greeting. He took their order himself.

Minutes later, all of her attention was devoted to her waffles topped with strawberries, then redirected to an oat bran muffin and numerous refills of coffee.

Doug quietly nursed his mug of black coffee.

When she sank back against the booth, a sigh of contentment from her lips, he demanded, "All right, feeding time's over. Now explain the marriage proposal—slowly and in detail."

She told him about the dinner at the Hartleys', followed by Jason's outrageous proposal.

"It was probably the worst evening of my entire life. Although," she quickly added, "last night was a close second. I was scared out of my wits." She smiled. "But, thank God it's over."

"Is it?" Doug looked glum. "You really should have asked the detective for police protection for the next few days. At least until your aunts return home."

"Nonsense. I'm not afraid of Jason. I'll deal with him later."

"Don't underestimate him, Erica. He's not the little friend you seem to remember, someone you can influence or coax to do the right thing. He seems to have developed some despicable habits. And he's obviously angry at you."

"I'll keep that in mind," she promised. "But I can't help being happy right now, knowing it was only Jason. And," she lowered her voice, "because I'll be spending the day with you."

"Agreed," he said and took her hand in his. "But there's something I want to tell you before we drop the subject. Friday night, my boss mentioned something about having a painting to show someone out on Long Island. Someone from this general area."

"So?" she asked, quizzically.

He laughed. "Mr. B's no art collector. Any works of art that come his way are either payoffs or stolen goods. He didn't mention any names, but he acts as a middleman for only two people I can think of—a high school principal who's a friend from the old neighborhood and Sherman Hartley."

"The principal's name isn't Jennings, is it?" she asked before she even knew what she was thinking.

He stared at her in amazement. "How on earth did you know that?"

She shivered. "Ron Jennings is Aunt Betty's boyfriend. She told me his wife's illness ate up all their savings. Now I'm beginning to wonder." She paused as her old habit of refusing to consider unpleasant possibilities took over.

"Go on," Doug urged none too gently.

"He stopped to talk to me when I was in town the other day. I didn't know who he was until he told me his name and that he was Aunt Betty's principal. I'd only met him a few times, and that was over three years ago." She bit her lip.

"And?"

"It was the same day someone pushed me into traffic."

"Did you see him at the scene?"

She shook her head. "No, but I can't help thinking he probably sees me as a cash cow, since Aunt Betty asked me straight out for money. And don't forget, if I die, she inherits millions. The fact that your boss is his art supplier tells me Mr. Ron Jennings doesn't hesitate to break laws to get what he wants."

He shot her a look of pure admiration. "I'm impressed by your observations and deductions about Jennings. I agree, he's a possible suspect, along with your Aunt Betty. But what about Sherman Hartley?" He scratched his chin. "Where's he getting all the dough to buy expensive artwork? Because if Mr. B's involved, you can be sure it's costing him a bundle."

"I don't know what you're getting at," she said primly. "Much as I dislike Sherman, he's compulsively honest. As for his money, he's a prominent lawyer with excellent connections. And he commands high fees."

"He's probably been making a pretty penny off your estate."

"Doug!" She was shocked. "Not Sherman."

"Well, someone's after your money," he said gruffly. "It would help if we could figure out who it is." He scooped up their check and left a tip. "Let's go."

He strode to the cashier, leaving her to follow in his wake.

They drove along the expressway without speaking. She sensed he was annoyed with her, but she was reluctant to ask why. Finally, he broke the silence.

"You're a gutsy, intelligent woman, but sometimes you act like a brainless fool."

"Thanks a lot," she said sarcastically, though his words cut her to the quick.

"Someone tried to kill you. Twice. You can't pick and choose suspects because of your past history with them, be it one of your aunts, Ron Jennings, Jason, his father, or Jason's step-mother."

Was he right? Was the fact that someone wanted her dead so difficult to accept that she'd resorted to the old habit of sticking her head in the sand?

He let out a mirthless laugh. "Isn't that how you managed to avoid finding out Terry was a gambler?"

"It is," she admitted. "I suppose part of me is so relieved that, last night, no one shot at me with bullets, I managed to downplay the other incidents, as well. Besides, looking at the situation with Aunt Constance's excellent sense of drama, if someone wanted me dead, I'd be dead by now, and I'm not!"

Doug frowned, apparently deep in thought. After a minute, he mused, "The key is finding out who Terry knew. Then we could be on our guard."

"And do what?" She put her hand on his arm. "Please, let's not talk about it anymore," she pleaded. "We keep rehashing, and nothing comes of it. Detective Sawyer will question Jason and look into the two attempts on my life."

"I do believe he'll do just that. He strikes me as a good detective."

For the rest of the ride, they made light conversation. She told him about the trip she was planning to take through Europe. To her surprise, he suggested many sites.

They crossed the Fifty-Ninth Street Bridge. He thought they might stroll along the Promenade, the lovely walkway that ran along the East River. She eagerly agreed. She hadn't strolled the Promenade since she was a child.

They parked near Gracie Mansion and walked south, down through the Eighties and Seventies. They passed elderly men and women sunning themselves on benches. Young mothers and nannies wheeled baby carriages and strollers, while preschoolers scampered just beyond their guardians' reach.

In spite of the No Dogs Allowed signs, there were almost as many dogs on the Promenade as there were people, of every size and breed. One Maltipoo pranced up to them to sniff Erica's sandals. She knelt to pet him.

"Dogs, children, people," she said, laughing. "Exactly what you find in suburbia, only here it all seems more glamorous."

They walked hand-in-hand. "You could live in Manhattan if you wanted," Doug said. He seemed to be waiting for an answer.

She thought a bit. "You're right, of course. I keep forgetting the many options suddenly open to me." She grinned. "I wouldn't mind having a duplex apartment in a luxury building. With a balcony overlooking the river. And a rooftop health club, where I could swim laps as I gazed up at the sky."

"Evenings at the theater and the ballet. Weekends in Europe," he teased.

She sighed. "It sounds exciting and, I must admit, very appealing. But it's not really what I'd like."

"It isn't?"

Did she detect a sigh of relief? Impulsively, she squeezed his hand. "What I want most of all is an old-fashioned life—husband, children, house. And work, of course. A good editorial position at a prestigious magazine, where I could freelance when the children are small."

As they walked along, she searched for the proper words. "I need love and stability and a sense of continuity. For me, that's what life is all about."

He smiled. "Sounds good to me."

They continued on in companionable silence, finally stopping to gaze out at the East River.

She brushed her forehead against his arm. "I hate to admit this," she said softly, "but I have to tell someone, and it seems that someone is you."

When she hesitated, he put his arm around her and drew her closer.

"I doubt I could have stayed married to Terry." She laughed softly. "He was handsome and sexy, but not the right husband for me. I know that now." She slipped her arm around Doug's waist. Standing like that felt comfortable. Right. "I feel terrible about what happened to him, and I do miss him. No other man had paid that much attention to me before. I was flattered and..."

"And?" he encouraged.

She laughed, suddenly amused. "And I thought how shocked my aunts would be if they could see me riding behind Terry on his motorcycle." She covered her mouth and looked up at him. "Isn't that awful?"

His answer was to take off her glasses and kiss her.

Afterward, he led her to an empty bench. "Let's sit here a minute," he said. "I've something to tell you. Something I feel you can handlenow."

Curious, she sat down and watched him expectantly. Was he about to tell her he cared about her, but they came from two different worlds...

"Erica, Terry said something else that Monday night before he died, something I didn't mention for fear it would devastate you. But now, I think you should know."

"Know what?" Her heart beat rapidly.

He took a deep breath. "Terry said he was paid to marry you."

"Paid?" she repeated stupidly. "Who would pay him to marry me?"

"Someone in Manordale. He wouldn't say who."

"But why would someone go to all that trouble?"

"To keep an eye on you."

She forcibly swallowed, afraid to ask her next question. "Do you think this person wanted Terry to kill me?"

He shook his head. "I don't think so, but I know one thing. Terry loved you, Erica. His decision to leave you was the noblest thing he ever did in his life."

Her eyes welled. "And he paid for it with his life." She sobbed softly, making no attempt to wipe away the tears falling on her lap.

"So, you see, sweet Erica, you were loved after all," he whispered, holding her close. "And you still are."

He reached in his pocket and handed her his handkerchief. "Next time, I must remember to bring two of these."

CHAPTER SIXTEEN

They left the Promenade and walked north along Second Avenue. Impulsively—because it struck them as appealing and was starting in five minutes—they stepped inside a movie theater to watch a foreign film about two unlikely lovers. It proved to be hilarious. Erica, not usually amused by slapstick humor, kept bursting out laughing at the clumsy advances of the inexperienced hero.

Doug held her hand. When the movie ended, he leaned over and kissed her firmly on the mouth.

She opened her eyes as the lights came on. The dozen viewers were exiting the theater. A few stared at them, but she felt no embarrassment. A deep contentment settled comfortably about her like a velvet cloak.

"Hungry?" he asked as they stepped into the glaring sunlight.

She blinked. "Definitely, now that I think of it," she said, and linked her arm in his.

"I knew I could count on your voracious appetite. We're right near a favorite restaurant of mine. Hungarian. They serve the best chicken paprika and nokedli outside of Budapest."

"Nokedli?"

"Noodle dumplings. You'll love them."

"Sounds terrific." She smiled, and couldn't help noticing how easy it was to go along with his suggestions.

At three o'clock, the small restaurant was empty except for a white-haired, elegantly dressed gentleman sipping tea and reading a newspaper at the corner table. The proprietress, a plump, middle-aged woman, came bustling over to seat them.

"Mr. Remsen! How nice to see you!" she exclaimed when she recognized Doug.

"It's nice to see you, too, Vera."

She shook his hand, then Erica's, and led them to a table. The starched tablecloth was immaculate. Tiny yellow flowers filled a vase at its center.

Minutes later, Vera beamed approvingly as Doug ordered stuffed peppers for their appetizers and chicken paprika, the house special. She sped away faster than Erica would have imagined her short, heavy legs could carry her, only to return with a complementary glass of Hungarian wine in each hand.

Doug raised his in salute. "To you, Erica. Happy twenty-fifth birthday." He kissed her lightly on the lips.

The kiss and the wine, whose name she couldn't pronounce, went straight to her head, and gave her the courage to speak her mind.

She leaned close to him, until their foreheads were almost touching. "You know practically everything there is to know about me, while you remain a mystery man." She took another sip and waved her hands expansively. "I don't even know how old you are. Or where you live."

"True enough. I turned thirty-five on March eleventh, which makes me ten years older than you. As for my address, I'll be moving soon, so there's no point in your writing it down. You'd only be crossing it out in a few days."

She gripped his arm in alarm. Her glasses slid to the tip of her nose. "You're moving? Where are you going?"

He took her hand in both of his. He seemed to be debating how to answer her. Finally, he shook his head and said solemnly, "I can't say for sure."

"What if I need to reach you?" She gave him a sharp look and frowned. "For all I know, your name isn't even Doug Remsen."

"My name's Doug, all right. I promise you that." He gazed at her with such naked adoration, she was the first to turn away. "Regardless of where they send me, I'll only be a phone call away. That's all I can say, except..."

"Except?" she prodded.

"Except..." Again, he seemed to be hunting for words. "You're very sweet," he finished. "Ah, here come our appetizers."

Vera set a steaming dish before each of them and wished them good appetite.

Erica thanked her politely, all the while, struggling to quell her rising anxiety. Doug was being sent away, which could only mean one thing. He was heading straight for danger.

She tasted her stuffed pepper and succeeded in burning her tongue. She set down her knife and fork, and faced Doug, who was relishing his first bite.

He caught her pained expression. "You don't like it? Or is it too hot?"

"I don't want anything bad to happen to you." Too late, she covered her mouth. She hadn't meant to say that.

"Nothing will. I promise." He was about to cut off another piece of his appetizer, but she reached across and held his hand down with her own.

"But they're sending you away. You're in some kind of trouble."

She waited for him to deny it. Instead, his jaw ticked. "I'll be all right. More restricted, but out of harm's reach."

Oh, no! To her, that could only mean one thing. "Poor Doug," she began. She stopped and took a deep breath. "Will they—I mean, can I come and visit you when...?" Again, she faltered, not daring to say what was looming in her mind.

"When I what?" he prodded, amused by her embarrassment.

"When you go to prison." There. It was out in the open.

"I'm not going to prison. What made you think of a silly thing like that?"

He reached for her hand again, but she rebuffed him. "Don't you dare take that patronizing tone with me. Like I'm some half-brained bimbo, too dumb to know what's going on." Although she kept her voice down, it seethed with anger and humiliation.

"I don't like your line of work. It's dangerous and illegal. But, damn it, I care about what happens to you, Doug! You're not the only person licensed to worry about someone else."

He was instantly contrite. "You're right, sweet Erica. I was being insensitive. But the truth is, there's not much I can tell you now." He leaned over to cup her chin in his hand. "Try to be patient."

She met his eyes. They seemed to be pleading for understanding.

"Please, Erica," he whispered.

Suddenly, the evasions sounded all too familiar. "I want to enjoy our outing today," she said, "so, I'll leave off questioning you for now. After that, I can't—no, I *won't*—be in a relationship with someone who keeps secrets from me."

He looked sad when he nodded. "I hear you."

She responded with a brisk nod. The situation was less than ideal, but at least she was being true to herself. And they still had today.

"Try your stuffed pepper again," he said matter-of-factly. "It must have cooled off by now."

"I will." She tasted, and smiled. "Delicious."

"See? What did I tell you?"

They managed to regain much of their earlier good spirits. When they'd eaten their cucumber salads, Vera brought out their main dishes.

"Enjoy!" she instructed in her lilting accent. "Would you like more wine?" she asked Doug.

"Erica?" He turned the question to her.

She nodded, her mouth full of chicken. It was heavenly—tender and delicately seasoned with paprika and other spices. She took another bite, putting all thoughts on hold. She hadn't realized how hungry she was.

Doug ate slowly, his gaze never leaving her. "Everything tastes better to me, knowing you're enjoying it."

"I do! I love it," she mumbled through a mouthful of food.

"Don't forget the nokedli."

She put a few in her mouth, discovered it to be a doughy marvel. She grinned, then ate some more.

"Ah, here's our wine."

He poured. She sipped.

For the moment, she was completely and thoroughly happy.

"I love this place," she said when she could speak again.

"In that case, we'll come back and try some other dishes."

For dessert, they ordered palascinta—crepes filled with apricot jam—and coffee.

"I'm stuffed," she admitted as she scraped her plate with the edge of her fork to get the last of the jam.

"Me, too," he said. "Let's sit a bit, then we can walk some of this meal off." He glanced at his watch. "We've about an hour before we have to start back."

"So soon?"

"I'm afraid so."

His closed expression told her all the pleading in the world wouldn't extend their outing one minute longer. She remembered what she'd told him earlier. If he continued to keep her in the dark, she would have to find the strength to end their budding relationship. She bit her lip and wished the day could go on and on, that Doug never had to leave her. She felt a connection to him she hadn't with any other man, and felt safe with him.

Why did he have to hurry back? What sort of plans did he have for this evening?

Stop it, she scolded herself. Then, she shook her head so hard, she felt dizzy. She refused to mull over circumstances she couldn't control. She would enjoy their remaining time together to the utmost.

On their walk back to the car, they peered into food stores and boutiques, commenting on items that caught their fancy. The streets were now crowded with Manhattanites returning from work, along with bike riders, dog walkers, and children playing.

They spoke little on the drive home. The stop-and-go traffic through Manhattan and most of Queens made her tense. Her uneasiness grew as they approached Manordale. When would she see Doug again? Why was he going away? Where was he going?

"Maybe one of my aunts has come home," she said brightly to camouflage the sense of doom weighing down her spirits. She shuddered at the thought of spending a night in the house all by herself. Not that she expected Jason to try anything else. He'd had his little joke.

It was seven-thirty when Doug pulled into the driveway behind her Honda. The sun had gone down, draining everything of color. The neighborhood trees and shrubs and houses were reduced to dark shadows, backlit by a pale gray sky.

There was no sign of Aunt Betty's car. No light or signs of activity came from the house. They hadn't returned. Her spirits sank even lower.

Doug took the keys from her limp fingers and unlocked the door.

"I'll come in for a glass of water, if you don't mind. I'm thirsty after all that paprika."

But instead of following her into the kitchen, he peered into every downstairs room and opened every closet.

"Do you want to check upstairs?" she asked sarcastically, although, secretly, she was relieved he was doing exactly what she'd intended to do the moment he left.

"Good idea." He took the steps two at a time.

"Find any robbers?" she called up when he reappeared at the top of the landing.

"Safe," he declared with a grin. "Now I'll take that water."

In the hallway, they kissed deeply and passionately, until he pulled away and said he had to get to work.

She clung to him shamelessly. "Not yet," she whispered.

He kissed her again, pressing her urgently against his hard body. He groaned. "If I don't leave now, I won't be able to go."

"Then stay," she said simply.

She felt him hesitate before he stepped back. "I'll call you later," he said, in charge of his emotions once again, "as soon as I catch a free minute. Keep the doors locked and the shades drawn. And, Erica, don't—for any reason whatsoever—leave this house."

"I won't," she promised.

"I'll stop by tomorrow with your present."

Before she could register her surprise, he winked and slipped through the door.

She watched him drive away, then wandered into the family room, dreading the long evening that stretched before her. She picked up one of Aunt Betty's crossword puzzle books, but soon tossed it aside.

She roamed the house aimlessly, noting signs of wear and neglect everywhere. The walls were in desperate need of a new coat of paint, the living room furniture was old and worn, the carpeting on the stairs was threadbare, and the hall wallpaper was peeling in several spots.

If I ever decided to live here, she thought, *I'd tear it all down and redo the entire house, room by room. Not that I'd ever live here*, she quickly amended.

She reflected on her conversation with Doug when they'd walked along the Promenade. Buying an apartment on the East Side and enjoying the Manhattan life would be more fun.

And then what? She supposed she could always find a job as an editor. Join a gym. Make new friends. Date.

Ick! She didn't want to play the dating game. She wanted Doug, and that didn't bear thinking about. Not when he was planning to leave the area without giving her a forwarding address. Despite his romantic protestations, he wasn't going to be part of her life for much longer.

Instead, she focused her attention on her aunts. She should have called Aunt Betty at school earlier in the day to make sure everything was all right. Not that she was terribly worried about her. She had her boyfriend, or whatever one called a person's fiancé who was still married to Wife Number One. Aunt Betty probably had moved out to get away from Aunt Constance's bickering, and had used their argument to make the break. Although, it would have been nice if she'd left a note letting Erica know where she had gone.

Aunt Constance was another story. She'd left the house in a state of emotional upset. For all her denials, she had a heart condition. But where could she have gone? Besides Aunt Betty, Monica Hartley was Constance's closest friend. But when

Erica had called Monica, she'd thought Aunt Constance was at home.

On impulse, Erica decided to try Monica again. The phone rang several times.

"Hello," said an impatient Sherman, obviously annoyed at being disturbed.

"Sherman?" she said hesitantly. "It's Erica. I was wondering—"

"Erica!" he broke in before she had a chance to explain why she was calling. "Where are you? I've been trying to reach you all day."

"I'm home," she said, puzzled. "Where should I be?"

"I couldn't even leave a message," he complained. "Your aunts must be the only two people in Manordale—in the state of New York—who don't have an answering machine!"

"You didn't call my...?" she began, then realized Sherman didn't have her cell phone number, and she wasn't about to give it to him. "Anyway, I was calling you because," she tried once more, only to be interrupted again.

"Can you come right over and sign some papers? They really should be taken care of immediately."

"Do you know where Aunt Constance is?"

"*Nooo*," Sherman said meditatively. "But I think Monica spoke to her today. She called here about noon, I believe."

"She did?" she breathed a deep sigh of relief. "Is she all right?"

"I assume so, since she's off visiting some distant cousin in New Jersey. Didn't you know?"

"I...I had trouble making out the note she left me," she improvised. "Is Monica there? I'd like to speak to her."

"Sorry, Erica. She just left for a meeting. I've spent the last two hours going over your papers. Are you coming over?"

"Well," she demurred, "I really don't want to go out alone. I had a very unpleasant experience last night, and I'm pretty sure Jason was responsible."

"Jason?" Sherman sounded concerned.

"Yes, Sherman. He scared me half to death. Probably because he was angry at me for turning down his marriage proposal." She gave a huff of exasperation. "I told the police about the first stunt he pulled. I'm sure they'll be speaking to him if they haven't already."

"The police! Erica, please come right over. We can talk about Jason and take care of the paperwork. I'd be happy to stop by your house, only I'm expecting an important call on our landline."

"Where's Jason? I'm not coming over if he's there."

"Don't worry. He's out with a friend. I think they were planning to drive into the city. At any rate, I don't expect him back for several hours. Rest assured, you won't run into him here."

"Good. I never want to set eyes on him again! He was horrible the night before when we went out for dinner. I had to take a taxi home."

"A taxi!" Sherman sputtered. "Jason never mentioned a taxi. I wish you'd come and explain everything to me."

"Gladly," she said. "It's time you learned a few unsavory truths about your son."

She grinned as she slammed down the phone. There was no point to her sitting alone in an empty house, waiting for the minutes to pass. She looked forward to her little chat with Sherman. After he heard everything, she had no doubt he would deal sternly with his contemptible son. Perhaps he'd cut him off without a penny. The thought pleased her that he might finally have consequences for his actions.

Humming, she threw a sweater over her shoulders and closed the front door behind her.

She squinted as she parked in the Hartleys' circular driveway. Why hadn't Sherman switched on the outside flood lights? As she climbed the wide steps, she decided he probably left such mundane matters to Monica, who must have left home while it was still light out. The only visible illumination came from Sherman's study, and that was muted by the curtains drawn across the window. But he must have heard her arrive, because the door flew open before she could ring the bell.

"Erica, dear, come in, come in. With as few insects as possible." With alacrity, he shepherded her through the dark hall and into his study. "Everything's all set up in here."

He spoke quickly and breathlessly while his hand gripped her upper arm.

Instinctively, she pulled out of his grasp.

Sherman released her abruptly. "Sorry."

She rubbed the sore spot, grimacing at the moisture his palm had left. He was undoubtedly upset about Jason, she decided.

"No need to be rough," she tried to joke. "I'll go quietly."

The study was next to the living room, across the hall from the dining room. Its dark, wood-paneled walls abounded with paintings of wildlife and country scenes. Her glance was drawn to the stacks of papers piled high on the large, old-fashioned desk that stood flush against the opposite wall.

"Sit down." He offered her his tan leather chair, which was the same color as the deep-piled carpet.

"The papers are all in order. But first, I'd like you to look this over. It's merely a statement declaring you're of sound mind, etc., and have received all properties as stated in your father's will. *Signnnn*," he held onto the word until he reached the last page, "here, here, and here."

She looked. There were several lines drawn for more signatures. "But this has to be witnessed and notarized," she pointed out.

He waved away her concern. "My dear, let's not trouble our-selves with such trivia. Your signature is what matters. I'll take care of the rest in the office. First thing tomorrow morning."

Once again, she noticed how breathless he sounded. It made her uneasy. "Are you sure?"

"I'm telling you not to worry." His voice grew sharp with annoyance. "If you insist, Monica will sign it as soon she comes home. Jason, too."

"Jason!" She leaped to her feet. "You promised he wouldn't be here."

Sherman urged her back into her chair. "Easy, Erica. Let's not get hysterical. I meant he could sign it when he got in later. After you're gone."

He handed her a pen. She placed it on top of the document and swiveled the chair around so she could face Sherman.

"First, let me tell you about your darling son. I want you to know exactly what happened so you can judge for yourself what kind of person Jason's turned out to be."

He pointed to the documents. Clearly, he wanted her to deal with them before they discussed Jason, but her look of determination seemingly made him reconsider.

"Tell me, by all means," he said, barely containing his impa-tience, "so we can move on to more crucial issues."

"I consider Jason to be a crucial issue," she said hotly, and proceeded to inform Sherman of what had taken place the last two evenings. "It was Jason, all right—in your Cadillac, using his old starter pistol to frighten me. It's the only thing that makes any sense."

He cocked his head and glanced at her thoughtfully. "If all you say is true, then Jason has been behaving most reprehensi-bly. But as for last night's incident, there's always the chance a car backfired or—"

"If you won't confront Jason, I'll tell the police what I know and have them question him." She wondered if Detective Sawyer had already questioned Jason about the incident at the park.

"That won't be necessary, my dear," he assured her smoothly. "I appreciate your coming to me instead. Believe me when I say that Jason will live to regret he ever lifted a finger against you."

He paced the room, his face glowering with pent-up anger. Finally, he came to stand before Erica.

"I had hopes Jason had matured and was ready to settle down. Ready to make something of himself instead of frittering away his life and what was left of his money. He led me to believe that you—ahem—cared for him, but were reluctant to make a commitment so soon after your husband's death."

He gave her a rueful smile. "I was so delighted with the prospect of having you for my daughter-in-law, I paid little heed to your protestations Saturday night when we had our little talk. I must admit, I encouraged Jason to propose to you, or at least to declare his feelings. I never expected he'd turn on you the way he did and scare you half to death."

She nodded, gratified Sherman finally understood just how badly Jason had behaved. "What do you plan to do?"

His voice turned harsh. Menacing. "Leave that to me, my dear. When I'm finished, my son will be very sorry he ever came back to Manordale."

His tone frightened her. Goosepimples rose on her bare arms. Had she gone too far? Undoubtedly, he planned to toss Jason out of the house and leave him to fend for his own. This was exactly what she'd hoped for, yet she discovered she felt sorry for her former friend.

"Now let's get back to business, shall we? Did you have a chance to look over the papers I gave you on Friday?"

She bit her lip. "I meant to, but with everything happening, I didn't get a chance."

He clucked his disapproval. He pointed to the papers before them. "Your father's will is on top. The rest are statements and records of everything you own. You can look them over here, then take them home and go over everything at your leisure. I'll be happy to answer any questions. But first, please sign this document. A mere formality that I am handing all records of your holdings over to you."

"Will do," she agreed. She scanned the four stapled sheets of barely comprehensible legalese, then scribbled her name beside the three Xs.

Sherman was at her elbow to scoop them up as soon as she was done. She hardly took notice, as she was staring at her father's will.

"I'd like to read this carefully, if you don't mind."

He gave her a magnanimous smile. "Certainly, I understand." He paused in the doorway behind her. "Why don't I make us some coffee and return in a few minutes to answer any questions?"

"Mmm," she murmured, already engrossed in her task. A wave of sadness washed over her as she studied the yellowing pages. Her father had made out a will as a matter of course, never imagining he'd die in the prime of his life and leave her, his only child, a large sum of money in his stead.

She waded through the long pages, ignoring the "thereof" and "hereby" as she gleaned the actual meaning and intent of the convoluted phrases. It was a bit like reading a foreign language. She read the terms of her dual guardianship, then the monthly allotment for household expenditures, so underestimated for today's economy.

A blow to the back of her head resounded, brutal and unexpected.

Pain and nausea sliced. She moaned as she slumped forward, senseless for the second evening in a row.

She came to not knowing where she was or how long she'd been out. A throbbing ache pierced her skull. She desperately wanted to rub the bruised spot beside her right ear, but she couldn't move her hand. Nausea rose in her throat. When she raised her heavy eyelids, the room spun and sideslipped away, so she quickly closed them.

She tried to move her hand and couldn't. Her puzzlement turned to terror. What had happened? Why did her head hurt so? This time, when she opened her eyes, the dizziness wasn't as bad.

"Come on, come on," Sherman said impatiently. "I didn't hit you that hard."

Hit me? Why would Sherman hit me?

Her mind couldn't grasp the situation. It sounded like Sherman, but everything was blurry and unclear. Of course! She wasn't wearing her glasses.

"I can't see," she croaked, then shut her mouth and swallowed to control her sickness. At the same moment, she knew her hands were bound behind her. And her feet were tied, as well. A groan escaped her lips.

Sherman picked up her glasses from where they'd fallen and thrust them on her nose. "We can't have that, Erica, dear. I want you to see what a fool you've been."

Mesmerized, she watched as he perched on the corner of his desk. He looked the same—paunchy and well-dressed in a gray-striped shirt and gray trousers. Only his eyes were different. They gleamed with a feverish excitement.

"What do you think you're doing, hitting me and tying me up?" she demanded, forcing herself to sound outraged when she was sick with fear.

It had been Sherman the whole time! Odd, how she'd never suspected him. Even now, part of her brain refused to accept the horrendous truth that he wanted her dead. Until he, quite deliberately, dashed all hopes she might be mistaken. He strode to the closet beside her. When he reappeared, a black Darth Vader mask covered his face.

She screamed, "It was you on the road to Montauk!"

He tossed the mask back on the closet shelf. "Don't shout again or I'll have to gag you."

She shuddered with terror. "How stupid of me not to have guessed," she whispered. She had considered everyone: Jason, Doug, Monica. Even her aunts and Mr. Jennings.

"You've been stupid and lucky," he agreed. "Until tonight."

She didn't bother to point out he'd been clumsy and unlucky until now. Her body trembled with fright. She had to clench her teeth to stop their chattering. "You...you didn't kill Terry, did you?" she asked hopefully. Maybe Terry's death had been an accident, after all.

"I'm afraid it was necessary. He was turning stupid, too."

She gasped, but Sherman ignored her and went on speaking. "He called that Monday night to tell me he was going to divorce you. I said it was a bad idea."

He peered at her, a glimmer of pity in his eyes. "You were well rid of the likes of Terry Parker, Erica. Frankly, I was a bit disappointed you ever married him. Even though I'd arranged it all."

"You did?" His words were like another blow to the head. "Why?"

"Your inheritance, silly girl. Terry owed me. I got him off on a drug charge and had his police record erased. With Terry as your husband, I could continue to control and—er—borrow from your estate. But he surprised me, all right." He let out a rueful chuckle. "Transformed himself into a regular knight in shining armor. He claimed he couldn't continue the charade. His big mistake was threatening to tell you the whole story."

She gasped again. The full impact of Sherman's words hit her with the force of a Mack truck. So that was why Terry had pursued her so ardently—taking her out every night and showering her with romantic attentions—until she'd had no choice but to fall in love with him. How flattered she'd been when Terry, so obviously a free spirit, had asked her to marry him.

What a fool she had been!

Her face boiled as all of the ramifications of her "arranged marriage" sank in. She was mortified and deeply wounded, as well as furious for having been manipulated once again. Terry had been sent to marry her as part of a business deal. A deceitful, despicable, criminal business deal.

And she was the bait, the mark. The patsy.

"But Terry loved me. I know he did," she insisted, hardly aware she had spoken aloud.

"Perhaps. Not that it matters."

"Of course, it matters!" she said, but Sherman's mind was obviously elsewhere.

A minute later, his attention returned to Erica. He pointed an accusing finger. "It's too bad you refused Jason. If you'd been a bit more cooperative, we wouldn't be in this nasty position, now, would we?" He smiled as if he were recalling a pleasant memory. "I was even pleased my earlier attempts had gone amiss." His eyes narrowed, his voice turning cold. "But you had to be difficult and spoil everything."

Her mouth flew open in anger as she momentarily forgot her plight. *What gall! He actually blames me!* But, for once, she had the good sense to bite back her words. There was no point in riling Sherman. At least, not while she was at his mercy.

"Of course, the one mistake I made," he went on conversationally, "was not going in with your father when he made all those killings."

She cringed at the word, but he seemed unaware of any irony. He had a faraway look as he reminisced about the past.

"I was too conservative then, too frightened to take chances." His eyes, fierce and shining, again bore into hers. "But nothing frightens me any longer. Taking risks is what life's all about."

He's mad! Wildly insane. The realization froze her with horror.

"Finally, after years of making money for your father's estate—money that kept doubling and tripling—I decided to put it to good use. Why not borrow the money to buy my paintings? My beautiful, precious paintings." He rubbed his hands together. "After all, they're an investment of sorts, aren't they?" His face took on a stern expression. "But enough babbling. We're wasting time."

She cringed as he bent down beside her.

"Ah, here it is," he said, reaching for her pocketbook.

He opened the clasp and unceremoniously dumped all its contents onto the desk. Eyeglasses case, wallet, keys, lipstick, and tissues tumbled out.

"*Mmm,*" he hummed softly, until he plucked the car keys from the heap. Then he looked up at her and smiled.

She held herself rigid to control her trembling.

"I'm going to bring your car around to the back of the house. I want you to sit here quietly until I return. If you move, it will be worse for you, I promise you that."

"Where are we going?" she asked, hating the high-pitched sound of her voice.

"For a ride."

"Where to?"

He stalked out of the room.

She remained where she was, too terrified to move. What should she do? What *could* she do with her hands and feet tightly bound?

The sound of the Honda starting made her hyperventilate. Chest tight, she gulped lungfuls of air and forced herself to breathe more slowly.

The one thing she couldn't do was wait around for Sherman to come back and kill her. She positioned herself upright, cursing the sling back high heels that would make it ten times more difficult to hop to the door on her bound feet.

How would she open the door with her hands tied behind her? Or get down the front steps without falling on her face?

You'll figure it out. Start moving!

The car sputtered twice, then blessed silence. Her old and trusty Honda had stalled! Heartened, she put every effort into moving herself out of the study.

It was proving to be even more difficult than she'd expected. She took tiny little steps that only gained her an inch or so at a time. She tried hopping but, with her hands behind her, almost lost her balance. Her glasses slid down to the tip of her nose. That was the scariest. If she lost them, she'd be blind.

Sherman switched on the ignition again. It didn't catch.

Erica, grateful for the unexpected reprieve, moved forward another few feet.

So did the Honda. Sherman bucked the car past the study window and turned the corner of the house. The motor made a rasping sound, then died.

She could hardly believe her luck. In a minute or two, she'd be out of the room. She'd cross the hall to the front door and slide down those damn steps on her rear. He'd never be able to find her in the dark, amidst all those trees and bushes growing wild outside the house.

The motor shut off, then a car door slammed shut. Was he coming for her now? She held her breath and let it out slowly when he, once again, tried to start her car. Fool of a man! He'd flooded the engine.

As she reached the study door, she heard the unmistakable sound of a key turning in the front door. Maybe Monica had come home! Surely, she didn't know that her husband was about to kill Erica. Or did she? The thought upset her, made her move too quickly. She stumbled and fell to the floor.

"Dad? I saw the light under the door and—"

The door opened and missed hitting her by inches.

Jason peered into the room. He spotted her lying on the carpet. "What the hell are you doing here? Why are you tied up?"

"Your father," she whispered. "He's going to kill me. Help me, Jason. Untie me before he comes back."

He stared down at her for what seemed like minutes. *It's funny how I never noticed they have the same watery blue eyes that turn icy when they're calculating.* Now Jason's were narrow, assessing.

"I think not, Erica," he said finally. "You had your chance Saturday night, but you're too good for me, aren't you?"

"That's not true. We were best friends growing up."

"Best friends, eh? Is that why you sicced that detective on me?" He laughed. "I told him I got rid of that starter gun ages ago. You know what? The sucker believed me."

She began to panic again. "Jason, you're not an evil person. You can't let your father do this to me!"

He grinned malevolently. "Why don't we just let things run their course? It's no skin off my teeth what happens to you, and it will give me something to hold over Dad for once." He chuckled as he shook his head in disbelief. "Who would have guessed the old guy had it in him?"

She twisted her aching neck to stare up at him, her eyes bulging in disbelief.

"You don't mean that, Jason. You can't mean that. Please untie me. Help me out of here."

He turned to leave the room.

"Don't go, Jason!" she pleaded. "Don't leave me like this! We helped each other through the worst times of our childhood. Doesn't that mean anything to you?"

He stopped to seemingly consider this. "We were close then, weren't we? But now, we aren't." He laughed, as if he'd said something amusing. "If Dad asks for me, tell him I'm in my room."

He slammed the door behind him.

CHAPTER SEVENTEEN

"Come back here, Jason! Come back!" Erica screamed at the closed door.

Hearing him bound up the stairs forced her to swallow the unpleasant truth. Jason was willing to let Sherman kill her so he could sponge off his father for the rest of his life.

The bastard! The rotten bastard!

Tears of anger and betrayal welled up and threatened to spill down her face. Furious, she blinked them away. She wouldn't waste valuable energy on sentimentality—not with Sherman about to return at any minute. She needed a clear mind and her wits about her if she expected to outsmart him and escape.

But first, there was the small matter of getting back on her feet.

She was rising to her knees when the door swung open. Sherman rushed in, cursing her and her car. He nearly tripped over her, and flung out his arms to keep his balance.

"So," he said between clenched teeth, "you didn't listen. Thought you could escape, eh?" He shook her roughly then pulled her to her feet. "From here on in, you do exactly as you're told." He moved out of her line of vision.

She adjusted her glasses with her shoulder as best she could. The shaking had brought on a new bout of nausea. She hated to think what Sherman would do to her if she suddenly were to throw up on his carpet.

He came around, pointing a silver-colored gun at her chest. "A little reminder to prove I mean business."

Her knees threatened to buckle beneath her. She'd never been this close to a gun before.

"This is a .38," he explained. "One wrong move, and I'll pull the trigger. I couldn't miss you if I tried."

Right. Like you couldn't miss me on the drive to Montauk, or finish me off in town, she retorted silently to bolster her courage. She shuddered when she remembered he *had* succeeded in killing Terry.

"Jason came in while you were gone," she blurted. She had to stop Sherman any way she could. Maybe he'd give up his plan to kill her if he knew his son was in the house.

To her dismay, he threw her a look of disgust. He must not have heard Jason drive up, and thought she was lying.

"Go upstairs," she cried frantically, "and see for yourself!"

"Your pathetic little ploys won't help you. Now, we're going to—"

"But it's true!"

He frowned. He placed the gun on the desk, then reached inside his trouser pocket and pulled out a large handkerchief.

"I see I'll have to gag you as well."

Before she could utter another word, the handkerchief was put in place.

Stupid, stupid, stupid, she berated herself. She nearly vomited at the thought of Sherman's used handkerchief over her mouth and shook her head until he managed to grab hold of her face. He squeezed her cheeks. The pain made her open her mouth. Quickly, he tied it behind her head. The gag hurt the corners of her mouth, but she was grateful it didn't affect her breathing.

He bent down and untied her feet. "Now, Erica, we're going through the kitchen and out to your car. You'll walk in front of me and do exactly as I say. Do you understand?" He was panting from the exertion of crouching down to get to the knots.

Her timing was perfect. As Sherman struggled to his feet, she kicked him squarely in the groin. He sank heavily to the floor, moaning in pain.

She sped out of the room toward the front door. If she opened it before Sherman got up, she'd be safe!

But the final hurdle proved more of a problem than she'd expected. With her hands tied behind her, she couldn't manage the front door. She turned around and twisted the knob the wrong way. The other direction!

Too late. Sherman came lunging at her, his face contorted with rage.

"You wise-ass bitch! Kick me, will you?" He raised his hand to smack her.

She cringed against the door.

The doorbell chimed, startling her.

His arm fell to his side. A moronic expression covered his face. He stared at her, then asked, "Now who the hell could that be?"

She didn't give a damn who was on the other side of the door. Whoever it was would save her! Her heart coursed with joy. She was about to be rescued!

She kicked the door behind her. "Help, help," she shouted through her gag, though her pleas came out as no more than muffled groans.

Her attempts to draw attention to herself roused Sherman to action. He yanked her away from the door and pushed her toward the study as the chimes rang again.

"Just a minute," he called out with false cheer. "Be right there!"

He shoved her again, and sent her stumbling into the study. "Get in there and be quick about it." He wound the cord around her feet and knotted it tightly. Then he thrust her inside the closet. "Not a sound," he hissed, and slammed the door in her face.

The shallow closet was crammed with shirts that all but smothered her. She could barely move. An upright coffin, she thought, then winced at the image. No need to have gloomy thoughts when help was but a few feet away.

She strained her ears, trying to discover who Sherman's unexpected visitor might be. Maybe Detective Sawyer decided to question Jason again. Or perhaps his investigation led him to suspect Sherman Hartley.

When she heard Aunt Constance's loud, anxious voice, she couldn't decide whether to laugh or cry.

"I'm so sorry to bother you like this," her aunt was telling Sherman as she blithely passed from the hall into the living room on the other side of the closet wall, "but when I called about forty minutes ago, the line was busy. I tried Erica at home, but no one answered.

"The truth is, I'm terribly upset. Too upset to stay in New Jersey. And," she paused, but only for a moment, "Monica did say, when I spoke to her today, that I could spend the night. So, when the train pulled in and I couldn't reach Erica or Monica, I took a cab and came right here."

Sherman offered halfhearted pleasantries as her aunt settled herself on the living room sofa.

"I'm so worried," Constance continued peevishly. "I don't know what to do. I tried calling Erica all day, but she's gone. And she didn't answer her cell phone. It's all my fault! I drove her away for a second time. Me and my big mouth."

Erica felt a pang of guilt as she realized she'd forgotten to turn on her cell phone that morning. To her astonishment, her aunt began to sob.

While Sherman made the obligatory soothing noises, Erica concentrated on ramming her elbow against the wall to get her aunt's attention. But the limitations of her bound hands were further restricted by the hanging clothes, making the sound too faint to be heard. She tried using her head, but that brought instant blinding pain.

When Aunt Constance spoke again, she sounded calmer. "Sherman, you seem on edge tonight. I hope I'm not disturbing you."

"Actually, tonight isn't the best evening for company," he said. "Monica must have forgotten about her meeting, and I've lots of office work to catch up on." He gave a little laugh. "There must be some other place where you can spend the night."

"Of course, there is," Aunt Constance snapped. "I've an entire empty house at my disposal, haven't I?" From the shuffling sounds and deep breaths, Erica knew her aunt was struggling to her feet. "I'll simply call myself another cab and leave you in peace."

"No, don't go into the kitchen," Sherman shrieked. "It...it's a mess!"

Erica noted his rising hysteria with glee. He was terrified Aunt Constance might spot her Honda from the kitchen window.

"I must say, Sherman, you're behaving decidedly peculiar tonight," Aunt Constance observed. "May I use the phone in your study, or is that room a mess as well?"

He was back on keel. "I'd be happy to call a taxi for you, Constance," he said smoothly. "Why don't you wait right here where you'll be comfortable? I'll only be a moment."

He hurried into his study and closed the door firmly behind him. He anxiously muttered as he fumbled through the phone book. He started to dial the number, then stopped.

The chimes were ringing again!

"Oh, my God," he moaned.

Erica's heart started pounding like a jackhammer.

Let's see how he deals with another uninvited guest, she thought as he scurried off to answer the door.

Her optimism grew. The more people in the house, the better her chances of staying alive. If only she could untie her feet! In his earlier haste, Sherman hadn't bound them too tightly.

She worked off her shoes. Then, using the back of the closet for support, she squatted and reached for the cord. Damn it! Just her index finger touched the knots, but it was a start. She focused all her determination on her only available utensil and poked away. One of the knots was loosening! Now, if only everyone would stay until she could get out of the closet and join them, she'd be safe.

Or would Sherman kill the whole lot of them? He'd already killed Terry, and he was desperate. By openly attacking her tonight, he'd gone well past the point of no return. Nothing he said could explain away her bruises and her bonds. Concentrating furiously on the knots and her thoughts, she paid little attention to the voices outside the study.

The new guest had joined Aunt Constance in the living room, an unfamiliar male voice. Probably a client, she decided as she jabbed and prodded, her finger already sore. Then a woman broke into the conversation, chirping happily about something. The gag turned Erica's chuckle into a muffled croak. What on earth had brought Aunt Betty here tonight?

"And so, Connie, dear," Aunt Betty was explaining, "I hope you'll forgive me for leaving, but I was distraught." She gave a simpering laugh. "As I say, things always work out for the best. I told Ron I couldn't bear any more of this secrecy, and last night, he had it out with his wife. She agreed to be reasonable about the divorce. We'll be getting married just as soon as the final papers are signed. Isn't that simply wonderful?"

Erica pressed her ear to the wall to take in every word of her aunts' tearful reconciliation. They rhapsodized about their long and devoted friendship, apologizing again and again for having quarreled. The joint sobbing rose to a crescendo, at which point, Sherman and Aunt Betty's fiancé made the duet a quartet in their attempts to quiet them down.

"Betty, how on earth did you know I was here?" Aunt Constance asked.

"I didn't. We stopped by the house to give you and Erica the good news, but no one was home. I wanted to tell someone, so we came to tell the Hartleys."

In spite of her past irritation with her aunt and her own dangerous situation, Erica felt tears welling up. Aunt Betty was courageous in her own way. She'd made every attempt to forget the man she loved because he was married. Then, when she'd realized they still loved each other after so many years, she'd fought for their relationship and won! It was very romantic in its own way.

If I ever get out of here, she promised herself, *I'll give Aunt Betty the money she asked for. She deserves to be happy.*

"By the way, where's Erica?" Aunt Betty asked.

Here I am! Erica screamed silently. She tried pounding her head against the wall. She only succeeded in making it ache. Nobody heard her.

"I think she's disappeared," Aunt Constance answered gloomily. "I'm terribly sorry, Betty, but I've gone and chased her off again." She told them how she'd argued with Erica on Sunday morning.

"Nonsense, Connie," Aunt Betty said. "You're making a big to-do out of nothing. Erica's a grown woman. She's probably out somewhere, that's all."

Sherman cleared his throat. "She—er—did call here earlier today. Said something to Monica about a date. "With—er—Doug Remsen, I believe Monica told me."

Rotten liar! Hypocritical murderer!

Angrily, Erica jabbed at the knots. She'd succeeded in unraveling one of them, but two remained. The minute she freed herself, she'd tell the world exactly what kind of a person Sherman Hartley was!

"Of course!" Aunt Constance exclaimed. "How stupid of me! He called her yesterday."

"See, Connie," Betty scolded her affectionately. "You worry all the time. Always imagining the worst for no good reason. Erica's out having a good time, and you're upsetting yourself and putting a strain on your heart."

"My heart's just fine, Elizabeth. Let's have that understood once and for all. I know you think I'm about to expire at the slightest sign of stress, but that's not the case."

"Well, well." Sherman cleared his throat. "I'm pleased to see you all, and thrilled about your news, Betty, and—er—Ron, but since I have all this work to do and since you've figured out where Erica is—"

"We're leaving, Sherman," Aunt Constance finished for him, her tone decidedly cheerier. "Sorry to have disturbed you. Tell Monica I'll call her in the morning. Betty, do you think Ron would mind dropping me off at the house? I have a suitcase in the hall."

"You do, Connie? Where have you been?"

"I'd be happy to drive you home," Ron gallantly offered.

Their voices grew softer as they headed to the front door.

"Don't leave!" Erica tried to shout, but her words gurgled in her throat. She struggled with the one remaining knot, the tightest of the three, her finger now sore and bleeding.

She bit down to bear the pain and jabbed frantically at the knot. Panic rose in her throat. *This can't be happening! My aunts are in the hall, kissing that demented man goodbye, the very same monster who intends to murder me the moment they drive away.*

No, he won't! I won't let him!

In a surge of outrage, Erica undid the knot.

She kicked her feet free of the cord, then remembered her bound hands and muzzled mouth. If only she could call out! Her breath caught as her aunts' voices faded away. Sherman was ushering them down the steps outside!

Her ankles tingled and felt unsteady, but she pushed through Sherman's shirts, then turned around so that her bound hands could grasp the doorknob. It opened easily.

Joyfully, she raced to the study door and was met with an unexpected delay. The long handle required a strong downward motion which her numb hands were finding difficult to maneuver.

Don't leave! Don't leave! she screamed in her head as she struggled to free herself in time. She reached the open front door just as the car's rear lights disappeared from sight.

She was a minute too late! She choked back sobs of frustration that threatened to overcome her. She couldn't fall apart now. She had to come up with another avenue of escape.

Escape! Her car was at the back of the house!

She slipped past the well-lit living room. If Sherman was planning to put her in her car and stage some kind of accident, he probably left the key in the ignition. She had to get out of the house before he discovered she was gone. He might shoot at her as she drove past, but that was a risk she had to take.

In the kitchen, she stopped dead in her tracks.

My hands. She moaned. *I must untie my hands in order to drive.*

Awkwardly, she jerked open the silverware drawer and, peering over her shoulder, selected a sharp cutting knife. She managed to grasp the knife between her bound hands, and nearly dropped it when she heard Sherman shouting from the study.

"Erica, where the hell are you? I told you to stay put."

She shuddered as he stomped about, slamming doors. Frantically, she set about cutting her bonds, but her hands were too close together and the knife barely touched the cord.

Sherman bellowed again.

I have to get out of here! She dropped the knife and ran to open the kitchen door.

Too late! Sherman came storming in.

"And where do you think you're going, young lady?" His angry fingers dug into her shoulders, making her recoil in fear and pain. "You're not getting away from me this time." His voice came in ragged, heaving breaths. "I can't have you blabbing all over Manordale that I've been borrowing from your estate to buy my paintings. There's my reputation to consider." He sent her a look of scorn. "Poor Erica. Your aunts came and went and never knew you were here. No one will save you now."

He thrust open the kitchen door and reached for the screen door.

Erica perched for flight. She would dash behind her car and into the bushes before he could pull the gun from his pocket.

"You go first," he ordered, "and no funny business. Straight to the car."

Instead of following her plan, she paused. There was a rustling in the grass. Was someone hiding out there? Probably a small animal, she told herself, annoyed she'd forfeited her chance to run.

Sherman was right. No one else was coming here tonight.

They both gave a start when the doorbell chimed again, loudly and insistently this time.

His fingers cut deeply into her arm. Her muffled shriek expressed both pain and hope. Maybe she had heard footsteps. Maybe help was on the way!

Sherman cursed, shocking her with his vulgar choice of obscenities. At the same time, it sounded as if the new visitor had a finger glued to the doorbell and was refusing to go away.

Sensing Sherman's distraction, she pulled away from his slackened grip and propelled her body forward. But this time, she had underestimated him.

"No, you don't!" He held her firmly and crashed the gun, butt down, on her head.

Though the blow was not as severe as the first one had been, it sent her sprawling on the kitchen floor. The nausea and dizziness returned, and she no longer had the strength to fight him.

He dragged her like a sack of cornmeal into the dining room, where he left her wedged between the table and the credenza.

The chimes ringing and ringing. They were soon accompanied by a heavy pounding that got mixed up with the pounding in her head.

"Stay here, bitch," Sherman hissed. "I'll be right back to take care of you." He hurried off to see who was hammering at the door.

She lay on the fringe of consciousness. The fight had been all but beaten out of her. She longed to drift off into peaceful oblivion, but she dared not. She didn't want to die. This was her very last chance to save herself.

Bruised and disoriented, she struggled to sit up. The effort took all of her energy. Heaving air, she rested her face against the seat of a chair, but the more upright position made her woozy and she started to slip. The gag caught on the corner of the chair and folds of it were forced up against her nose.

She couldn't breathe! Terror focused her mind. She shoved her face up against the arm of the chair, pushing the wood hard into the hollow of her cheek as she forced her head even higher.

The handkerchief came free of her nose. She drew long, grateful breaths, which cleared her head somewhat and made her aware of her terrible thirst. The gag was loose! She could push it down, away from her mouth! While she worked at it, she became aware of the voices in the hall.

Sherman was striving for his pompous lawyer's manner, but his pitch was high, almost strident.

"—several times, she's not here. Now leave quietly, Remsen, and take your friends with you, or I'll have to call Mr. B. He won't be very happy when he finds out you've been harassing me."

Doug! Doug was here! Her spirits soared. Adrenaline pumped through her body. She forgot her many aches, the dreadful thirst. She maneuvered herself around the table and peered into the hall.

A wondrous sight greeted her eyes. The door flew open, and Doug strode into the hall. In one fluid motion, he grasped Sherman, pressed his back against the wall, and lifted him so that his feet dangled inches above the floor.

Shaking him, Doug said, "I'll kill you if you've hurt her, Hartley."

She wanted to laugh, to call out, to run to Doug. She tried to stand, but when she rose to her knees, the room began to spin.

"That's enough, Vern—er, Remsen. We'll deal with Mr. Hartley." The voice was familiar. The speaker stepped into the house and announced himself. "Detective Sawyer, Police."

Two officers in uniform closed rank behind him.

She smiled contentedly, allowing lassitude to overtake her for the moment. If her hands were free, she would have applauded. She was being rescued, after all!

"Oh." Sherman was obviously shaken. "Come in, Detective. Gentlemen."

At that moment, Jason came downstairs and joined the group. "What's going on? How can my father and I be of service?" For once, he seemed to possess the composure his father lacked.

For a moment, Sherman stood gaping at his son. "These men are looking for Erica. I've already explained that she isn't here, but they pushed their way right in."

Even now he sounds aggrieved. Just like Jason, she thought, stifling the urge to chuckle.

Her head was clearing, but she still felt too groggy to stand or call out. Besides, she was content to remain silent and watch the scene unfolding before her. It was like being in a movie she knew would end with happily-ever-after.

"Hello again, Jason," Detective Sawyer said. "We have a witness who saw you racing down Mrs. Parker's street after hearing what sounded like a gun."

"I don't know what you're talking about," Jason mumbled.

"Really? He managed to write down the license plate number of the car you were driving. It belongs to your father."

There was a soft rapping at the door. Detective Sawyer opened it. A young, uniformed policeman whispered in his ear. Detective Sawyer followed him outside, closing the door behind him. He reappeared a minute later.

"Her car's out back. On an unpaved road behind the house," he told Doug. He turned to Sherman. "We're going to have to search the house, Mr. Hartley."

"Where is Erica?" Doug said through clenched teeth. He raised his arm, ready to strike Sherman.

"Easy does it," Detective Sawyer said. He eyed Sherman. "Now, perhaps you'll tell us where Mrs. Parker is," he said mildly. "It would be better for everyone involved."

That was her cue to make her grand entrance, but her legs were still too wobbly to support her. "I'm here," she said, her voice no more than a whisper.

Nobody heard her. Nobody looked in her direction. All eyes were glued on the front door, concentrating on the key turning in the lock. Still as statues, the six men watched as Monica entered the house.

She, in turn, stared in astonishment at the men forming a semicircle before her. "Good evening," she said. Her eyes sought and found her husband. "What's going on, Sherman?" She sounded both puzzled and annoyed. "You told me you had work to do tonight. That was the only reason I agreed to go to that boring meeting. As it turned out, I left before it ended. I simply couldn't sit there another minute."

When she didn't answer, she became agitated. "Who are these men? Why is a police car in our driveway?"

Erica stumbled to her feet.

Sherman struggled for composure. He put a reassuring arm around Monica. "Sorry to distress you, my dear. These gentlemen are looking for Erica. I've told them repeatedly—"

"I'm here!" Erica huffed, finally strong enough to step into the hall.

Sherman was the first to reach her.

"So, you are here, after all!" He tried for a laugh. "Heh, heh. Just arrived, I bet. And used the back door, as usual."

"Sure, Sherman. I drove here with my hands tied behind me." She turned around for everyone to see.

Doug rushed over and untied her. Tenderly, he rubbed each of her sore wrists. "You foolish, foolish woman. I told you not to leave the house."

As happy as she was to receive Doug's attentions, her gaze sought Detective Sawyer's. "Sherman was planning to kill me. He hit me over the head twice, then tied me up and gagged me."

"Erica, dear," Sherman said soothingly. "How can you invent such lies? As for your hands, I have no idea..."

Erica ignored him. "He has a gun in his pocket."

Detective Sawyer nodded, and the two policemen closed in. "Let's have it, Mr. Hartley," one of them said. "There are cars outside and men stationed in back, in case you're thinking of making a run for it."

Sherman's gaze darted from one to the other, as he thrust his hand in his pocket. His face was flushed and glistened with perspiration.

The others waited.

So, she *had* heard someone out back, she thought. In spite of the tenseness of the moment, she felt safer than she had in weeks.

"Come on, Mr. Hartley," the same officer urged. "Hand it over."

Sherman gave him the gun. He hunched up his shoulders and let his head fall to his chest.

The officer handcuffed him and led him outside.

Monica trailed after them. "Sherman, what's happening?" she cried. "What did you do?"

He paused to give his wife a wan smile. "I'm sorry, my dear. I'll send Frank Reynolds over first thing in the morning to look after you." Head bowed, he got in the back of the police car.

"I had nothing to do with this," Jason declared as soon as the door closed on his father.

"Of course, you did!" Erica glared at him. She took pleasure in watching his face crumble.

"Tell them the truth, Erica," he pleaded. "Tell them my father was using your money and couldn't afford to have you find out. Explain that I had nothing to do with it, at all."

She resisted the impulse to slap his face. "You were going to let him kill me. I'll testify to that in court."

She turned to Detective Sawyer. "It was Jason who frightened me half to death last night. I want to prosecute to the full extent of the law."

The detective gave Jason a grim nod. "I intend to speak to you, Mr. Hartley. Either here or down at the station."

"I'll wait in the kitchen," Jason mumbled and slunk away.

Someone tugged her arm.

"Erica, dear, what's happening?" Monica's mascara-smeared eyes brimmed with tears. "Sherman didn't try to hurt you, did he?"

An unexpected surge of pity rushed over Erica, checking her other emotions, and she found herself hugging Monica. "I'm afraid he did. There's a side to Sherman that none of us knew about."

From the corner of her eye, she caught Doug and Detective Sawyer exchanging glances. She was surprised they seemed to be in perfect accord.

The detective lifted his chin toward Monica.

Doug gently detached the sobbing woman from Erica's embrace and led her into the living room.

Detective Sawyer fixed his eyes on Erica. They were bloodshot from obvious lack of sleep. Wordlessly, he escorted her into the dining room and sat her down in a chair.

Erica took the glass of water he handed her a minute later. She finished it and asked for more.

"Are you feeling better?" he asked.

"Much better."

"Hartley struck you. You should be seen by a doctor."

"I suppose you're right. I still feel woozy and my head hurts."

"In that case, we'll drive you to the Emergency Room, and take down your story tomorrow."

"Tonight," she said firmly. "Let's get it over with." She cocked her head and looked at him quizzically. "What time is it? I've lost all track of time."

"It's ten minutes past ten."

"That's all? I feel as if I've been here for days."

"I'm sorry about that." He sounded sad, the way he had last night. "I should have listened to my instincts and assigned someone to follow you, especially after looking into your husband's death. Our I.T. genius did some digging and found a link between your husband and Sherman Hartley, who I knew was Jason's father. I told him to dig further."

She gave him a small smile.

"When he texted me to say he'd discovered Hartley was handling your father's trust," the detective continued, "I drove over to your house. I saw no one was home and called the station."

"A good thing you did." Doug glided past Detective Sawyer to stand beside Erica. "Those fellows down at your precinct didn't believe one word I was saying. I told them Erica had to be here, that if they didn't get a move on, there'd be hell to pay. Anyway, I was about to leave and handle it on my own when I heard them mention your name, and I realized they had you on the phone."

Detective Sawyer laughed. "What kind of a reception did you expect, with the credentials you're carrying?"

"Still, they should be able to tell the good guys from the bad."

They grinned at each other as though they were sharing a joke.

"Obviously, you two know something I don't," she groused.

They turned to beam at her, openly amused by her show of exasperation.

"You'll know, too, soon enough," Doug said. He turned to the detective. "Mrs. Hartley's resting in the living room. She took a pill to calm her nerves."

"I'd better see her," Detective Sawyer said and left them alone.

Erica stood and found herself in Doug's strong arms. They kissed gently at first, then fervently with the relief of averted danger. She clung to him. He had saved her life. They leaned back to gaze into each other's eyes, too full of emotion to speak.

It was him who broke the silence. "Don't ever scare me like that again. Never, ever." He traced her nose with his finger. "I was terrified we wouldn't get here in time."

She pulled him close and smiled. "I have to see a doctor, then go down to the police station," she said.

"I know," he said, a silly grin on his face. "And I'll be driving you." He kissed her forehead, then each cheek.

She grinned back. She couldn't remember ever feeling this happy. "It's a funny way to see my birthday in," she commented.

"True, but think of what a great story it will make to tell the grandchildren."

CHAPTER EIGHTEEN

Minutes later, they were on their way to the Emergency Room of Manordale Hospital, escorted by Detective Sawyer's unmarked car and a police cruiser, its siren going full blast.

Erica placed her hands over her ears and grimaced. "Isn't this a bit much?"

Doug grinned. "A survivor's tribute. Enjoy it."

Detective Sawyer accompanied them into the hospital. He disappeared inside an office, leaving Erica to fill out forms. She and Doug had just sat down in the half-empty waiting room when the detective returned with a young doctor at his side.

"Dr. Patel will look after you, Erica. See you later," he said and left.

The young woman led her and Doug to a tiny examining room. "Does this hurt?" she asked as she gently prodded Erica's head.

"Ouch!" she exclaimed. "Sorry," she immediately apologized.

"No need," Dr. Patel replied softly.

She arranged for a CAT scan.

"No internal bleeding or skull fracture," she announced afterwards. "You have a concussion. Go home and get some rest."

Erica yawned. "I could sleep for a week. Police Power," she muttered as they passed the many people still waiting to be treated. She yawned again. "But I sure appreciate it tonight."

Doug helped her into the car. He got in and leaned over for a brief kiss.

"Mmm," she said, pulling him tight.

Gently, Doug disentangled himself. "Later, my darling. I promise. But now, it's on to the precinct!" he declared with a flourish, and they drove off.

She studied his handsome profile, pleased to see he wasn't suffering from any signs of fatigue. In fact, he seemed lighthearted and thoroughly enjoying his role as chauffeur.

In spite of the tablet the doctor had insisted she swallow, she felt achy and terribly tired. She was beginning to regret not having taken up Detective Sawyer's offer of postponing her visit to the police station until the following day.

She had never been inside the station before, and nothing about its grim appearance inspired the desire for a return visit. The old stone building was poorly lit, and reeked of greasy French fries.

Doug, a supportive arm around her shoulders, delivered her to Detective Sawyer. His office was a small cubicle just large enough for a desk and two visitors' chairs. She spotted the tape recorder immediately.

Doug gave her cheek a peck. "I'll be back later."

"Aren't you staying?" she asked, dismayed. She'd assumed he would remain with her for moral support.

"Sorry. I have to settle some unfinished business."

He and Sawyer nodded to each other, and the detective slid behind his desk. He reached for a white Styrofoam cup and downed whatever was left of his coffee.

"Like some?"

She nodded. "With milk, please."

He pushed a buzzer, and a uniformed officer appeared in the doorway. "Some more coffee, Bill, if you'd be so kind. Cream for Mrs. Parker."

"Right."

Detective Sawyer rubbed his eyes. For a moment, he rested his head against the bridge formed by his thumb and forefinger.

"You look beat," she observed with concern.

"It's all right. Tomorrow's my day off."

With what appeared to be a superhuman effort, he roused himself and studied her intently. She felt the force of his powerful concentration. He flipped on the tape recorder.

"Now," he said gently, "I'm going to ask you some questions. Take all the time you need to answer them. Feel free to elaborate. Give me as much information as you can. I want to know everything. Every little detail you can remember, even if you think it might be silly or unimportant."

She spent the next two hours telling and retelling her story until she couldn't think straight. Detective Sawyer was a stickler for facts. He wanted dates, times, details. He asked her about her childhood, her parents, their relationship with Sherman Hartley, her relationship with Sherman and with Jason. He asked about her life with Terry.

She held nothing back. She was glad to tell her story to Detective Sawyer. It helped put it behind her and gave her a sense of release. She'd been lugging around a heavy burden of doubts and guilt and fears, the weight of which she was finally beginning to realize. And there was heartfelt relief, as well, because the detective believed every word she uttered.

She was grateful that his tone remained matter-of-fact. It helped put the world back in perspective. Not everyone was out to harm her. Only Sherman, and perhaps Jason, although it was still difficult to accept that they had actually wanted her dead.

Detective Sawyer's calm voice droned on and on.

He's a coffee freak, Erica decided, watching the empty cups pile up beside the tape recorder. Only his red-rimmed eyes and an occasional sigh revealed how moved he was by what she was saying.

It was one-thirty when he switched off the machine and said they were done "for now."

Erica struggled to her feet as Doug entered the office. He, too, appeared exhausted.

"There's an all-night coffee shop across the street," he told her. "Let's go there. We've a few things to talk about."

"Can't it wait?" she asked, covering a yawn.

"It's important."

"Oh, okay," she agreed, too weary to argue.

Much as she liked Doug, she'd just finished off a gallon of coffee, and a coffee shop was the last place she wanted to go to. Besides, this had been the longest, most arduous day of her life. She was willing to save any further revelations for the bright sunshine, after a good night's sleep. But if he felt he had to bare his soul...

Her pulse quickened. Perhaps he'd decided to abandon his criminal career, after all!

In retrospect, she decided she wouldn't have missed their conversation in the coffee shop for anything! It proved to be the highlight of her day. Her week. Her year! All she had to do was listen, ask an occasional question, and grin like the lucky kid who'd bought only one raffle ticket and went home with the ten-speed bike. At one point, her relief had her shrieking with delight. The two off-duty cops sitting in a nearby booth threw them dirty looks, but their waitress never blinked an eye.

Doug's manner grew easier with each revelation. "Erica, sweetie, I never wanted to keep anything from you, but I had no choice."

"Speaking of which," she said, suddenly remembering, "who was that woman I spoke to on the phone, the time I called you from Montauk? Was that your sister?"

He chuckled. "My partner."

She looked at him. "Is she very pretty?"

"Her husband sure thinks so, but Roxy's a bit too plump for my taste."

She sank back, content.

Outside, on the dark and desolate street, he took her in his arms and kissed her. "Besides, you're the one I can't stop thinking about," he said as he nuzzled his face against hers.

"Me too."

They strolled arm-in-arm across the street to Doug's car. He kissed her again. "Happy birthday, darling."

She grinned. "Thanks. I almost forgot what day it was." In the car, she said, "I'm glad that kind detective offered to drive my car home for me."

He took her hand. "It was the least they could do, after nearly letting you get killed. I tried telling them you needed police protection, but would they listen?"

She brushed her lips against his knuckles. "Yesterday, you weren't exactly someone they could trust."

They laughed, delighting in their shared knowledge.

The house was dark when they pulled into the driveway. Erica unlocked the front door and Doug followed her into the hall.

"I'll say a quick good night and let you get to sleep. I know you're exhausted."

She giggled. "Don't go. I'm so overtired, I could never fall asleep. Besides, with all that's happened, I feel like I'm in a wonderful dream that I never want to end."

She placed a possessive hand on his arm and led him into the family room. "You won't want any more coffee. How about a drink? Some soda?"

"A drink would be in order," he said, then quickly added, "though I don't think you—"

"I wasn't planning on having any."

"Who's there?" Aunt Constance called sleepily from the top of the stairs. "Is that you, Erica?"

She hurried into the hall. "It's me, Aunt Constance."

Slowly, Constance lumbered down the steps. "Erica! I was so afraid you'd gone off again, but you're really here!" Tears streamed down her wrinkled face. She tripped and caught her balance.

"Wait, I'm coming up!"

She dashed up the stairs and steered her aunt back to the second-floor landing. "Everything's okay," she murmured again and again as her aunt gripped her fiercely. It was the first time she'd seen her cry since Uncle Leonard's funeral. Erica hugged her tight. "We were both so silly, weren't we?"

Constance nodded like an obedient child. Her sobs subsided, and she allowed Erica to walk her to her room.

"Put on a robe," Erica told her aunt. "There's someone I want you to meet."

"Are you out of your head, Erica? It's past two in the morning." Constance sank onto the bed. "It's been a crazy two days. I went straight to Cousin Molly's."

When Erica looked blank, her aunt explained. "Our cousin from New Jersey. You met her years ago. Anyway, I couldn't stop thinking about you. I had no business running off like that, leaving you on your own. I tried calling here all day and got no answer. And you weren't answering your cell phone. I was so worried you'd gone off again. I took the train home this evening and tried you from the station, but still no answer. So, I went to the Hartleys'."

"Yes, I know," Erica said.

Constance seemed not to have heard. She sniffed. "Monica said I could stay there if I wanted, but Sherman seemed put out. Betty stopped by, too. She didn't know where you were, either. Sherman thought you were probably out with Doug Remsen."

"I was out with Doug just now."

Constance sighed deeply. "Silly of me to get so upset. Betty was right when she said I worry for no good reason. She's getting married very soon. To her old love, Ron Jennings."

"Yes, I know," Erica said again.

This time, her words registered. Constance stared at her. "How can you know? They've only just decided. She said they stopped by the house, but you weren't here."

She answered by squeezing her aunt's hand. "Put on a robe and come downstairs. I'll explain everything, I promise." Impulsively, she kissed her aunt's cheek. "It's good to have you home."

So that's the way to handle her, Erica thought as she traipsed down the steps.

Doug met her in the hall and kissed her. "You were gone much too long," he murmured in her ear.

"Sorry," she said, not sorry at all. She liked being missed. "Come into the kitchen. I know there's a bottle of Scotch someplace."

She rummaged around in the cupboards until she found what she was looking for. She took the bottle and two glasses and led Doug back to the family room. They sat down, and she popped up again.

"Oops. I forgot the ice."

"Relax. I'll get some," he said, and was away before she could stop him.

"Erica!" Aunt Constance appeared, clutching at the neck of her robe. "There's a man in our kitchen. I hope it's not who I think it is."

Erica grinned as Doug came into the room, a bowl full of ice cubes in his hand. "Aunt Constance, I want you to meet Doug."

Before Constance could open her mouth, he was embracing her warmly. "It's a pleasure to meet you, Aunt Constance."

Female vanity vied with moral rectitude and lost. "Isn't this your gangster friend?" she sputtered. "How could you, Erica? You know how I feel—"

"Sit down, Aunt Constance, and have a drink," she ordered, practically pushing her aunt onto the couch. "The evening's just begun."

Dumbfounded, Constance sat and stared up at her niece.

It gets easier and easier, Erica thought. Her fatigue had all but disappeared, leaving her clear-sighted and full of vitality. *All I have to do is out-manage her, and Aunt Constance becomes as docile as a lamb.*

Erica placed an ice cube in each glass, which Doug then filled with a shot of Scotch.

"To Erica's birthday," he said, lifting his glass.

Aunt Constance barely hesitated, then did the same. "To Erica," she seconded.

"Thank you."

Erica pulled over one of the large chairs and sat facing her aunt.

Doug perched on the arm of her chair.

"First of all," she said, "Doug's last name is Vernon, not Remsen, Aunt Constance."

Aunt Constance looked puzzled.

Erica went on. "What I'm trying to say is, Doug's not a gangster."

He smiled. "On the contrary. I was working undercover for a federal task force on organized crime." His smile turned to a grimace. "I was, until tonight, when I blew my cover." He shook his head. "My boss—my real boss—gave me hell. Fifteen months of hard work down the drain."

Erica put her arm around him and kissed his cheek. "He did it to rescue me, Aunt Constance. From Sherman Hartley. Doug went to the police, but they didn't believe him because he had no proof. So, he finally had to tell them who he really is, but by then, Detective Sawyer—"

"Police? Sherman?" Constance gawked at the two animated faces before her. "I don't understand what you two are getting at. And I'm afraid I'll like it even less when I find out."

Erica sighed with exasperation. "Remember I told you Sunday morning that someone in Manordale was out to hurt me? Well, that someone turned out to be Sherman. He was about to kill me. He had me tied up and stuffed in his study closet when you stopped by."

"Tonight?" Aunt Constance's mouth fell open and remained so while Erica related her evening's adventures.

"The police are holding Sherman and won't let him out on bail. At least, not yet." Erica's eyes narrowed. "Unfortunately, Doug thinks Jason will be out tonight. That bastard."

Aunt Constance threw her arms around Erica and squeezed her until she could hardly breathe. "My poor baby," she crooned. "Did Sherman hurt you?"

"Just a few bruises," she admitted. "They should heal in a few days."

Doug looked at her with concern. "Isn't it time for you to take another pill? The doctor said every four hours."

"She said only if my head hurts, and I'm fine. Really."

He and her aunt exchanged a brief but meaningful glance.

Aunt Constance cleared her throat. "Well, Erica, dear, perhaps you should—" she began, but Erica stopped her.

"You don't like it when I interfere with your medication, do you?"

To her surprise, Aunt Constance gave a deep guffaw. A minute later, her face was grim. "How's Monica? I hope to God she wasn't involved in this business."

"She wasn't," she told her. "Detective Sawyer said Monica nearly fainted when he explained what Sherman was planning to do to me. She was horrified to learn he'd killed Terry and stole from my trust fund to buy paintings. Her sister and brother-in-law came to pick her up. She'll be staying with them for a while."

"To think that Sherman wanted to kill you because of his stupid paintings." Constance shook her head. "Betty and I trusted him so. Why, we'd go to him for advice on just about everything. And all that time, he was taking your money and planning..." Her voice broke, and she covered her face with her hands. "I've been wrong about everyone—you, Sherman, Betty."

She got up to comfort her aunt. "Don't be so hard on yourself, Aunt Constance. You meant well." She smiled impishly, unable to resist. "But you have to learn to let people handle their own lives."

Doug moved closer and put an arm around Erica.

Aunt Constance, her eyes blurry with tears, gazed into his handsome face and tried to smile. "I was even wrong about you, wasn't I? And you only had Erica's best interests at heart."

"True," he admitted, "but I had my work interests at heart, as well." He grinned at Erica.

They sat down, and she slipped her arm around his waist. *He fits so comfortably*, she thought. *So right.*

Aunt Constance must have thought so, too. "You two—is there anything else I should know?" she demanded. "Erica, are you sure you haven't left something out?"

She burst out laughing. "I knew a drink would revive you," she teased, knowing full well she was dodging Aunt Constance's question. "As a matter of fact, I have a surprise for you. I'm giving you this house. It's yours, Aunt Constance. As soon as we can go to a lawyer and get the paperwork done."

Her aunt stared at her in wonderment, eyes shining with tears. "Do you mean that, Erica? Really?"

"I do. And don't worry. I'll make sure you have enough money to fix it up and redecorate to your heart's content."

"I can hardly believe it!" Aunt Constance clutched her hands to her ample bosom. "I can hardly believe anything you've told me tonight!" She stopped when she noticed Erica's look of concern. "What's the matter? What are you keeping from me?"

"It's just that I'm worried about your health. Aunt Betty said—"

"Pay no attention to your Aunt Betty." Constance sniffed. "She just felt guilty about her love affair, and convinced herself I was too sick to live alone."

"But the doctor—?"

"What about him? I see Dr. Harris twice a year. My heart's as good as can be expected. Of course, he'd like me to lose some weight. And to watch my diet because I keep getting indigestion. He tried to send me to another specialist, but I refused to go."

"Perhaps you'll change your mind after we discuss it in the morning," Erica said firmly.

Aunt Constance pursed her lips, but said nothing. "Anyway," she said finally, "I have you. You'll come and live with me, won't you?"

"I'm afraid not, Aunt Constance," Erica said, beaming with her secret.

"But where will you live?" her aunt wailed. "This is your house, Erica. You're welcome to live here as long as you want. I don't want you to feel—"

"Don't worry about me. I'll be living in the city. Isn't there anyone who could come and share the house with you?"

"Cousin Molly from New Jersey," was Constance's prompt reply. She leaned conspiratorially toward Erica, as though afraid someone might overhear them. "She never came to visit me here because she can't abide Elizabeth. But she hates her little apartment. I just know she'd love living here."

The crafty vixen! Erica chuckled. She had it all worked out.

Aunt Constance met Erica's level gaze. "You will come and visit, won't you, Erica?"

"Of course, we will," Doug said.

"We?" Constance stared from one to the other.

Erica poked him. "For an undercover man, you sure can't keep a secret."

He grinned. "I can when I have to. Go on, tell Aunt Constance our news."

"Doug and I are moving in together," she announced, beaming with joy. "We're thinking sometime in the next few months.

"If not sooner," he chimed in.

Aunt Constance gasped. "But, Erica, honey, don't you want to give this more thought? I mean, it's all so sudden. You and Doug hardly know each other, and you've been through so much."

She placed a finger over her aunt's lips. "Sssh," she instructed. "Not another word. I'm more sure about this than I've been about anything in my life."

Aunt Constance thought a bit, then hugged them both. "I suppose I can't argue with that."

CHECK OUT THESE OTHER TITLES FROM ROWAN PROSE PUBLISHING!

A former Spanish teacher, Marilyn Levinson writes mysteries, romantic suspense, and novels for young readers. Her Golden Age of Mystery Book Club series was a King Rivers Life Magazine's "Best of 2014," and on Book Town's 2014 Summer Mystery Reading List. She's an Agatha nominee, a Library Journal "Pick of the Month," on Goodreads's list of the 200 "Most Popular Books Published in 2017," a Suspense Magazine Best Indie, and was on Book Town's Summer (and) Fall Reading Lists. She also writes under Allison Brook. She is co-founder and past president of the Long Island chapter of Sisters in Crime. She resides in New York with her family. www.marilynlevinson.com